Hoboman
The Higham Cut

Liam Higham

First published in Australia by Aurora House
www.aurorahouse.com.au

This edition published 2024
Copyright © Liam Higham 2024

Cover artist: Daniel Greenhalgh (https://cargocollective.com/danielgreenhalgh)
Cover design: Donika Mishineva (www.artofdonika.com)
Typesetting and e-book design: Amit Dey (amitdey2528@gmail.com)

ISBN number: 978-1-922913-64-7 (Paperback)

A catalogue record for this book is available from the National Library of Australia

Distributed by: Ingram Content: www.ingramcontent.com

Australia: phone +613 9765 4800 |
email lsiaustralia@ingramcontent.com

Milton Keynes UK: phone +44 (0)845 121 4567 |
email enquiries@ingramcontent.com

La Vergne, TN USA: phone +1 800 509 4156 |
email inquiry@lightningsource.com

Dedication

For you, the reader – in the knowledge
that anyone can be a hero.

Just, please, not like Hoboman.

Acknowledgements

If I may be so bold, I would like to start by acknowledging myself – firstly, Liam *circa* 2007, who initially came up with the idea for *Hoboman*. Of course, that Liam – being a dumb teenager without any understanding of the real world – thought it would be in keeping with Australian sensibilities to have an unlikely demographic to represent us on the superhero front. He didn't quite understand the seriousness of homelessness and the myriad factors that contribute to this, such as trauma and abuse, mental health issues, financial difficulties, and so on. So, I'd like to acknowledge that boy who just wanted to tell a fun story, but perhaps did not properly think things through. There was certainly never the intention to make light of the plight of the homeless – and, in fact, the story might inadvertently bring the topic to the forefront, particularly in the current housing crisis.

Or maybe only three people will read it. I dunno.

Secondly, I'd like to extend an acknowledgement to Liam *circa* 2017, who went through the process of having *Hoboman* published for the first time. Now, there are a lot of expenses associated with self- and independent publishing, including cover design, editing and proofreading. Let's just say that Liam *circa* 2017 may not have had the funds to bring this first *Hoboman* effort up to the standard our superhero deserved. Liam *circa*

2017 was convinced all his jokes were funny and that people would simply lap it all up.

But patience is a virtue – and hindsight brings wisdom. Which is why Liam *circa* 2023 felt the need to re-release the story as *Hoboman – The Higham Cut* (cheeky little Snyder Cut reference there, just in case you didn't catch it) – cutting the jokes that just weren't funny, polishing the writing, and clarifying some points. A true director's cut, I guess ... but of a book, not a movie. (Is that a thing?) Also, to add footnotes – I originally wanted to have jokes written as footnotes because they just make my brain ping! We can all learn lessons from the past, and it's important to be compassionate towards our younger selves – but, like, past Liam's dicking around has necessitated that I release the true vision of *Hoboman* without studio interference!

I would also like to acknowledge Kat, one of my best friends, who has been so supportive and uplifting throughout the whole process and given me lots of constructive feedback; Hanna, who always gets 'mad excited' when I bring up *Hoboman*; Troy, who doesn't get as excited but still says, "Sounds good, mate"; Tanoa, whose sense of the ridiculous is very on par with mine and who, therefore, revels in my attempts at absurdist humour; and the real David Muter, who I would like to point out envisioned the plot and fate of his fictional counterpart himself – so any criticism about that character should be directed his way. Also, maybe Travis ... although he probably won't even read this unless an audiobook is made. With what money, dude?

My thanks go to Anne, my editor, for all her work on this story (even although I'm sure it wasn't her usual preferred genre!) and to Linda and the rest of the team at Aurora House for taking a chance on Hobart Mann.

My gratitude also to Daniel Greenhalgh, for his amazing work on the cover. You've been incredibly patient with all my to-ing and fro-ing with design elements and for listening to my suggestions, even although I'm sure you had other ideas! It was a pleasure.

Finally, thanks to *you*, the reader, for picking up this book and giving it a go. I hope to entertain you. If not, please don't crucify me.

Cheers,
Liam

Table of Contents

Man of Steal

If you have chosen to peruse these pages, I am obliged to offer you a warning. The contents of this extraordinarily true and completely non-fabricated story will blow your mind so hard it will escape your skull and splatter on the wall, and only intense scrubbing for four to seven days will be able to get those little bits of grey matter out of the skirting boards.

In this epic tale of not-so-epic proportions, I am the suave, smooth-tongued narrator. Devilishly handsome, too, if I'm being honest. It is my sworn duty to tell you all about our eponymous hero, for I know everything there is to know about him. (But not in a creepy way. In a healthy way.)

What follows is a legendary story of romance, thrills and political intrigue; of comedy, horror and science-(non-)fiction; of martial arts, high-seas hijinks and animated adventure.

Don't believe me? You wound me. Fine. You want a corker of a sneak preview? If you will, I implore you to use your thinkbox to create those moving pictures in your head – and then you can come to a decision.

* * *

The dirt-cheap hatchback continued to idle for longer than necessary as his trembling hand struggled to turn the ignition key.

"Tim? Why are you so nervous?" laughed the woman in the
passenger seat, watching him wrestle to kill the motor. "It's just
Dead Man's Cliff. What's the big deal?"

"You're always saying how much you love making out at this
place," Tim replied, his voice catching in his throat.

"It's just so romantic," the woman replied. "Since they put the
fence up."

Tim nodded a little too enthusiastically. He fumbled with
his seatbelt, managed to extricate himself from the car, tripped
over his feet and unceremoniously faceplanted. "Want to join me
on the bonnet, Tam?" he asked, wiping grass from his person as
he stood.

She found the high pitch of his voice adorable. It was almost
like he was a teenager again, asking her out for the first time. Tam
followed her boyfriend to the hood of the car where they sat as
best they could, as the near-negligible surface barely accommo-
dated them.

"I was thinking—" Tim began.

"Did it hurt?"

"Tam, I'm serious! I was trying to figure out what makes us
so perfect together." He could barely look her in the eye, and she
couldn't help but smile at his cheesiness. "We just complement each
other, you know? What do you love most about me?"

"Not your looks," she answered immediately, and he slipped
off the hood of the car in surprise. "Just kidding, you idiot. It
would have to be your optimism. You've got big plans, and you
aren't afraid to follow your dreams."

Sighing, Tim leaned back and gazed up at the stars. "Just you
wait, Tam. Just. You. *Wait*. One day, my poetry will make me

famous, and we'll be rich, and you'll have everything you've ever wanted."

"I already do," she replied.

"I can just feel it. Once I send my latest portfolio to the publishers, they're bound to take me on."

"I know they will."

"This last lot has all been about you."

"You're a loser, Tim Arnott. But you make me smile."

"Maybe I can make you smile ... for the rest of our lives?" Before Tam could register what was happening, Tim was on his knee and reaching into his pocket. "Tam, you're the chocolate to my biscuit—" he began, and immediately dropped the ring, only just managing to catch it before it was lost in the grass. "Would you make me the happiest man in existence by becoming my wife?"

"Yes! *Yes*, you idiot, of course!" she cried, her eyes glistening with tears. Tim promptly sighed with relief, as if he had anticipated the opposite answer. The two embraced. "I'll love you forever," Tam whispered into Tim's ear.

And as the years passed, Tim knew this to be true. He was a very perceptive man who was never wrong about anything. When you know, you know, right?

* * *

Now, ever since he'd been a wee lad, Tim had known he was destined for great things. And while nothing overly important had happened to him for years, except perhaps his marriage and kids, he knew it was just a matter of time before the world saw him for what he truly was.

When his alarm clock woke him on this particular day, he had no idea how big a turn his life was about to take. He brushed his teeth in the mirror and took the time to notice just how average he was. What I'm saying here is: imagine the most average person out there and you've just imagined Tim. Average haircut, features, height, weight – you name it. His parents should have called him 'Joe' but, alas, by the time they realised how average he was, they were too underwhelmed by him to do anything about it.

'Uneventful' would be the best word to describe his life. He wouldn't say he was unhappy; after all, he had it way better than most people. He worked a steady job, nine to five, and had a lovely wife and three children.[1] But together, all these aspects served only to make him feel one thing: unfulfilled.

After cleaning his teeth, Tim went about the rest of his preparations on autopilot. His life was so routine, he didn't need to pay attention to what he was doing. He changed the nappy on the bin, threw the baby in the skip, ate the same boring breakfast, and read the same boring newspaper.[2] As he spooned another mouthful of bland bran into his mouth, he looked up at his wife. "I'm thinking of writing some more poetry," he said.

"Where's the baby?" Tam replied.

"Darling?"

"What?"

"I said I'm thinking of taking up poetry again."

"Have you ever thought you should just … end it?" she asked.

"My poetry?"

"Sure."

She paid him no more mind, instead choosing to rant about having to get the kids ready for school, even though the baby

---

[1] Probably the only aspect in which he deviated from being completely average, as opposed to the snooty Jenkinses next door, who had to go and have the average one-point-nine-three kids.

[2] Which was a bit silly, as news updates daily.

had disappeared again. Tim ignored her grumbling, used to hearing the same thing every day. He straightened his ill-fitting suit and fished the keys out of the fruit bowl. Tam had always thought it would be quaint to have a fruit bowl filled with keys; however, Tim was not the adventurous sort and this organised chaos filled him with anxiety, although no one respected his feelings on the matter. He climbed into the same old hatchback from years ago, pulled out onto the freeway and was immediately stuck in gridlocked traffic.

Fast-forward several hours and Tim was pulling into the alley next to the office, cursing that damn John Jenkins for stealing *his* allocated parking space. He glanced at his watch and swore at the stupid traffic, as he now had precisely one minute to get to his office and clock in. As he dashed up the office stairs, he lamented the fact there was no other feasible way to make the two-block drive to work quicker. If only he didn't live so far away, he might have walked.

Tim arrived in the office at one minute past nine, which meant his boss was on his case from the get-go. The boss's second-in-command, Jane Jenkins, berated him for half an hour. The time could have been better spent on work, but Tim was too average to assert himself. Maybe less-average people with more impulsivity would have found the urge, but not average old Tim. "If I could just talk to Miss Omen," he stammered, "I could explain—"

"She's much too busy, I'm afraid."

When at last he was excused and allowed to start work – now expected to work half an hour of overtime without pay to make up for the time spent being yelled at – he took a seat at his desk and sighed. The same old paraphernalia adorned his work surface, unchanged for years: his stapler, his notepad, the novelty drinky-bird thing that broke last year and was stuck in the bowed position.[3] It was all same old, same old ...

Tim had no idea just how much his life was about to change.

* * *

Wowzers, I bet that got your heart pumping, right? What do you mean, it didn't really explain anything? I don't want to spoonfeed you everything straight away. I said 'sneak preview'. I never said I was going to give you the entire plot. I mean, yes, I *will*, but that will eventuate from the natural flow of the narrative. Whatever. I don't need your approval. Except I do. Look, if you doubt my credibility, I strongly urge you to take a long, hard look at yourself in the mirror and reflect on how you became so cynical. Also, there's a bit of spinach stuck in your teeth.

Depending on your philosophy, a superhero may be a product of the times they live in, forced to rise to the challenges of their modern world in order to overcome the adversities rampant within it. Alternatively, their very existence may inspire the hordes of supervillains that swear to destroy them and everything they stand for. Hoboman's origins are sort of a mix, really. Allow me to elaborate ...

* * *

The smoke from a cigar curled into the air as it was exhaled. The cigar's owner sat in a chair facing the window. The top floor of the high-rise, formerly known as Slim's Shade Cloths and Sunnies, granted a picturesque view of the city below – when the smog had blown away. Despite the curtains being drawn apart, the figure was

---

[3] Which one could argue was a metaphor for the current stage of his life.

steeped in shadow. Because that's just how dramatic lighting works and I will not be challenged on the subject.

Two men entered the room, eyeing the chair almost reverently. "Sit" was all the shadowy figure said as he heard them approach.

The pair took their places obediently on the other side of the desk and waited. The shadowy figure puffed on his cigar and continued to look out the window. Down on the street, a dog was attacking its reflection in front of Backscatter's Mirror and Meditation Emporium. The watcher was mesmerised, as although you saw that sort of stuff all the time on the internet, seeing it in real life was something else. When the dog finally ran at its mirror image and knocked itself out, the man deigned to turn around and acknowledge his guests properly.

"Mario. Luigi," he wheezed. "You come to me on the day of my daughter's high-school graduation. And what is this? Whadda you doin', comin' in here, lookin' like that, uhh?" He gestured at their fluoro suits. "Casual Friday isn't for another three days. Jus' fogedda 'bout it."

Mario was immediately defensive. "It's not our fault, Godfadda, it's not." He plucked at his pink suit jacket uncomfortably.

Luigi, shifting awkwardly in his turquoise version of the same outfit, added, "We went to the dry cleaners to pick up our suits, and they gave us these!"

"Didn't even get my colour right," grumbled Mario. "Everyone knows purple complements my eyes." He let everyone know how he really felt by spitting on the floor.

The Godfather stared at the spit on his recently lacquered floor, then at Mario, without changing expression. Deadpan, he ordered, "Clean that up. Spittin' is a disgustin' habit."

"Sorry, Godfadda."

Mario crouched down and went about cleaning his spit with his sleeve. In the meantime, Luigi continued, "I think the dry cleaners ain't too happy on accoun' of we whacked their cousins last week. Think they're tryin' to make us look like a couple a mooks."

"Makin' *you* look like a mook, more like," Mario hissed, returning to his chair with a flushed face, smelling distinctly of lacquer.

"Why, I oughta ..." Luigi raised a hand to slap Mario across the back of the head.

"Clam it, chowderheads," the Godfather interrupted, before any other fluids ended up on his floor.[4] "Are you tellin' me? That the dry cleaners? Dressed you two up like this? I was unaware of this deceit."

"That's right, boss! Should we whack 'em?" Mario and Luigi asked in unison.

The Godfather's face was impassive. Then he began to laugh, all the while retaining the same deadpan expression. "How amusing."

Mario and Luigi exchanged uncertain glances and reluctantly joined in.[5] "So ... we aren't whackin' 'em, then?" Luigi asked.

The Godfather wiped a tear from the corner of his eye. "Ah, funny. But no. Whack the dry cleaners."

"Sure thing, boss," Mario said. "Say, boss, I gotta ask: why d'ya sound like Marlon Brando with his mouth stuffed with cotton balls?"

"I had my wisdom teeth removed today."

---

[4] Not after last time. Not again.

[5] Because, as we all know, it is good practice to laugh with the boss, regardless of how funny (or unfunny) the situation is, providing the jokes aren't inappropriate in any way. If they are, your boss is probably flouting several ethical guidelines and should be reported immediately.

"Yeesh. That'd explain the cotton balls, but maybe you shouldn't be smokin' cigars. Don't wanna end up with dry socket. But what about soundin' like Marlon Brando?"

"That I cannot explain." The Godfather leaned back in his chair and flicked a hand towards the door. "You may go."

Mario and Luigi left the room, leaving the Godfather to attend to further business. In the ensuing silence, he reflected on the recent events that required him to interview the family to screen for a mole.

"They are clean," said a voice from the shadows.

"Of course, they are, Stavros – they just got back from the dry cleaners," the Godfather explained, while he stubbed out his cigar.

Stavros, a bespectacled Greek man, pirouetted his way out from behind the drapes, where he'd been hiding. Even though Stavros was of Greek descent, he was still a part of the Giovanni Crime family, as the Godfather took the view that 'family' was not strictly restricted to blood relatives.[6]

"Perhaps we shouldn't have scheduled these interviews while you are off the planet on Endone?"

The Godfather pondered this. "Perhaps."

Stavros coughed delicately into a handkerchief before examining the notes on his clipboard. "I don't believe the threat comes from within the family, Godfather. Do you have any enemies?"

The Godfather made to bring his cigar to his mouth then remembered he had crushed it out already. "There is ... one man," he said mysteriously, as he staggered out of his chair and approached the window.

Stavros waited patiently, but it soon became apparent that prompting was required. "But, Don, who have you offended so

---

[6] Plus, it also added to the Mafia's family-friendly, non-discriminatory image.

badly they would leave such a gruesome thing in your bed? I am by no means a squeamish man, but …" Stavros could not go on. He raised his handkerchief to his mouth and had to resist the urge to retch.

"Do you have it with you?" the Godfather asked, his expression as neutral as ever.

Stavros pulled a transparent clip-lock bag from his pocket, doing his best not to look at the contents. He placed it on the Godfather's desk. The Godfather turned and examined the bag, his face inscrutable. "There is only one man I believe would send me this. It is a message."

Memories of dancing fire flickered in the Godfather's mind's eye. He gazed upon the severed head of the potato, dribbling blood and saliva onto his lovely, lacquered floor as he breathed, "He wants revenge!"

*   *   *

At this point, I bet you are asking, "Is Tim the Hoboman to whom the title of this book refers?" And my answer to you would be: "No, are your stupid?" Tim is lacklustre. What qualities make him a great hero? None! Oh, he's a dreamer? Get stuffed. Heroes take action. But the take-home message is, Tim isn't homeless. And then you'd all be like, "But surely Tim is indebted to the Mafia? Possibly gambling loans as a release from his boring life?" This is where I'd begin to question your intellect. But then you'd all be saying, "How about *this?* Tim incurs the wrath of the Mafia; they come to his home and shoot up his house, killing his family. This breaks him and results in his homelessness?" And it would be at this point I'd walk away to have a more fruitful debate with a garden gnome.

You see, our hero is one of the kind that many tend to overlook. He is not a billionaire who lived in a mansion and fell into a cave one time, and all the bats were like, "Get out ma cave", and as a result he was so mentally scarred that it made him fight crime, ironically dressed as the very thing that traumatised him. No. The streets are our hero's home, and the closest thing he could fall into would be a sewer. And if he was inspired to fight crime dressed as the contents of one of those bad boys ... well, we'd be dealing with a completely different superhero.

No, Hoboman is the type of hero who is ready to clean up the streets, which is beneficial for him as it is the equivalent of having a big spring clean, because he lived among the back alleys of a perfectly respectable city called Uptown.

* * *

Hobart Mann began his day in one of the aforementioned back alleys in the usual fashion, waking up in the morning feeling distinctly like P Diddy, whatever that meant. The fumes from the cars wafted down the corridor, causing him to inhale deeply. Suburban smog hit him like a blast of fresh air, clearing his head. It probably, maybe, potentially wasn't healthy, but the stark reality was he could wake up with pneumonia tomorrow, so what the hey?

Hobart had no idea that this morning would be a turning point in his rather uneventful life. But, then again, he had no idea about most things, and he never let his ignorance get in the way of having a good time. Besides, at one stage, he'd taught himself cold fusion and nobody had paid him any attention, so why be clever if there was no extrinsic reward?

Hobart regained consciousness inside his fort of garbage bags and forty-four-gallon drums, canopied by a tablecloth. He inched his way outside using a technique he colloquially referred to as 'the grub shuffle', given his raging hangover prevented the functioning of his arms and legs. His stomach rumbled and, although that was a regular occurrence, on this particular occasion, it was worse as it was what he called 'the alcohol munchies'.

Back in the old days, he would have been able to scrounge something from the bins; however, a new recycling initiative introduced by the mayor had led to everyone becoming 'environmentally friendly' and composting their scraps. Hobart countered that they weren't being very 'Hobart-ily friendly', but no one listened.[7] The mayor declared the initiative had resulted in progress, but Hobart scoffed at this, purely because he didn't know what 'progress' meant. Then again, hipsters scoffed at things, and they seemed like they had their heads screwed on.

Now he was up, Hobart set about getting breakfast together. He didn't actually *have* anything to get together, but he was ever the optimist. Rummaging through his 'cupboard' inside the fort, he unearthed a flat piece of metal to use as a hotplate. He picked at the funky mushrooms crusted to it from a previous meal and danced along to the colour purple as he carried it to the crackling bonfire-in-a-drum that all back alleys seem, magically, to have.[8] Once the plate started to warm, Hobart picked a random direction and headed out, hoping to encounter some food along the way.

Before he knew it, he found himself in the middle of Grand Slightly Off-Centre Park. The only people around were a couple of early morning joggers and a man who looked mysteriously like God feeding the ducks by the pond. Hobart seriously considered jumping in front of the ducks and stealing their bread, but past

---

[7] Mainly because it was a made-up word and made no sense. It could also have been a result of him shouting it at anyone who would listen, which gave the impression he was raving.

[8] Does that drum not seem suspicious to you? How many people are just casually dropping drums, but never food? And lighting them on fire? I dunno. Seems kinda hokey.

experience told him both the ducks and the humans feeding them became quite incensed by this sort of behaviour. As if able to sense Hobart's thoughts, the man who looked mysteriously like God turned and stared at him – a penetrating stare that seemed to look deep into his soul. But Hobart was used to stares, so he turned away and minded his own business. He was too strung-out to play the "What are you looking at?" card just yet.

Hobart's hobo senses alerted him to the presence of food in a nearby tree. The stray cat slinking about, judging whether it could reach the bird's nest cradled in the branches above, was also a dead giveaway, but now you're just splitting hairs. The cat's swishing tail stiffened when it became aware of Hobart, and the two locked eyes, each sensing the competition. For most people, an alliance would have been the natural next step – a truce between human and feline so both could eat.

But Hobart was a selfish jerk.

The cat waited for the tiniest flicker of movement from Hobart. It came in the form of a twitch of the hand.[9] The cat sprang up the tree and began scaling the trunk as fast as it could. Hobart waited patiently, using the time to crouch down to pick up a rock from the path. With surprising and sheer-chance precision, Hobart threw the rock, hitting the nest of eggs and knocking it out of the tree.

He had been aiming for the cat.

In the heat of the moment, the cat lunged for its prize, even though this meant leaping from the tree – which was huge, in case I haven't already mentioned this. Has it already been mentioned? It was a *huge* tree, and this cat just, like, jumped. What a freak. What I'm trying to say is, both the cat and the nest of eggs

---

[9] He wasn't sure if the twitch was hereditary, a result of countless years of trauma, or from alcoholism. But wondering about it didn't solve the problem.

were falling. Hobart leapt underneath the plummeting bounty to ensure the prolonged safety of the delicious, nutritious food-stuffs within. The cat wasn't extended this same courtesy. Every-one knows cats land on their feet, right? And this cat did. But have I mentioned the tree was huge? The cat landed on its feet from such a height, survival was extremely unlikely. (Of course, Hobart could have caught the cat too, but the fact he was a selfish jerk remains unchanged.)

"Are you all right, my son?"

Hobart turned, unaware his actions had attracted the atten-tion of the old man who looked mysteriously like God. There was compassion in the old man's eyes, once you navigated past the bushy beard and thick, white eyebrows. Suspicious, Hobart instinctively clutched the nest to his chest and, without speaking, ran away. He paused, then ran back, suspicion still in his beady eyes. He grabbed the loaf of bread from the hands of the man who looked mysteriously like God and fled again.

On the return trip to his alley, Hobart considered what an amazing haul he had made today, and also stopped to vomit because the strenuous activity didn't mix well with his hangover. Once he was sure he was up to it, he continued on his merry way.

By now, the hotplate had warmed up nicely, and he could smell the funk from those funky mushrooms diffusing in the air. Inhal-ing deeply and sighing with satisfaction, Hobart set about cook-ing his delicious, nutritious meal of delicious, nutritious eggs and delicious, nutritious bread, all the while sampling the taste of car horns through his feet.

Hobart thought he was still tripping when he looked down the alley to find the man who looked mysteriously like God stand-ing at the entrance. He bit into his egg on toast and, as yolk slowly dripped onto his shirt, quickly began formulating reasons to justify stealing the man's bread. When nothing came to mind, he shoved the entire sandwich in his mouth, because his mother had always told him it was rude to speak with your mouth full.[10]

The man who looked mysteriously like God, with His flowing white beard and flowing white robes, smiled benignly. "Have you heard the Good News?"

Hobart swallowed all his food in one great gulp, instantly regretting it as the toast crust cut his oesophagus up pretty nastily in the process. "Nah, not yet. My radio is out of batteries, if you know what I mean."

"Of course," replied the man who looked mysteriously like God, nodding sagely. "Your faith is running dry, and you need more charge in order to believe."

"I just mean my radio is out of batteries," Hobart said in response, nodding sagely back. He had recently discovered the joy of using batteries to make circuits. His favourite experiment to date was completing the circuits on other hobos. "If you've got any spare ones, I won't say no."

The man who looked mysteriously like God rummaged about in the deep pockets of His robe and came across a couple of AA batteries. "Here you are, my son," He said, gently lobbing the batteries towards Hobart, who missed completely and stooped to collect them.

"Hey, thanks bud."

Hobart turned around to find his radio and stuff the batteries into the relevant receptacles, but something felt wrong. "Missing something?" expressed the voice in Hobart's head. Which made

---

[10] At least he assumed she would have if she and his father hadn't ditched him on the streets after they won a holiday for two in a raffle. Children were not included.

sense, of course, as he had a lot of voices in there. This one, however, was unexpectedly female, which Hobart was definitively not. It also appeared to be coming from above.

Regardless of the fact he was hearing voices, Hobart was horrified to learn his radio was gone! More importantly, the shopping trolley that housed said radio was also gone! No hobo who wants his name known should be without their trusted trolley. Rage and grief roiled inside Hobart's chest like a pressure cooker. He could no longer hold himself back. Falling to his knees, he put his hands to his head and shouted a curse word this writer dares not articulate. To give you some context, this particular curse word was so terrible and so powerful, everyone in a five-block radius who heard it fell to the ground, writhing in agony as their brains melted out of their earholes.

Hobart ran past the man who looked mysteriously like God, who had been cleaning His ears with His pinkie fingers at the time and had not heard the swear word, and began frantically checking the nearby streets for anything that looked like a trolley. To his exasperation, all he could see were lots of prostrate bodies with what appeared to be brain matter leaking from their earholes.

"What in God's name do I do now?" Hobart shouted to the heavens, falling to his knees.

The answer to his prayers did not come from above, however. It came from the alley. The man who looked mysteriously like God approached him, gently clasped his shoulder and helped him to his feet. "Perhaps I can help, my son."

"Yeah? Just who are you, anyway?"

"Me?" the man who looked mysteriously like God asked with a slight chuckle. "Oh, no one special …" He leaned backwards slightly and was suddenly enveloped in golden light. "Only God!"

*   *   *

Tim heard his car alarm blaring and looked out the office window into the alley below. Two men seemed to be having a conversation, and the one who looked mysteriously like God had apparently leaned back onto Tim's car, setting off the alarm. Tim opened the window, pointed the key at his car, and the alarm stopped. When quiet had resumed, he shut the window and went back to work.

As mentioned earlier, Tim had no idea how much of a turn his life was about to take. Because it didn't take a turn at all. Tim isn't the hero of this story. Tim continued his life of being average and inadequate and died empty and unfulfilled after his children put him in a nursing home and never spoke to him again. I guess they all just moved on with their lives, found other people, had families of their own, and there just wasn't time for old Timmy anymore. Quite sad, really. But we're here for Hoboman.

* * *

The light behind God suddenly disappeared, along with the annoying alarm, so Hobart counted his blessings. God also stood down from His tiptoes, which He had apparently gone up on so as to look taller and more majestic.

Awkwardly, Hobart stuck his hand down the neck of his shirt and scratched his back, his face scrunching up with distaste as he did so. "I dunno, mate. I don't wanna be *that* guy, but I'm not sure I believe you are God. I've always believed in Santa Claus, sure, but God? Bit of a stretch. Plus, religion sort of divides people, hey. I'd rather not alienate my readers, to ensure I sell as many books as possible."

"What?"

"You know, like, everyone is your friend, then one day you reveal you're a Muslim and bam: instant shunning!"

"No, the book thing."

"Oh, I just meant for when I write my memoir."

"But how can you deny what is right in front of you?" asked the man who looked mysteriously like God, because He allegedly was.

"I want proof," Hobart said simply, folding his arms adamantly.

"You can't just test God!"

"Yes, I can."

"No, you can't!"

"Yes, I can. And I can do this all day, buddy. I literally have nothing better to do with my life."

God balled His fists repeatedly and sighed. "Fine! But only because this is important. Try this on for size."

God raised both His hands like a madman in one of those castles the moment lightning strikes behind them – although the madman is usually cackling evilly, and God wasn't cackling evilly: He just did the hand gesture. As God raised His hands, a hobo who had been sleeping peacefully in the alley burst into flames. God allowed this vision to sink in before lowering His hands, causing the flames to disappear. The hobo remained asleep, although the shoulders of his coat were smouldering.

Hobart raised a single eyebrow, unconvinced. "That's nothing. He catches fire all the time. We call him 'Flaming Eddie'. I mean, how do you think we light the bonfire?" Hobart gestured towards the forty-four-gallon drum that was crackling merrily away. "I don't have matches, so we just shove Flaming Eddie in there for a bit and let him work his magic. He's renowned for dousing himself in whiskey and setting himself on fire, claiming he's a Christmas pudding. Legend says Flaming Eddie is the Santa Claus of hobos and jumps from drum-to-drum lighting fires for all the good boys and girls, though we have no proof to confirm this theory."

"So, how am I supposed to prove I *am* God?" asked the man, who looked mysteriously like God, in exasperation.

"That sounds like a *you* problem."

"Want me to send a flood?"

"You could try. Hey, can you curl your tongue?"

"I hardly see what relevance—"

"Can you?"

"No, but—"

"You mean you *can't* curl your tongue?" Hoboman was shocked. "But you're allegedly *God*. Surely you can do everything?"

A voice called to Hobart, seemingly from the heavens. He was transfixed as the heavenly female voice called, "Hobart!"

"Are you my conscience?" Hobart asked aloud, more for the benefit of the readers than anyone else.

"Um … sure. Let's go with that," the voice replied. "Look, you have to listen to me, Hobart."

"Obviously. You're my conscience."

"Your trolley going missing is a sign."

"Yes, yes!" Hobart exclaimed, falling to his knees, his mouth agape with rapturous ecstasy. "It's a sign!"

"The catalyst for your transformation!"

"Yeah, that thing. Transformation and stuff," Hobart echoed.

God rolled His eyes. As the voice wasn't in Hobart's head, it wasn't as if the conversation was private.

"You must become something more than a mere human, to ensure what has happened to you never happens to anyone else!"

"More than a human? Like … a mutant?" asked Hobart, a tad uncertain. "I've heard they have a pretty rough time, and I'm not about that life."

"No. You must become … a superhero!"

"Yeah, that sounds a lot better. I have to become a superhero who stops other people having their trolleys stolen!"

The female voice faltered slightly. "More of a superhero in general. Like, stopping supervillains, natural disasters ... that sort of stuff."

"But there aren't any supervillains in town," Hobart reasoned. "Plus, how am I supposed to reverse natural disasters?"

"I can. Just saying," God interrupted.

"I didn't ask you." Hobart scowled at God. "Seriously, think about it. A cyclone comes; I can't beat up a cyclone."

"Will you let me finish?" asked Hobart's conscience.

"Go ahead."

"Thank you. To bring justice to this city, you must go by a name that strikes terror into the hearts of evildoers. And that name ... wait for it ... is Hoboman!"

Bet you didn't see that coming, eh? 'Hobart Mann' becomes 'Hoboman'. What clever wordplay. Almost as though his name was *made* for it.

"That makes perfect sense," Hoboman replied enthusiastically, nodding his head vigorously. "I can't believe I didn't see it before. But then again, you *are* my conscience, so I guess I *did* see it, it was just never at the front of my mind. Gosh, I'm smart."

God, bored by this point, entertained Himself by setting Flaming Eddie alight again and warming Himself against the glow. He raised a hand to interject. "Uh, Hobart: why is your conscience a woman?"

Hoboman whipped around, scandalised. "I'll have you know that we live in Australia: the land of opportunity! My conscience can choose whatever gender it relates to best! Hell, my conscience should have the right to marry whoever it wants. You're just being sexist. You can't be the *real* God. The real God wouldn't be sexist."

"I am not sexist!" God shouted back defensively. "And I *am* the real God. Probably should have led with that," He added. "All I'm saying is you're getting your knickers in a twist, thinking your conscience is making you become a superhero, when I can see the woman responsible in the window up there. How does that make me sexist?"

God pointed to the window, which just so happened to be directly above Tim's office. The woman quickly pulled her head inside and slammed it shut, so by the time Hoboman turned around to look, his conscience had gone. "I think someone is just making stuff up now. And I mean you, by the way."

"I gathered. Hobart, listen: I need you. The forces of darkness are gathering. I need your help to stop them."

"Look, God, if that *is* your real name ... I'm a superhero now." Hoboman rummaged through his possessions until he found his beanie. As he tugged it over his ears, he shrugged. "I just don't have time to mess around with the forces of darkness, you get me? I'm sure you understand."

Frowning, God concluded, "Okay, I'm not going to get through to you right now. But I'm going to call on you again when you've grown tired of playing the hero. When I do, I pray you will be ready."

"You're God, supposably. Praying is what you do."

God gave Hoboman one last, grave look and exited the alley ... before yelling at a driver who nearly wiped Him out as He hadn't been watching for traffic. Hoboman merely shrugged, the significance of the meeting having had no effect on him, and set about finishing his costume.[11] He stuck his hands into his pair of fingerless gloves and scratched the stubble on his chin, deep in thought.

---

[11] For merchandising purposes.

Something was missing. At last, it came to him. He grabbed the red-and-white-checked tablecloth sheltering his fort, dusted it off and tied it around his neck, striking a mighty pose.

And that, my friends, is how our hero was born.

I am being figurative here, I might add. He was, of course, born as a baby in a hospital. He didn't magically get born as an adult. I just thought it would be a good way to end the chapter. Shall we try that again?

And that, my friends, is how our hero—

You know what? I've ruined it. Just go to the next page.

CHAPTER **2**

A Little Snag

"I'm a Bolbusta," the man shouted at his son. "Just like my father and his father before that. And every other male on the Bolbusta side of the family tree, come to think of it. And much to my dismay, so are you. So, if I can't disown you, the only option I have left is to force you to toe the line."

"You just don't get me," was the muffled response from Mister Bolbusta's son as he sobbed into his pillow.

Mister Bolbusta sighed and rubbed his temples, his patience wearing thin. "Ozzie, get up. I'm not going to tell you again."

"Don't call me 'Ozzie'! 'Oswald' is my preference."

"Oh, here we go again with your fancy *preferences*. Look, I let your mother call you 'Oswald' because she thought it sounded fancy. The only reason I was cool with it was because I could call you 'Ozzie', which sounds like 'Aussie': the name for a true-blue, dinky-di bloke who watches footy and drinks beer with the boys."

Oswald Bolbusta finally pulled his face out of the pillows. His father recoiled at the sight of running mascara, as if it might burn his flesh away if any landed on him. "I'm sorry I can't be what you want me to be!"

"You could. The problem is you *won't*."

"Why can't you accept me for who I am? Are you threatened by what you don't understand?"

"Oh, I understand you perfectly well. You're just gross. My almost-adult son, prancing the streets dressed up as a she-male."

Oswald's mother chose this moment to come to her son's aid. She entered the room and floated gracefully down onto the bed, caressing Oswald's rumpled hair delicately. "Why do you have to be so hard on him?" she reproached her husband.

"Oh, you too? He's a man, *allegedly*. He was born with all the bits a man has. Isn't it about time he started acting like one?" Mister Bolbusta retorted.

"You make it sound like such a big deal," Missus Bolbusta scolded. "So, he wears a bit of mascara? So what? Do you remember when he was a toddler and got into my makeup? We all laughed so hard, Grandma Bolbusta wet herself."

"She was incontinent, anyway," Mister Bolbusta shrugged.

"How about the time when he was little and found my dresses and high heels? The dress was so long, he kept tripping over it all the way down the hall!"

As the memory resurfaced, Mister Bolbusta chuckled to himself. "Heh, what an idiot." As soon as the words escaped, he shook his head as if rattling his brain around his skull would permanently remove the recollection. "That's not the point! When you're a child, it's different. At this age, Ozzie should know better."

"I'd just like to say—" Oswald began.

"Speak when spoken to!"

"Yes, sir."

Missus Bolbusta threw her hands in the air. "All he did was say he was hanging out with his boyfriends! It's just like how girls say they're hanging out with their girlfriends."

"Exactly!" Mister Bolbusta shouted back, mimicking his wife by throwing his hands up, too. "Like a girl!"

"It doesn't make him a homosexual or anything."

"Yeah," contributed Oswald. "In fact, I'm still trying to figure out my sexuality. I really don't know where I sit in terms of—"

Dark splotches coloured Mister Bolbusta's face. "Stop! Stop right there! Quite enough of that, thank you very much!" He paced his son's bedroom, trying to think of what to do next. He stopped mid-step, having reached an epiphany. "I've got it! We'll send you away to boarding school. That will straighten you out ... in multiple senses of the word!"

Missus Bolbusta's face screwed up in confusion. "Dear? Isn't sending him to a school filled exclusively with other males ... the *opposite* of what you want him to be doing?"

"Nonsense," Mister Bolbusta blustered. "I went to boarding school and met all of my closest friends there." He reached for a catalogue on Oswald's bedside table and flipped it open to a spread showing muscular underwear models. "There was Handsome Harry. Gorgeous Georgie. Cutiepie Guy. Sexy Tex." He lingered on the models' bulging biceps and oil-coated thighs. "Real men's men."

He wrenched his gaze reluctantly away from the magazine so as to give his son his undivided attention. His smile mutated into a leer, to the point where he would have been reported to the police if he had looked at a stranger the same way; even a family member was grounds for concern. "You have a big choice to make, *son*: the military or the police?"

Oswald sighed and buried his head in his pillow again.

* * *

In a few blinks of a perfectly defined eye, several years flew by. Missus Bolbusta sat in the audience, watching her son standing proudly in his uniform among the other graduands. "Oh, isn't this exciting?" she nudged her husband, who was sitting beside her. Mister Bolbusta glanced up briefly from his male underwear catalogue and grunted in a non-committal fashion.

"Bolbusta, Oswald," announced the officiator of the graduation ceremony, and Oswald dutifully stepped forward. "Raise your right hand and repeat after me," the officiator instructed. "I, Oswald Bolbusta ..."

"I, Oswald Bolbusta ..."

"... do solemnly swear to uphold the law ..."

"... do solemnly swear to uphold the law ..."

"... until such a time that a superhero hobo ..."

Oswald faltered at this part. He raised an eyebrow and the officiator nodded solemnly. "... until such a time that a superhero hobo ..."

"... helps me to realise the benefits of vigilantism, thus causing me to have a moral crisis regarding what is right and what is law."

This time Oswald couldn't proceed any further. "Does that actually happen?" he whispered.

"As a matter of fact, it does."

"To the point where it's necessary to be included in the oath?"

"You'd be surprised."

"Hmm, interesting," Oswald noted. He cleared his throat and finished. "... helps me to realise the benefits of vigilantism, thus causing me to have a moral crisis regarding what is right and what is law."

Silence fell across the venue. After a moment's hesitation, the audience took this as their cue to applaud. The officiator shook

Oswald's hand, passed him his graduation certificate and congrat-ulated him. Oswald fell back into line as the rest of his class took the oath and were handed their degrees.

After the ceremony, Missus Bolbusta ran from her seat and hugged her son tightly. "You must be so proud," she beamed, tears in her eyes. "Valedictorian and all."

Oswald stood tall, his chin slightly raised, with eyes only for his father. Mister Bolbusta remained impassive as he held his son's stare. Both said nothing.

"Well ..." Mister Bolbusta began after a while, and Oswald's heart filled with pride as he anticipated his father's next words. Finally, he would gain his father's acceptance!

"... have you got a job yet?"

*   *   *

I'd like to draw attention here to something you may not have thought about at great length. Y'all've probably seen at least one superhero movie or read at least one superhero comic. I'd also wager that after you watched/read it, you were like, "Holy rusted metal, I am *super*-inspired to become a hero right now." So, shall we take a moment to dwell on why we aren't all dashing about in our undies, saving the world?

Answer: because we're all lazy as shit.

Hoboman, who had spent most of his life aimlessly indulging in brainless shenanigans, was no exception. He knew he should be out finding troublemakers, but once he left his alley, the grandeur of fighting crime diminished somewhat. Besides, there was already an institution known as the Uptown Police Department that was *paid* to apprehend said troublemakers – and those guys actually had the legal authority to do so.

Our hero had encountered Uptown's finest on several occasions, and each had gone down like a sack of hippopotami.[12] The only way Hoboman would be able to get his name known would be to help those who were in need of assistance, while also meeting the specific criterion of reaching them before the police arrived. This was problematic due to the fact he did not have a police scanner to locate crimes in progress; he had no transport to get to crimes across town; and there were currently no souls in need of saving nearby as they had all collapsed on the pavement, their brains mysteriously leaking out of their ears.

Hoboman fell to his knees and, in sheer frustration, screamed the terrible curse word again – only to have the paramedics arriving on the scene drop dead, *their* brains also leaking out of their ears. "Oh, what's the point of being a somewhat macho superhero if there isn't anyone to save?" whined Hoboman.

He realised if there was no one in need of assistance in the general vicinity, he'd have to look elsewhere for someone to help. If that failed, he supposed, he could always commit a crime, run round the corner, pretend he was a bystander and run back to help. But that, of course, would be highly unethical. And if there was one thing Hoboman was about, it was ethics.

Steeling himself, he decided he'd be able to see better from the middle of the road and ran straight out without looking both ways.[13] As luck would have it, there were absolutely no negative repercussions from this action as there was no traffic, the police having already cordoned off the area to investigate the mass occurrence of death-by-brains-leaking-from-ears. Ten metres out, Hoboman

---

[12] Messily.
[13] A big no-no in the world of traffic safety.

came to a halt, out of breath. Maybe people could come directly to him instead, he mused, because running was really hard work.

Just then, someone started screaming. Even though that someone was on the other side of the city, Hoboman was able to hear it. This was not a coincidence. It has been scientifically proven that noise carries in polluted cities due to the high levels of particulates in the air. The sound wave vibrates one particulate, and it passes the reverberations to the next. Thus, a polluted city is the perfect medium for noise to travel. Science.

The scream was so long and protracted, Hoboman had to cover his ears. "Why the hell are you screaming so loud?" he called out.

The screaming stopped long enough for a girl to reply, "Because I'm in trouble!"

"Why don't you find someone who gives a damn?" Hoboman shouted back,[14] before doubling over with laughter. "That was a good one," he congratulated himself. "I need to write that down. I need to learn how to write first though."

The girl took a deep breath before she screamed her response. "I wouldn't want your help, even if you were some kind of super-hero! God, nobody understands me. Why am I surrounded by idiots who have no idea what it's like to be a teenager? Even the adults who used to be teenagers! I think they hit adulthood and got some sort of amnesia!"

"Retroactive!"

"What?"

"Retroactive amnesia is the inability to recall past memories. It would explain why adults don't remember what it was like to be a teenager!" Hoboman elucidated.

"Don't care!"

---

[14] Obviously, this conversation could occur, as already explained.

"Ooh, I really don't like her," Hoboman muttered to himself. "But wait … isn't that the superhero code?'Help everyone, including the douchebags'? Yeah, I'm pretty sure that was it. This could be my big chance! Hoboman … away!"

In a dramatic twist that would rank at least a solid eight on the Shyamalan scale, the screaming endured for the entirety of the time it took Hoboman to get across town and locate its source. This took Hoboman roughly an hour, as he had to stop to use the toilet twice, and was then entranced by the display of meat in a butcher's shop window. After managing to drag his attention away, disappointed by the lack of sausages, he finally arrived at his destination, which was just next door.

Hoboman took in an apartment building, sussing out the place before making his entrance. It was a typical modern complex: tidy, neat, organised. There was a perfectly serviceable door that led into the lobby, but a fire escape running up the left-hand side of the building enticed him with its sexiness.

Not wanting to break the superhero tradition of doing things the hard way – especially on his first day on the job – Hoboman opted for the fire escape. He jumped up to the first ladder and began his ascent. It was not long before he began to realise just how tall the apartment complex was, so when he reached the fifth storey, he ended up commando-rolling through a terrified old lady's window so he could take the internal stairs instead.

On reaching the top level, Hoboman was easily able to pinpoint the source of the screaming, as the pollution had seeped through the cracks in the windows, which meant the sound was still echoing. Before searching for the distressed person or persons, Hoboman puffed out his chest importantly. He strode casually down the hallway like he owned the place, which he most certainly did not. If you still haven't clicked that Hoboman is a hobo and, therefore, does not own real estate, I highly recommend you stop reading right now and stare at the sun for a good hour.[15]

The door to Room Eleventy Hundred and Eleven was locked, as Hoboman had expected, but his heightened hobo strength was more than enough to gain access.[16] The owner, who bore the distinct demeanour of one whose vitality has been sapped as a result of parenting a teenager, did not even look up from his cereal as Hoboman strolled on by; he simply grabbed blindly until he found his mobile phone, dialled a number and said, "Hello, police? Yeah, another hobo got in. I'm Room Eleven-Eleven, Folded Arms Apartments."

"We don't have that address," the operator advised.

He sighed. "Eleventy Hundred and Eleven."

"Perfect. Can you describe the culprit, please?" the operator asked.

"Um, fingerless gloves. A red-and-white-checked tablecloth."

"Can you please describe what he is doing with the tablecloth?"

"I'm sorry?"

"Is he using it to cover a table?"

"No, he's tied it around his neck."

"Well, that certainly isn't regulation usage of a tablecloth. A squad has been dispatched. Officers will be with you directly." The operator hung up and the man went back to his cereal without another word.

Meanwhile, Hoboman had found himself before a door with a One Direction poster plastered on it, which utterly baffled him, given the five teenage boys were not looking in one unified

---

[15] Disclaimer: please do not do this.
[16] Meaning he tried the handle, found it wouldn't budge, took a run up and 'fell' through the door.

direction but in five *different* directions. He gently rapped on the door and pushed it open.

On entering, he was met with a teenage girl who was flailing her hands around as a tyrannosaurus might, should it ever attempt to make a bed. "Oh. Em. Gee! Like, this cannot be happening!" One might assume this was in response to having an intruder enter her room. It was not. She glanced at him, rolled her eyes and huffed. "What do *you* want?"

"I'm here to save the day!" our hero cried, jumping across the threshold and striking a heroic pose.

The teenager raised an eyebrow and sighed, "Whatever. I doubt you can help."

"What's the problem?" Hoboman asked, his inferiority complex making him seem a bit desperate. "Deadly meteor that will wipe out all of humanity so robotkind can thrive? Radioactive spider? Bombs placed at strategic points below the city, rigged to detonate so the populace is cut off from any outside support while we wait six months for me to come back and whoop some heinie? Stop me if I guess it."

The teenager relented. "Okay. So, like, there's this one totally weird girl at my school, right?"

"I never went to school," Hoboman admitted. "I don't follow."

"Oh. Em. Gee. Shut up, I'm telling a story! You're just like Jenny. God! She always interrupts me when I'm trying to tell a story. I'm like, 'Jenny, Oh. Em. Gee. Just shut *up*, will you?', and she's all like, 'God, Trish, stop being a screw-on!', and I'm like, 'Oh no, you didn't!'

"Anyway, so there's this weird chick at school. We, like, totally thought it would be hilarious to mess with her. Like, she's got no friends, right? So we were all like, 'Hey, you can totally come sit with the cool group. We'll be your friends.' So, like, we were going to get her hopes up and when she went to sit with us today, we were all going to get up at the same time and leave. Like, that's funny."

Hoboman stared in horror as Trish explained the situation. He hadn't been to school, but sometimes people would watch movies in the office above his alley, and if they had the window open, the sound would carry on the pollutants and he could listen. The plan Trish was laying out sounded just like the teen movies he'd heard being played in the office. And teen movies sickened him to the core.

Hoboman paced the room. He began fiddling with Trish's makeup box as he said, "We haven't talked about me in a while. What am *I* supposed to do?"

"The weird chick, like, totally squealed to her mum, saying something about us always picking on her. As if! Like, I have other stuff to do, so it's not *all* the time. Anyway, her mum called up the school, who then called all our parents, and now we *have* to sit with her, and if we don't, we'll get suspended for bullying or something stupid like that. I mean, I wouldn't care usually, but my dad seems to have it in his head that, like, I actually *do* bully people, and that is totally not true, but he said he would take away my phone. And how am I supposed to stay popular when I can't stay in contact with my squad, y'know?"

Somewhere during Trish's explanation, Hoboman had dissociated. He had realised this was not a crime that needed to be prevented but a normal job, and that was something that Hoboman could not do. Superjobs, yes. Normal jobs? Heck, no! He had a reputation to uphold.

"Sorry, I'm just here to solve crimes and steal your things, and I've already stolen everything of value in this house …" He trailed off as he looked around the room for anything he might have missed. "Yep, I'll be going now."

"Wait, I thought you were going to help me," Trish protested. Then she saw what he was holding. "Hang on, is that my Gucci handbag?" That was going too far. She had a reputation to uphold. "Give that back!"

"No!" Hoboman screeched, holding the handbag out of reach. "Finders, keepers."

The girl stamped her foot and balled her hands into fists. She opened her mouth and released a scream loud enough to rival those of the banshees from Hoboman's ancestral homeland. Being superstitious, Hoboman was terrified Trish may actually *be* a banshee in disguise and set about taking steps to hush her so as not to die – or at the very least, stop her from piercing his eardrums. Hoboman swung the handbag at her.

In his terrified state, his grip slipped and the bag sailed across the room, collided with Trish's makeup shelf, and caused it to collapse on top of her. Powders and polishes exploded in a rainbow. Trish groggily extricated herself from the rubble. Her face bore the semblance of a crazy, creepy clown, and Hoboman had a flashback to a time when dressing like that was a thing. This freaked him out even more, so he made a run for it, breaking the doorknob off for good measure.

"That should keep her trapped. Job well done," a satisfied Hoboman said to himself as he dusted his hands, having protected the city from another clown.

In dire need of a break after so much hard hero-ing, he stepped back into the lounge room and, when he saw the television was on, took a seat on the couch. He ignored Trish's dad, who reciprocated.

"Oh, this is one of those shows where you can figure out the plot if you actually pay attention," Hoboman noted.

A handsome reporter with parted hair and thick-rimmed glasses shuffled a sheaf of paper as he dramatically turned to face the camera. "Good morning. I'm Gabriel Messenger and if you're watching this, you're watching Channel 4 Shadowing News. If you're not watching this, it doesn't matter, because you will have no idea I even said that." Gabriel faked a laugh, but his eyes betrayed his disgust with his writing staff.

"Our top story today – a testament to how slow the news is – yet another butcher's shop has been robbed. A note was left at the scene reading, and I quote, 'You should keep a tight grip on your sausages'. Police have sought the assistance of experts from Uptown University to try and analyse the meaning of this. Here is what highly esteemed English language scholar, Professor Obie Views, had to say on the matter."

The video feed cut to Professor Views examining the note. He adjusted his glasses, frowned and sighed. "In my professional opinion … this *might* be a double entendre."

The footage flashed back to Gabriel Messenger in the newsroom. "Sources from Double U later confirmed it *was*, in fact, a double entendre. While a butcher's shop was robbed earlier this morning, police did not make it to the scene in time. Leading criminologists believe the culprit may be hiding in the Folded Arms Apartment complex next door to the shop; however, there are no leads as to who the culprit may be. Hungry, hungry hippos, or just someone who likes sausages? You decide."

Hoboman was about to change the channel to the cartoons, which he felt conveyed much more important messages to the youngsters than the drugs and violence so prevalent on the news, when he heard sirens. The sirens were so high-pitched they shattered the glass all through the apartment building.[17] Our hero ran

---

[17] Including the lenses of the glasses belonging to the little old lady whose window he had commando-rolled through.

to the window to double-check if the police were here for him, as sirens never boded well in his experience.

"Oh, bugger!" he exclaimed.

At the foot of the apartment building were at least twenty police cruisers. They were parked in a jumbled mess, almost as if the drivers had come to a stop by crashing into the other stationary cruisers.[18]

One of the officers raised a megaphone and an amplified voice rang out. "My name is Sergeant Bolbusta of the Uptown Police Department. Exit the building with your hands up! Do not resist arrest!"

Before Hoboman could protest, one of Bolbusta's colleagues raised his own megaphone and screamed, "He's resisting arrest! Get in there and cuff him, boys! Use excessive force if need be."

"That's not how we do things here," Bolbusta reprimanded.

"Sorry," apologised the other officer. "I've just transferred from the States."

Hoboman turned towards the door of the apartment to make his daring escape, only to find the entire police squad lined up in the hallway, blocking the exit. "Don't move or we'll shoot!" ordered the officer from the States.

"How the hell did you all get up here so fast?" Hoboman asked.

"We ask the questions around here!"

"But—", Hoboman began, lifting his hand to scratch himself.

"I said, don't move!" screamed the officer.

"All I was doing was—"

"The criminal has a weapon! Open fire!"

The squad squeezed their triggers in unison. They shot-up the place, screaming war cries above the sound of the gunshots. They

---

[18] Although that would be *completely* unprofessional, and police would never do such a thing ... would they?

kept their eyes firmly shut and their heads turned well away from their target for added accuracy. Hoboman was able to dodge all the bullets using the ancient technique of running and ducking, aided by the fact they were all being shot at chest height. He sought refuge in the apartment he had just tried to exit, hiding behind the bathroom door, as no one ever seems to check behind the door first anymore.

Trish's father, meanwhile, had kicked down the door to his daughter's room (as it was without a doorknob) and was doing his best to reorient his daughter to the present. He glanced up in horror as the squad, having lost their target, decided they needed a better vantage point.

"What are you doing?" he screamed. "My daughter needs medical attention and you're shooting up my apartment?"

"Sir," the American officer placated, "you called for the police, not for an ambulance. How about you let us do our job and we'll let you do yours?"

The squad squeezed into the bathroom, looking around desperately ... yet not one officer checked behind the door first.

"Where could this sick freak have gone?" hissed the American officer.

"Have you tried behind the door?" Bolbusta suggested.

"Yeah, right."

"Maybe he went down the fire escape?" Bolbusta offered reasonably.

The American officer bestowed on Bolbusta a look that suggested he had said the stupidest thing in the history of stupid things. "That's exactly what this psycho *wants* you to think. No. No, he's definitely still in the room." He looked suspiciously at the curtain dangling in front of the shower cubicle. "Yes, he's right ... here!"

Whipping the curtain back, the officer prepared to uncover our hero, probably cowering at the foot of the shower and begging for mercy. He didn't. "Ah, he's a cunning one. It's clear he has made his escape down the plughole! We need our skinniest officers to give chase!"

With the police now satisfactorily occupied, Hoboman slipped out from behind the door and ran out of the apartment, which was no mean feat considering there were, like, twenty people in there. Emerging into the hallway, he heard the elevator doors open with a ding at the far end. Hoboman's ADHD dictated he make a dash for it, even though he had never been in an elevator before and had no clue as to how it operated. Once inside the lift, he stared at the grid of buttons before him, dancing from one foot to the other in an attempt to kick his little grey cells into action.

He nearly lost his cool when, glancing up, he saw the police squad had given up on the idea of fitting down the drain and were congregating in the hallway to devise a new plan. They possibly wouldn't have noticed him but, at that moment, he let out a squeal like a stuck pig ... which *was* sort of noticeable. The squad lined up in formation and opened fire once again. Bullets sprayed the hallway and elevator but, luckily, the bullet-to-hit ratio was zero.

In a last-ditch effort to escape, Hoboman frantically prodded his fingers across all the buttons on the grid. The doors closed and the elevator began its descent. An automated voice over the intercom recited, "By pressing all the buttons, you have indicated you wish to travel to the secret basement of this building. If you have done this accidentally, or you are just a stupid child who always touches everything, press any button to cancel."

Hoboman had rammed his left pinkie into his left ear to try and clean out some earwax and did not hear this message. After the allotted time to cancel his request had expired, the elevator rumbled and the descent picked up speed. The automated voice returned. "You are now entering a restricted area. Defence protocols will now be engaged." This time, Hoboman didn't hear as he was cleaning out his right ear with his right pinkie.

"Screamo will now be played. Some people are into that, but this track contains expletives so vulgar they cause your brain to melt out of your earholes. We apologise for any inconvenience." Even as the screamo blasted away, Hoboman remained blissfully ignorant; both of his pinkie fingers were now jammed in both of his ears as they worked at an earwax build-up. He could hear the music faintly, though, and hummed along to the tune. When the music died down and the elevator shuddered to a halt, the voice on the intercom said, "You have reached your destination. Have a lovely day."

Hoboman arrived in a rather cramped basement. It was only dimly lit by a fire in a boiler off in the corner of the room. Conduit pipes fed out from the boiler and traced the building's veins on the ceiling above. One of the pipes had cracked, resulting in that incessant dripping sound. With the heat and moisture, the humidity made the air suffocating to breathe. Hoboman was suddenly anxious. The sound of maniacal giggling bouncing off the walls didn't help matters. It was then that he realised he was not the only one here.

The extra someone was hunched over, yet was still amazingly tall and sickeningly red.

"Well, well, well ..." The figure stood up and Hoboman breathed a sigh of relief when it turned out the stranger was simply a man dressed up like a giant sausage. He'd seen worse. "It looks like we have a ... wiener."

"Hey," Hoboman warned, "that sort of talk makes me uncomfortable. I am more than just my body, okay?"

"You are clearly a worthy adversary." The sausage man observed his worthy adversary belch and scratch his arse. "You somehow survived the music from my experimental college band, 'Linkin' Pork'. What did you think? It's a *banger*, wouldn't you agree?"

"I think it's a copyright lawsuit waiting to happen."

The sausage man hesitated. "Yeah," he admitted. "That's kind of why I had to put a stop to it."

"That, and you're shithouse."

"Yeah, that too."

Hoboman grimaced awkwardly. "Right. Do you think you could point me towards the exit? I'm a little lost."

"Don't try to ... string me along." The sausage man laughed, pulling out a chain of link sausages and devouring half of them. He smiled, revealing a mouthful of yellowing teeth. There was even a bunch of masticated meat spilling out, which was just gross.

Hoboman almost gagged at the oil rolling down the man's face, which he had initially mistaken for sweat. "Ugh, where are you from? Grease?"

"Germany, actually." The sausage man perked up. "You want to know my backstory?"

"Not really."

"It's quite tragic, really," the sausage man sighed, ignoring Hoboman completely. "It all started one Christmas ..."

* * *

Picture in your mind, if you will, this scenario from some thirty-odd years ago. Maybe you aren't thirty-odd and struggle to do this. Just pretend. The scene is thus ...

'Tis a cold day in Germany. Specifically, Frankfurt. It's probably snowing. I've never actually been to Germany, so I don't know if it snows there. Even if it does, I don't know if it snows in Frankfurt.

I feel like it probably does. And I mean, yeah, I *could* Google it, but let's not allow facts to get in the way of a good story.

We focus on a small cottage. The roof is covered in powdery snow. Icicles hang above the front door, which is aesthetically pleasing, but now when you open the door, it either jams if you don't apply enough force, or it rains down icicles of deadly doom if you apply too much. The windowpanes are frosted opaque, but only in the corners, so you have those little circles that allow a glimpse of the warm orange light from inside.

Bathed in the glow of a roaring fire sits a young boy. (To alleviate your fears, this fire was contained within a fireplace. He wasn't just casually sitting in front of a raging house fire. That would be terrible.)

He was dressed in a pair of red footsie pyjamas, giving the impression he was a fluffy little sausage. The look of delight on the boy's face as he roasted bratwurst on a skewer could have suggested Christmas had come early. It had not. Christmas had come at the regular time. And the sausage was his Christmas present. Most children would have thought that was a pretty awful present, but Werner Münch was not most children.[19]

There was no explaining Werner's fascination for wieners. It had been just a stroke of luck his parents had called him 'Werner' in the first place, sounding as it did sort of like 'wiener'. Ever since he was little, he had loved them. Wieners, not his parents. He ate so many different types of sausages! (I'd say you'd be surprised by all the different types, but we all react to processed meat in our own way, and I honestly couldn't tell you how you'd feel.) He became known for it at school. The other kids beat him up and

---

[19] Literally and metaphorically.

called him the German word for 'wiener'.[20] It was yet to be determined whether they called him that because of his diet or simply because they were terribly cruel children.

As Werner sat there happily, his parents entered the lounge room. His father looked at him and smirked. "Is that you or the chipolata cooking, wiener?"

Werner's father's bullying had evolved from minor taunting every so often to a daily occurrence, slowly intensifying as the years progressed. You would think Werner would eventually become desensitised, but Mister Münch's words still stung. A single tear rolled slowly down Werner's cheek; since it tasted salty and delicious, he licked it up.

Missus Münch gently placed a hand on her husband's shoulder. "Be careful. Remember our last child you bullied? Remember him snapping, so we had to take him outside and shoot him?"

Mister Münch knocked his wife's hand away. "Relax. What's the worst this little wiener can do?"

Werner inhaled deeply and breathed out slowly. This was his father's favourite game: antagonise him, and then punish him if he reacted. All he could do was stare at the raw sausage in the dancing flames, transforming into a tasty treat before his very eyes.

Mister Münch approached his son and wrested the skewer from his hands. "You don't want this, fatty. Let me help you." He threw it into the fire and leered at his son's slowly reddening face. "What are you going to do about it?" he challenged.

Werner did nothing to retaliate. Mister Münch shook his head in disgust and turned his back. Werner was so offended by what had transpired, he found it difficult to process. But a rage was building inside of him, a rage he felt powerless to control. Never in

---

[20] Which is probably just 'wiener'.

his life had he suffered such an indignity. His heart was shrivelling like the sausage shrieking in the fire; he felt like he was going to explode from his intestinal casing.

Mister Münch had lost all interest in his son. He turned to his wife and was saying, "What a wussy. I told you—"

"Holy bratwurst!" shrieked Missus Münch. "He's got a bratwurst!"

By the time Mister Münch turned, it was already too late. So consumed with hatred was Werner, he had plunged his hand into the fireplace, removing the glowing hot skewer with his bare hands. He seemed not to feel a thing. He slid the sausage off the skewer and ran at his father, slapping him so hard in the face that boiling oil burst from that tiny little air pocket sausages always seem to get when they're cooking. Blinded, Mister Münch fell to the floor and Missus Münch just lost it, freaking out as her husband and child tussled on the floor.

Mister Münch managed, "Get the gun!" before a slap from the sausage unhinged his jaw, preventing any more orders.

"I don't think so, Papa," Werner replied. "Who's the little wiener now?"

Mister Münch's shrieks of terror mingled with the whistling of the cooked sausage until it was hard to tell what was producing what noise. Werner did not know how long he beat his father, but as the sausage in his hand began to cool, he started to come to his senses. It appeared his mother was so stunned by the sight of her husband being brutally murdered, she had watched it all unfold without even attempting to go for the gun as instructed.

Werner slowly looked up at her, a murderous look in his eyes, and smiled a rather seedy smile. With the sausage held in his tiny little hands, Werner dipped it in some of his father's blood and took a bite, savouring the taste.

Missus Münch shook her head in disgust. "Oh. That is festy."

*   *   *

"And that's how I became a trained killer," Werner finished.

"Yeah, I could have done without that," Hoboman huffed. "And would you really call yourself a trained killer if you killed your dad in a fit of passion? Who *hasn't* been there?"

"The police have been looking for me, but they have all failed," Werner reflected. "What makes you so different? Are you a plain-clothes officer? Or some sort of detective? If you're here to arrest me, I'm afraid you have another think coming." He raised his arms above his head, swinging link sausages like nunchaku.

Hoboman couldn't comprehend why this dude was being so totally not rad. "I wasn't lying for once. All I want to do is get out of here. The cops were chasing me, too. What do they want you for?"

"Robbing butchers," Werner answered, lowering his weapons when it became obvious Hoboman wasn't fighting back. "What about you?"

"Meh, probably for being a hobo, I guess," Hoboman shrugged. "How do I work the machine that elevates me?"

"The elevator?" Werner looked deflated. Perhaps he'd been hoping for a bit of nunchaku action. He pointed to the elevator compartment nonetheless, instructing, "Go in there and press the button with the letter 'G'. It will take you to the ground floor."

"Thanks!" Hoboman turned to leave, but as he stared at the open elevator, something clicked. The news footage replayed in his head: the robbing of a butcher's shop, a note that *might* be a double entendre, and now, a man with a string of sausages. It could only mean one thing!

"Wait a minute!" Hoboman shouted, pointing a finger accusatorily at the sausage man. "You're no hippo! You're no hippo at all!"

Werner grinned and lifted his chin proudly. "You finally figured it out! Do you find it hard to believe that I, Werner Münch,
have managed to elude and outwit even the most intellectual—?"

"I want those sausages, Wiener Munch!" Hoboman shouted.

"No, no: it's *Werner*," Wiener Munch corrected.

It took one punch to the stomach to wind Wiener Munch.
Hoboman then grabbed the string of link sausages, wrapped them
around Wiener Munch's neck and pulled tight, strangling the man.
"You're the worst!"

"Heh, sausage pun. Nice."

"What?"

"*Wurst.*"

"I'm gonna frigging kill you!"

Wiener Munch's face went so red it matched his costume.
"No!" he choked. "Will the instruments of my destruction be
those that I love the most?" Unfortunately for him, his soliloquy
was brought to a premature end when his airway was completely
closed off by the sausages. His red face turned purple, then blue.
Wiener Munch went limp.

And that was that.

Hoboman's first supervillain had been taken out rather anti-
climactically, but he had ended up with a pocketful of sausages – a
reward in itself. He grabbed his fallen adversary by the scruff of
the neck and dragged him into the elevator. Confused by the buttons and unable to read the 'G', Hoboman shook Wiener Munch
until he regained consciousness. "Would you mind?" he asked, and
Wiener Munch groggily obliged. After pressing the right button,
Wiener Munch had his head smashed into the wall and lost consciousness once more.

The elevator ascended with no defence protocols being acti-
vated (as Wiener Munch had not foreseen anyone surviving to

make the return trip). When the doors opened on the ground floor, Hoboman was greeted by the raised guns of the entire Uptown Police Department (as it seemed this was the biggest case of the day, and any other ongoing crimes just didn't matter). Everyone stood still, waiting for someone else to make the first move. The tension was building. Someone would have to do something! Suddenly, Hoboman threw Wiener Munch into the lobby. Not as evidence he had apprehended a culprit. But because his arm was sore from holding him. Plus, he smelled, even by Hoboman's standards.

"And just what do you call this?" Sergeant Bolbusta asked our hero.

Hoboman glanced from Bolbusta to Wiener Munch and back again. "A man in a sausage costume."

"Why, pray tell, is this man in a sausage costume?"

"I imagine he's quite fond of sausages," Hoboman replied. "Pretty sure he's the bloke knocking off the butchers."

The officer from the States scoffed. He looked around at his comrades as if asking them to get a load of this guy. "What makes you say that then?"

"The guy *is* dressed like a giant sausage," Bolbusta reasoned. "It gives this half-hobo, half-man's statement some credence. Besides, there seems to be a confession in one of the pockets." Bolbusta pulled out a scrunched-up piece of butcher's paper that, indeed, had a confession written on it, although it was dubious as to whether it was written in grease or sweat. Bolbusta visibly recoiled and attempted to handle the scrap of paper with as little contact with his skin as possible.

"Wait a minute? You mean, I did it? I just busted a bad guy?" Hoboman did his 'just busted a bad guy' jig. "I'm a proper superhero!"

Bolbusta's eyes clouded as he remembered his oath. He advanced intimidatingly towards Hoboman, poked him hard in the chest, and leaned in so they were inches apart. "I hope you don't expect to get out of this scot-free. Vigilantism is not the right option! Among other things, you are up for breaking and entering, *and* resisting arrest!" The edge disappeared from his voice ever so slightly. "You'll have to be reprimanded."

Bolbusta proceeded to pat Hoboman on the bum, winked, and left to oversee the arrest of Wiener Munch. Hoboman shivered violently, not because it seemed Bolbusta was into men as Hoboman respected people's sexual preferences, but because unwanted sexual attention was simply not on, especially from those in a position of power. Feeling slightly violated, Hoboman fled to the streets, his cape flowing heroically behind him in the breeze.

"Do we have to chase him?" asked another officer.

Bolbusta watched Hoboman's retreating figure. "We have to chase him. Because he can take it. Because he's the hero Uptown deserves—"

"No, I mean do we actually have to chase him?" The officer glanced at his watch. "It's nearly morning teatime."

"Morning teatime? Ah, forget about him. I'm sure we'll see him again later. Guy as impulsive as that, he'll probably try to break into the station," chuckled Bolbusta. "Ah, that'll be the day."

Hoboman returned to his alley a happy boy, pleased to have saved the day, but even more pleased to have a pocketful of sausages, which was like having a pocketful of sunshine, only tastier. Knocking off for the day, he untied his cape and moved his hotplate onto the fire to cook his meal.

In the building overlooking the alley, Hoboman's conscience watched him with a smile on her face. Gabriel Messenger could be heard on the TV in the background reporting on Wiener Munch's arrest. Hoboman's conscience began to cackle.

Everything was going according to plan.

CHAPTER 3

Training

Hoboman couldn't lie; he was disappointed. After his exhilarating encounter with Wiener Munch, he thought things would start looking up. True, he was a household name. But that name was 'the hobo who keeps breaking in and stealing our stuff in broad daylight'. And, yeah, the kids loved him, but the parents had concerns about their children's role model being a homeless man who beat up sweaty people dressed as sausages. Hoboman's main grievance, however, was that the town's butchers weren't giving him free food, seeing as how he had saved their businesses from mild financial inconvenience.

Following the superhero story layout, we now come to the part where the superhero *really* gets noticed. The much-publicised showdown between Hoboman and Wiener Munch had revealed Hoboman to the world – even though, in the grand scheme of things, his debut had been smallish. The butchers were happy, but they were the only ones who really cared. Hoboman realised he would have to stop a supervillain who threatened more than the niche market of those who cut up and sell meat in a shop.

Our hero was strolling aimlessly around the streets (this may have been related to his ADHD) when he heard running footsteps behind him. He tensed, thinking he was about to be mugged; then it occurred to him that he was the one who did the mugging. His muscles relaxed and he nonchalantly turned around.

A woman stopped in front of him, doubled over to catch her breath, and clutched at Hoboman's arm to hold herself up. Hoboman shook her off.

"Just who the hell do you think you are, buddy?" he asked, frowning.

The woman raised a hand to indicate Hoboman should wait.

"Jeez, I need to run more often. Let me catch my breath. Okay, I think I'm better now." Her breathing was still ragged, but less so. "Hoboman, don't you remember your conscience when you see it?"

Hoboman was embarrassed now.

"Oh yeah, sorry. I didn't recognise you for a second there. Been busy, you know?" He clapped his hands together and exhaled awkwardly. "So … how are things?"

"Have you seen the news?" his conscience asked urgently.

Hoboman threw his head back for a good chuckle. It took a while for the laughter to subside. "Do I look like the kind of guy who *legally* owns a TV, hmm?" he sneered.

"Listen up! This could be your big break!" Hoboman's conscience leaned on our hero again and was not brushed off this time. As Hoboman assumed it was a physical manifestation of something that was all in his head, where was the harm?

"On the other side of the city is a suburb called Deddrich. There is a monorail project under construction there, but someone put the train on the tracks before the work had finished."

"That sounds like a very silly thing to do," noted the man who often electrocuted things with a battery and bits of wire.

Hoboman's conscience nodded in agreement. "The worst part is they actually powered up the train as well. A lone engineer has been monitoring the monorail and keeping it on a closed loop. It completes the same circuit without going onto the unfinished tracks and driving off into the middle of the suburb."

"What's the big deal then?"

"In an engineering faux pas, the switch has been designed in such a way that it needs to be manually held to keep the loop closed. When it's in default position, the loop is open. This worker has been monitoring the train for almost five days straight now, and he is only on a flat rate of fifteen dollars per hour, so he is threatening to boycott his duties."

Hoboman was confused. "Why does he need to be holding it in? Why can't he just use, like, a bungee cord wrapped around a cinder block? I've got some spare ones if he wants."

Our hero turned to go and search for his belongings. His conscience held out a hand to stop him, which reinforced the notion that this was indeed a manifestation of his conscience as Hoboman didn't like sharing, but it didn't count if you were giving it to yourself.

"The engineer doesn't have the resources. And none of the Deddrichians will bring him what he needs as they think it will take too long, and time is money." Hoboman's conscience hesitated. "What do you do with a cinder block and bungee cords, anyway?"

Raising an eyebrow and smirking knowingly, Hoboman told her, "Please. You're my conscience. You know *exactly* what I do."

"If you don't tell me, I can't be held legally liable," his conscience shrugged. "Anyway, the engineer said he would switch the tracks and let the train crash into the town square."

Our hero scratched his chin idly while he mulled over the dilemma. "That seems reasonable, I guess. I mean the train may crash into the town square, but if everyone evacuates and the authorities set up a safe zone, the loss of life could be zero. You can replace buildings, but you can't replace life," he informed, wisely parroting a quote he had heard on a life insurance ad.

"It *would* be a reasonable thing to do. Except the residents of Deddrich have all decided to assemble in protest in the very town square the monorail would crash into." Hoboman's conscience shook her head in exasperation. "The people of Deddrich believe if they amass a large enough crowd and stay there, the engineer will relent and allow the monorail to crash into a poorer suburb, so they don't have to pay for the repair work."

"They are rich, which makes them stupid. Us socioeconomically challenged folk have never made a poor decision in our lives," Hoboman advised. "I guess it's my duty to save them, huh?"

"Yes. And the monorail will be arriving at Deddrich station in an hour. You need to get there by then and stop it."

"Righto, then. Hoboman away!"

Running to the corner, Hoboman came to a halt at the bus stop and waited for it to arrive. A couple of minutes later, the bus veered over to the curb so Hoboman could jump aboard. He immediately pulled out a switchblade, threatened the driver and screamed at everyone to get off the bus. He was doing this so they wouldn't be dropped off in the middle of a suburb that was about to be destroyed, but he was not very good at articulating his reasons. He urged the bus driver to get off, belatedly realising the folly of his actions when he stared at the controls and remembered he didn't have a licence.

Hoboman hastily jumped off the idling bus. "Oi, get back here!" he shouted after the driver, who was running off down the street. When the driver failed to stop, only turning to see how much distance he had put between himself and the armed hobo, Hoboman growled. The driver's eyes widened in fear when he saw our hero begin to chase him down. He didn't see Hoboman tackle him, but he certainly felt it when he hit the ground. He blacked out and found himself back in the driver's seat of the bus in the blink of an eye.

"Please, don't hurt me," he whimpered, as mucus streamed from his nose into his mouth. "I have a wife and kids. I can't die!"

"We all die in the end, mate, but I'm not here to kill you. Although, you *are* tempting me." Hoboman squinted at the bus driver, hoping to convey how mad he was, but it just looked like the sun was in his eyes, or he was trying to have a good look at something on the driver's face. "I just need you to get me to Deddrich, like, right now. Can you do that for me?"

The driver sniffed and nodded his head like a child who had just recovered from being scolded. He put the indicator on because he wasn't a massive ignoramus, shifted gears and merged back into the traffic. He tensed when Hoboman took the seat directly behind him. His next words were littered with sniffles, but he did his best to say what he was paid to. "Next stop ... Deddrich. Estimated ... time of arrival ... fifty-five minutes."

"Fifty-five minutes, eh?" Hoboman pondered. "That won't give me much time to stop the train. Onwards, good bus driver!" Hoboman hummed along to nothing in particular but stopped short at the sight of an ice-cream shop. "Hey, pull over, I want to get a delicious cold treat."

"I thought you said you needed to get to Deddrich in a hurry. Won't stopping to get a snack ruin your schedule?" the bus driver asked. His tears had mostly gone but the tracks still stained his face.

"That's assuming the train is on time and, let's face it, that's being pretty optimistic. Public transport, amiright? We can take time out for ice-cream."

"But—"

The switchblade was at the bus driver's throat again. "I said. We. Can make time. For ice-cream." The tears began rolling down the bus driver's face again, but he obediently pulled over. "Grab the money from your fares," Hoboman urged. "I'm light on cash."

"I can't take the fare money. The company will kill me."

Hoboman's hot breath dampened the inside of the bus driver's ear as he leaned in and breathed, "And if we don't get that ice-cream, *I'll* kill you. Got that?"

Once they'd stopped for the ice-cream, Hoboman settled down and they continued on their way.[21] "How long have you been doing this job for?"

"About ... about twenty years," the driver replied, trying to muffle his sobs.

"Enjoying it?"

"I guess so."

"That's good. It's rare to see someone who actually enjoys the profession they're in."

"Uh-huh," the driver said as he wiped his eyes. "And what about you?"

"What *about* me?"

"Do you have a job?"

"Good one, mate. It's *Hobo*man, not *Working Class* Man. I'm not Jimmy Barnes."

The driver had nothing more to say, so he kept on driving. They finally pulled up at Deddrich town square and Hoboman alighted, but not before giving the driver a friendly but firm pat on the back in thanks. The driver waited until Hoboman had left

---

[21] Hoboman got rum 'n' raisin. The bus driver settled for mint choc-chip because he didn't want to be charged for drink driving, as well as embezzling company money.

before finally letting go of his emotions, curling up in a foetal position on the floor and bawling his eyes out.

As his conscience had informed him, the residents of Deddrich had gathered for a protest rally right underneath the scaffolding of the incomplete monorail track, which was an OH&S nightmare. Hoboman made his way through the crowd, the locals stepping aside to allow him through; not because they knew who he was, but so he didn't brush them with his homelessness.

"Good heavens!" cried one rich lady. "Everyone, look at this homeless man! What a sight! And he smells absolutely *putrid*! The shame! The shame of it all!"

Hoboman was feeling extremely self-conscious at this point and needed a way to pass the time as he walked to the makeshift stage erected for the event. He studied his fingerless gloves and his forehead creased in deep concentration. "I wonder how I could make these warmer for winter. Maybe I could add fingers? But then what would I call them? *Fingered fingerless gloves?* No. That's just silly." He was so vexed by this puzzle he lost his spatial awareness, banged his knee on the stage and swore, much to the displeasure of the refined and cultured audience.

"Wait a minute," someone called from the crowd. "Isn't he the homeless man from the slums they keep saying is a hero? Maybe he can save our great – not to mention, rich – suburb from almost certain doom. Just don't let him into your house! He'll probably steal everything. He has that look in his eyes."

Clambering onstage, Hoboman took his place behind the podium. He tapped the microphone tentatively (this was down to nervousness rather than expertise, as he had no clue how microphones worked), then physically jumped like a cat seeing a cucumber when his tapping was amplified across the square. Everyone fell silent and stared at him expectantly, and for the first time in his life, Hoboman discovered what stage fright was. Suddenly anxious, he tried to imagine the crowd in their underwear but couldn't bear to do so for a prolonged period of time as the crowd was filled with old – not to mention, rich – people, and picturing them in their underwear made him gag.

Deciding he may as well have a fair crack at this public speaking malarkey, Hoboman yanked the microphone out of its stand, causing harsh feedback in the process, and began strutting up and down the stage like a celebrity.

"What's up, people?" he asked and waited for a response. When none came, he continued, "My name is Hoboman. I'm the new superhero in town, and my conscience told me I should save you all from a train."

From the crowd, an old lady called, "This district is incredibly wealthy, and therefore great; how do you intend to save us from this psychopath holding our fair suburb to ransom?"

"To stop this engineer character, I have a secret weapon at my disposal, which is ..." Hoboman rummaged around in his pocket and removed the first thing he could find: a coupon for a weight loss clinic. "This!"

Seeing this as a personal attack, the old lady promptly fainted.

"Sir," another citizen called out, using this term of address very loosely. "Not that it surprises me, but I don't think you quite understand our plight. A train is going to kill us all if that engineer isn't stopped."

A high-pitched whistle sounded, and Hoboman suddenly broke out in a sweat. The support beams of the scaffolding began to rattle and shake, and dust drifted down from above. "Wait, that's what a train is? Bugger this! You're on your own!"

Someone in the audience began to clap nervously but ceased almost immediately when no one else joined in.

Hoboman dashed through the crowd and made for the road, but his escape was foiled when a car screeched to a halt in front of him. His conscience got out of the car, pinned our hero's arms to his side and shook him violently. "What do you think you are doing, Hoboman? You MUST stay and save these people!"

"Hey, you never mentioned anything about a train!"

Dumbfounded, his conscience stuttered. "I think I mentioned it *several* times. I *know* I mentioned it several times," she amended when Hoboman raised a finger to argue the choice of words.

"Fair point, you probably did, but not in terms I understood. If you had said 'big, long clickety-clack', I would have been on your wavelength. Plus," Hoboman added, "these guys aren't being very nice to me."

"It's a superhero's duty to protect everyone, no matter how not-nice they are. Remember the superhero code? 'Help everyone, including the douchebags'! Go and ... I dunno ... 'Spider-Man 2' the situation."

"Get hit by a train because someone is using the power of illusion to disorientate me?" Hoboman queried.

"No, that's Tom Holland!" his conscience corrected.

"Put a coin into a subway station and find my father's research in a disused carriage?"

"No, that's Andrew Garfield!"

"*Oh,* jump in front of the monorail and shoot webbing all over the buildings to gradually bring the carriage to a stop *just* before it reaches the end of the scaffolding, all the while pulling a face that lends itself well to memes?"

"Something like that!" his conscience confirmed.

"I wouldn't know, I've never watched those movies."

"But ... how did you know the relevant plot points involving the trains in each movie?"

"I don't *own* a television. I told you already!"

"Hoboman, stop that monorail and help those douchebags!"

Hoboman was about to refuse, citing no douchebag was worth his life, when a crane from a nearby construction site swung around, hooked his cape, and promptly sent him skywards.[22] Gaining altitude, Hoboman was launched into the air and sent soaring when the crane hook tore through his cape.

"I can't believe it! I'm flying! I'm actually flying! This is the greatest experience of my life!" Unfortunately, he had no real control over his flight. Conveniently for the plot, he just so happened to crash through the train station window. "I can't believe it! I'm bleeding! I'm actually bleeding! This is the worst experience of my life!"

Brushing shards of glass from his coat, Hoboman recovered what was left of his shattered dignity and looked up to see what he assumed to be his foe, gazing upon him from the comfort of a revolving chair.

"Are you okay?" the villain asked. "That has to be the most spectacular entrance I have ever seen in my life. Be that as it may, I'm more concerned about your wellbeing. You might have a concussion. Do you know your name?"

"I'm Hoboman," our hero cried.

"I think we can confirm the concussion."

Hoboman squinted at a tag on the fluorescent safety vest the engineer was wearing. "What does *that* say?"

"What? This? It says 'Hi-Viz.'"

"Hi-Viz?" Hoboman tasted the name. "You're a pretty stupid supervillain to just blurt your name out."

---

[22] The crane operator had ingested cough medicine before operating the heavy machinery.

Hi-Viz furrowed his brow. "This isn't a nametag."

"An admirable attempt at backpedalling, however, it won't work with me!"

"I have no idea what you're talking about. You aren't making any sense," Hi-Viz spluttered. "Look, you're all scraped and bloody. I have a first-aid kit—"

"Don't even think about attending to my wounds," shouted Hoboman, pointing a bloodstained finger at Hi-Viz and splattering the office with specks of blood. "You just want to hear me scream when you pour alcohol all over everything. I've got news for you, buddy. I'm no idiot! I see you for what you are, you filthy hippogriff!"

"Pardon?"

"You pretend to be nice to me, but you don't care about the lovely – not to mention, rich – people below us!"

Hi-Viz left his seat and began pacing. "I told them not to begin construction on a monorail before the Christmas holidays. I told them it would never be done in time. But no one listens to a lowly engineer. I don't know what they want from me. The monorail is automated. It drives itself. There are no passengers. If everyone had listened to me, there wouldn't have been anyone in the town square. No one is forcing them to stay there. I've been working impossible hours, but they don't care so long as *they're* not inconvenienced. It's cheaper for me to work for the minimum wage than to halt construction. It's like I'm nothing to them."

Hoboman advanced on Hi-Viz until their faces were inches apart. "I'm going to go out there, hold in the switch that makes sure the train stays on the loop, and there isn't a thing you can do to stop me!"

Hi-Viz shrugged and replied, "Fine, then. You do you."

Having expected more defiance, Hoboman did nothing. After a moment, he stammered, "You're ... you're not going to try and stop me? Not even a little resistance?"

"Why should I?" queried Hi-Viz. "I just want to go home. It's not like I'm some sort of supervillain."

Hoboman snapped, tackling Hi-Viz so they both crashed through another window. The pair fell onto the tracks. Groaning, Hoboman rolled away and staggered unsteadily to his feet. Hi-Viz stood up and gingerly held the small of his back.

"What are you doing, pushing both of us onto the tracks?" Hi-Viz called. "This is suicide!"

"No," Hoboman corrected. "It's *murder*-suicide."

Hoboman leapt at the engineer again, but Hi-Viz was ready this time and only had to step out of the way to dodge him. Hoboman found himself sprawled on the tracks with a mouthful of blood. Woozy, he looked up and saw the train in the distance, rushing towards him. "Hell."

"Maybe I can override the computer systems with voice commands!" Hi-Viz wondered aloud, shouting over the noise of the oncoming train. He palmed Hoboman to one side as he bravely stepped closer to the train and shouted, "Brake! Brake!"

Even if he had just fallen on his arse, Hoboman wasn't taking the engineer sitting down. "Break? You want them to break? What is wrong with you?"

"Have you stopped that psychopath yet?" a young man yelled at Hoboman, but in a dignified manner. "Time is money, you know?"

Hoboman looked to the crowd, then at the train, then at Hi-Viz, who was still shouting and flapping his hands about. "What would Flaming Eddie do in this situation?" our hero asked himself. An idea came to him. A flamethrower! Of course! He leaned over the scaffolding and asked, "Anyone have a can of deodorant?"

"I do," replied the young man. "Though I'll have you know, it isn't *just* deodorant. I'm much too good for *regular* deodorant. I wear Cologne-in-a-Can, thank you very much."

"Yeah, just chuck it, mate!"

The young man looked offended, though Hoboman was too far away to see this. "You want me to just *give* you my Cologne-in-a-Can?"

"It's sort of a necessity right now, so yeah!"

"But it's the best money can buy."

"I'm sure, but I need it, like, thirty seconds ago!"

"We could barter?"

"Nah!"

"Imported from France, Cologne-in-a-Can uses only the choicest of scents for the choicest of taste. 'Dipstique'. Why would I just hand it over?"

"Put it this way," Hoboman growled. "If you don't throw it to me, you're all going to die. And then I'll climb through the wreckage, find you, jumpstart your heart with a battery and some wires, and kill you again! Got that?"

It wasn't in Hoboman's best interests to be so blunt with the young Deddrichian. It seemed he had made the man so afraid he threw the Cologne-in-a-Can with absolutely no warning. All Hoboman saw was a thin, metallic tube filled with cologne flying at his face, and instinct made him duck for cover. The cologne flew up between two railway sleepers, reached the apex of its arc, and fell back to whence it came. By the time Hoboman realised he was supposed to catch it, the opportunity had passed.

"That's it! I'm done!" Hoboman screamed. He stalked up to Hi-Viz, whose attention was still on the train, and grabbed the villain by the collar of his shirt. With one great heave, he sent Hi-Viz crashing onto the tracks, where he lay spreadeagled.

"Why do you keep doing this?" Hi-Viz asked. "I'm trying to save us, and you seem to have a death wish!"

Hi-Viz now had his back to the unfinished tracks overhanging the town square; Hoboman faced Hi-Viz with his back to the monorail. Hoboman began to windmill-punch, swinging both of his arms in circles, walking steadily closer towards his enemy. Hi-Viz backed away, barely dodging Hoboman's flying fists between checking to make sure he wasn't putting his feet through the gaps in the sleepers. With the two men fast approaching the drop, Hi-Viz would surely plunge to his death if he could not find a way to stop Hoboman.

It seemed like a miracle. Hoboman halted abruptly, his arms frozen mid-swing. Hi-Viz was just wondering why, when without warning Hoboman sneezed a particularly mucousy sneeze all over him. Taken aback by this unexpected manoeuvre, Hi-Viz hacked and spluttered in an attempt to ensure he didn't swallow any. He was so surprised he took a step backwards with little regard to his footing. Solid ground failed to materialise beneath him. He felt as though his stomach had dropped out of his backside. Screaming, Hi-Viz thought he was surely doomed, but at that moment a crane swung around and hooked him by the belt loops of his pants.[23]

Hoboman didn't stop to watch his enemy's death. He had more important things to do. "I'm here to stop trains and pick my nose," he reminded himself. "And I'm all out of boogers."

With an almighty roar, Hoboman placed his feet apart in a fighting stance and extended his arm, ready to block the train

---

[23] After ingesting the cough medicine, the crane operator had promptly fallen asleep at the controls, and the crane had been spinning continuously for about ten minutes.

with his fist. He quickly changed his mind, however, and opted instead to run back to the station, grab the lever responsible for switching the tracks and yank it with all his might. The tracks changed with a heavy clunk. Hoboman wiped the sweat from his brow and punched the air with his spare hand. The train would continue on its loop, and the people of Deddrich were safe. He had saved the day!

Applause broke out beneath the monorail scaffolding as the crowd cheered for their hero. Hoboman blushed a little at all the ruckus they were making for little old him. "Hooray!" they shouted. "The smelly homeless man has saved our great – not to mention, rich – suburb!" On hearing the next sentence though, Hoboman's smile devolved into a frown. "Now *he* can hold that lever until after the holidays!"

Hoboman released the lever immediately, and it reverted to its earlier position. The train resumed its natural course for the town square, speeding past the station in a flurry of noise and rushing metal. It quickly passed the point of no return and derailed. The locomotive shot off the unfinished track, plummeted into the town square of Deddrich and killed everyone. Not a soul survived. Not one. In the resulting explosion, the Cologne-in-a-Can rocketed into the sky, destined for unfamiliar places.

Hoboman smiled, proud of his latest achievement. The people of Deddrich were dead. He had saved the day. And there were no witnesses to dispute this.

By the time he managed to climb down the scaffolding, Hoboman found his conscience surveying the carnage. Having driven to safety after coercing Hoboman to stop Hi-Viz, his conscience had rushed back the moment she'd heard the huge explosion to find smoke billowing from the twisted metal. Counting her blessings, Hoboman's conscience was spared the sight of the mangled bodies because the monorail had collapsed several of the nearby buildings, covering the evidence.

"Hoboman," his conscience stuttered. "What have you done?"

"Destroyed Deddrich," our hero answered.

"You can't do that!" his conscience rebuked.

Hoboman stood in the rubble and looked from side to side at the devastation. "Clearly I *can*," he corrected his conscience. "I just really *shouldn't*. Plus, I don't hear any Deddrichians fussing." He cupped his ear and, as he'd pointed out, there was a serious lack of complaining from the dead – not to mention, rich – bodies of the townsfolk. "I guess you could say it's the end of the line for them."

Hoboman's conscience shook her head gravely. "I think you may have gone too far this time, Hoboman."

"What do you mean *this* time? My only two outings have involved me beating up a sausage man and crashing a train into a rally of douchebags. There isn't really much to compare."

Hoboman's conscience bit her lip. "Everyone will see you as a villain now," she mused.

"Relax." Hoboman waved a hand casually, not in the slightest bit worried by his actions. Instead of reflecting on the destruction he had caused, his attention was drawn to the metal barrel his conscience was holding. "Hey, conscience, why are you carrying around a tub of baby formula?"

"What? What are you talking about?" his conscience asked, a little too quickly, hiding the container behind her back. Luckily, Hoboman lacked a sense of object permanence, and out of sight really *was* out of mind, so he immediately dropped the interrogation. "Hoboman," his conscience continued, "you may have just ruined any chance you had of becoming a superhero. I pray for both of our sakes I'm wrong."

Hoboman's conscience hopped back into her car and took off in a hurry, awkwardly avoiding eye contact so Hoboman would not ask her for a lift. The tyres screeched as she peeled away, although no police tried to pull her over because the officers stationed at Deddrich were pretty crushed over the ruined monorail.

"What if my conscience is right?" Hoboman asked himself, resuming his aimless meandering after it having been interrupted earlier. "Maybe I need to learn how to control my emotions, as sissy as that sounds. What if … I actually need training?" He stopped. "Wait a minute. Training. *Training!* And there was just a giant train. Oh, I still got it." He doubled over in response to his gnarly puns. Recovering, he concluded, "With puns as funky phresh as those, who needs to train? Not this guy!"

Hoboman looked around and remembered he wasn't in his own neck of the woods. Hoping to fly like he had before, he stuck out his fist and jumped. Nothing. Figuring he had to be in the heat of the moment to unleash his latent abilities, he worked on devising an alternative plan to get home. Ahead of him was a comforting sight: a bus shelter. He skipped down the street and stopped at the shelter. After about ten minutes, a bus indicated to pull over.

Hoboman flicked out his switchblade.

CHAPTER 4

Jean's Genes

A dull glow shone from multiple computer monitors. The basement did have a light, but the lone occupant was unwilling to use it. He said he liked the darkness, but it was more that he was just too lazy to climb the stairs and switch it on. The poor lighting made it difficult to make out the youth's pasty face and lank, black hair.

Clips from various news broadcasts played on a loop. They all concerned themselves with the increasing crime rate in Uptown. Newscasters like Gabriel Messenger spoke of moral panic; how people were reluctant to walk the streets for fear of being attacked; how petrol prices were going up and what a pain that was, because half the time they were sitting at a standstill in traffic jams anyway, but couldn't risk turning the ignition off because the light might change to green, and then someone might honk their horn at them if they didn't drive off immediately, and one shouldn't have to deal with that kind of pressure.

The young man in the basement laughed as the clips began another cycle. He switched the monitors off, no longer needing to listen as he knew the speeches off by heart. The basement was instantly plunged into darkness – something he had not considered. He staggered blindly across the room, knocked his shin on the basement stairs, and proceeded up them so he could find the light by the door. He flicked the switch and instantly reeled when the light blazed into life, contrasting painfully with the darkness; again, something he had not considered. He shielded his eyes and descended the steps again by gripping the banister. Having no idea of his relative position to the furniture in the room, he connected with his desk and toppled over.

"Jean, honey, are you okay?" the man's mother called from upstairs.

"I'm fine, Mum! God, leave me alone! Is that too much to ask?" Jean called back angrily.

"Do you want me to bring you some sandwiches or something? It's nearly lunchtime."

"I said I'm fine! What more do you want from me? Just leave me alone to plot!"

"Oh, the things you say make me laugh," Jean's mother said. And true to her word, she laughed.

Jean paused, waiting to make sure his mother wasn't going to interrupt him once he began soliloquising. When it became clear that wasn't going to be an issue, Jean rubbed his hands together and began talking to himself – a trait many consider to be a problem.

"The city of Uptown is in turmoil. It is a festering wound, and the villainous scum are bacteria infecting it. But with this ..." Jean whispered, pulling a pen-like device out of his desk drawer, "... with this, I will be able to sterilise the wound. Kill the bacteria!" He paused, not quite knowing how to extend the metaphor any further. "And then I will be a superhero!" he finished lamely. "Should I have said I would be a doctor? Seems a little ambiguous."

Thankfully, he was saved from having to come up with a better example when his phone alerted him to a breaking news report.[24] Jean quickly grabbed the remote for the television and switched the news back on.

"Good evening, my name is Gabriel Messenger and you are watching Channel 4 Shadowing News," the report began. "This just in: police have apprehended the culprit responsible for robbing local butcher shops. Werner Münch, reportedly going by the alias 'Wiener Munch', was arrested outside Folded Arms Apartments, where he had been hiding for some time. Sources say a vigilante by the name of 'Hoboman' played a substantial role in his capture. Here is what Wiener Munch had to say for his actions."

The footage cut to Wiener Munch, still dressed in his giant sausage costume, being ushered towards a police cruiser. "It's *Werner!*" he screamed at the camera before he was forced inside the car.

The bulletin was cut short when Jean switched the television off. He was furious. Seething. This had been *his* time. *He* was supposed to be the superhero! And now what? This ridiculous 'Hoboman' was trying to invade his territory. He would not have a bar of it. There was only room for one superhero in this town!

"I must destroy Hoboman!" he raged.

The sound of the news playing on his mother's television drifted down from upstairs. Jean clenched his fists and stormed up from the basement. In the lounge room, he found his mother parked comfortably on the couch. Back in the newsroom, Gabriel Messenger was pointing to an opinion poll, which showed an overwhelming proportion of viewers voting for a particular option. "As

---

[24] Because if one were to be a superhero, they needed to be up to speed with current affairs and not simply rely on random women to update them.

you can see, despite popular opinion, Wiener Munch was *not* a hungry, hungry hippo."

Fuming, Jean grabbed the side of the television and flipped it off its perch. It fell to the carpet with a muffled thump, tugging the power cord from the socket as it did so. Jean's mother half-rose from the couch, gawping at her son with thinly veiled disgust. "Jean, dear, why on earth would you do such a thing?" she asked, barely able to maintain her demure composure.

"You don't need to be watching that filth, Mum," Jean ranted. "It's poison, every bit of it! Talking about heroes like Hoboman." He spat on the floor. "This city needs *me*, even if they don't know it. And if I have to kill Hoboman to make them see the truth ... so be it!"

"Jean," his mother said, hands on her hips, "I have to kill cockroaches for you."

"No, you don't," denied Jean immediately, avoiding eye contact.

"You were scared it was going to attack you, so you ran and hid. I don't know how you can even put up with your little ant farm—"

"Mum, stop! You have no idea what you're talking about! Just shut up for once!" he ordered, tearing up.

"Oh, I forgot, I don't know anything," his mother remembered. "I'm just an idiot."

"That's right!" Jean ran from the room and sought refuge in his basement. Tears ran down his face, but they were tears of passion, not because he was a little wuss.

Jean's mother waited until Jean slammed the basement door, listening hopefully for the distinct sound of her son missing a step, toppling down the stairs and sustaining a serious injury. When this failed to eventuate, she lit up a doobie and set about cleaning up the broken television. "I should kill him. I really should," she muttered to herself after taking a large hit. "They would never find the body." As she swept up the shards of broken screen, she dwelled on the name of the vigilante from the news. "Although … maybe *I* won't have to."

* * *

Hoboman woke up, his stomach growling, thinking it would be another day of struggling to get by – and then he would get sick of struggling to get by and resort to robbing a servo. But boy howdy, instead he had rolled over and, like a gift from above, spied a trail of doughnut pieces right in front of his nose, leading him onto the streets.

Because of his one-track mind, he paid no attention to where he was going. All that mattered was that he pick up as many of these doughnut pieces as possible before the pigeons beat him to it. Imagine: he might even be able to fit them together to make a full doughnut! Now *that* would be a productive day. Much to his surprise and delight, there were more than enough doughnut pieces to make two of them! What. A. Day! It never occurred to him that maybe someone had left the trail on purpose.

The string of doughnut pieces came to an abrupt end at an innocuous-looking house. The last few chunks led right to an open door, something Hoboman frequently found hard to resist. Without a second thought, he walked inside. There was no one in the kitchen, so he started rummaging through the contents of a compost bin. It didn't take him long to find a quite fresh-looking potato nestled among some other degrading vegetable matter.

"First doughnuts, now a potato. Oh, Hoboman, what *will* you find next?" he wondered out loud.

"Excuse me?" a woman called.

Hoboman instantly tensed up, as usually people who found him pilfering in their house were not too happy about it. He straightened up and readied himself to run at a moment's notice.

The woman stood at the doorway to the living room and seemed indifferent to his misdemeanours. "Are you one of Jean's friends? He said he was looking for someone who matched your description."

Hoboman made sure to pocket the potato before its absence was noted (one never knew when a potato might come in handy).

"That depends." He looked the woman up and down, went to lean his elbow casually on the kitchen counter, missed, and stumbled slightly. "Is there food?"

"I can make sandwiches if you like," the woman answered.

"Then, yes, I *am* Jean's friend."

"It's so wonderful you've come around. He rarely has any friends over, and he spends an awful lot of time in that basement. He's always going on about how he is going to defeat Hoboman. I'm assuming you two do a lot of role-playing? You must be Hoboman, of course." Hoboman shrugged half-heartedly, more interested in the promised sandwiches. "I'm Jean's mother, of course. Miss Ettic."

"*Miss* Ettic, eh?" Hoboman asked. "Not Missus?"

"No, Jean's father left when he was quite young. It could explain why the boy is so messed up. Lack of a father figure. Inappropriate attachment styles." Hoboman nodded as if he had the faintest clue what she was talking about. "He's always had a thing for animals. Not in a good way; aggravating bees to set them on other kids, kicking ants' nests, pulling wings off flies. Really sick kid."

"About those sandwiches," Hoboman butted in.

Miss Ettic directed him to sit at the dining table and began buttering the bread. "I worry about him sometimes. He doesn't get enough vitamin D. Do you know I have to buy Jean vitamin D tablets? It's because he doesn't get any sun, hanging around in that basement all day. Back in my day, we used to run around outside until it was dark. We didn't have TV back then."

"With these sandwiches," Hoboman interrupted, "would it be possible to cut the crusts off them? I'm not picky, but I like having only one texture for the bread. Plus, I get to keep the crusts as snacks for later." Hoboman licked his lips and rubbed his hands together, salivating at the thought of beef and pickle sandwiches, or maybe she would make soldiers and he could dip them in egg. That would be positively swell. "You could even cut them into little triangles."

Before long, Miss Ettic was piling a plate with sandwiches cut into little triangles with the crusts cut off. "Jean is just in the basement," she informed him. "As usual," she added in an undertone.

Hoboman hurriedly took possession of the plate of sandwiches, swept half of them into his pockets once he was out of eyesight, and headed for the basement. He could kill some time entertaining a little kid if food was involved. Hell, it might even be better for his image if he was seen to be child-friendly … although not *too* friendly. He stopped at the basement door, hearing voices from inside.

"In other news, the Deddrich Monorail Project ended in disaster yesterday when the train plummeted into the Deddrich town square, killing hundreds. Citizens of Uptown applaud the efforts of new superhero, 'Hoboman', who was single-handedly responsible for ensuring the train ran off the rails. After the break, we speak to Sergeant Bolbusta of the Uptown Police Department to discuss the repercussions of this event. And coming up: one bear has had a grizzly encounter with a Member of Parliament after being arrested for possession of maple leaves. I'm Gabriel Messenger, and you're watching Channel 4 Shadowing News."

"That sounds like me!" Hoboman exclaimed with delight, bursting into the basement. "Your friendly neighbourhood Hoboman! Not the bear."

The sudden blaze of light caused Jean to flinch, smash his leg on his desk, and topple off his chair. The commotion startled Hoboman to the point where he overbalanced on the top step, fell heavily down the stairs, and came to rest on his back. Both he and Jean lay on the floor, groaning in pain.

"I want my mum," Jean moaned.

"I want your mum, too," Hoboman moaned back.

Jean sniffed and a pungent smell filled his nostrils. "You stink so bad." He stiffened as realisation hit him like a brick, or perhaps like knocking your head on the basement floor after falling out of your chair. "Wait ... are you who I think you are?"

"I already said: I'm your friendly neighbourhood Hoboman," our hero replied, covering his eyes with his arm to block out the glare from the monitor.

Not content with this answer, Jean crawled up the stairs like a soldier who had sustained a serious leg injury. He managed to flick the light switch, despite his extensive aches and pains. "Aha! It *is* you! I should have known you would find me before too long! You must have heard you have competition!" Seeing his mortal enemy before his very eyes reinvigorated Jean. He managed to get to his feet and make his way back downstairs to leer over Hoboman, even though he had the *worst* limp that no one would ever be able to relate to.

Hoboman uncovered his eyes and slowly opened them, allowing light to filter through. The face he saw made him cry out in terror. "Oh, God, no!"

"That's right, pray to your god!" Jean sneered.

"I'm not sure I really believe in any gods."

"You have looked upon the face of your enemy and know escape is impossible. Don't try to resist; it's futile."

"So ...ugly ..." Hoboman mumbled indistinctly. "What have you done to little Jean?"

Jean cackled evilly, but he really shouldn't have because his voice was all high and squeaky and didn't lend itself to cackling evilly. Like, Patrick Stewart can totally get away with cackling evilly because his voice is so deep and rich. But not Jean. Jean should not cackle.

"I. Am. Jean."

"You killed him, didn't you? Why do they always kill the kids? You monster!" Then, when what Jean had said sank in, Hoboman propped himself up on his elbows and steeled himself to look at Jean directly. "Wait, *you're* Jean? The way your mum was talking, I thought you were a kid. What are you? Twenty-five?"

"Twenty-four, actually," was Jean's offended response. He racked his brains for a brilliant comeback. "How old are you? Probably old. You *look* old. My joke is that you look old."

But Hoboman wasn't listening. Silent tears were rolling down his cheeks and his head was bowed in deep sorrow. "I will never forgive you for what you've done." Jean followed his gaze to the shards of broken plate but, more importantly, the sandwiches littering the basement floor, having been dropped when Hoboman fell. "You are a monster, Jean Ettic!"

"Only to the uneducated! When I enact my masterplan, the world will see me as an unstoppable super-genius, and no longer just a hideous recluse who hides in his basement!"

"Your words, not mine." Hoboman finally stood up and dusted his trousers down. "Is this a kidnapping, by the way? This feels like a kidnapping."

Jean scratched his chin thoughtfully. "I suppose it is. I never really thought of it like that."

Hoboman groaned loudly. "I feel an exposition coming on. Mind if I sit down?"

"How did you—"

"Your type is like that."

"I don't have a type!"

"Yeah. Your type says that a lot." Hoboman ignored Jean's frustrated pouting. He crossed the room, righted the computer chair, sat down and folded his arms. "All right. Impress me. Where are the palm cards stashed?"

Jean blushed deeply before hesitantly opening a desk drawer and removing the palm cards and a pen-like device. He cleared his throat nervously, wiped sweat from his forehead, and mumbled, "I haven't really done this in front of an audience before."

"Try your best."

"Okay. The moment of my apotheosis is nearly upon us. Soon, using this," he indicated his pen-like device, "I will transcend the bounds of humanity and become the superhero worthy of saving Uptown."

Hoboman raised his hand. "I'm already a superhero, which makes you redundant. More would probably just decrease my productivity."

"The superhero worthy of saving Uptown ... from *you!*"

"How are you even going to become a superhero?" scoffed Hoboman. "You probably don't even have a trolley for someone to steal."

"I will become a superhero with my gene splicer!" Jean raised the pen-like device for Hoboman to see. It resembled a clicky-pen with a minute LCD screen built into the barrel and a hypodermic needle replacing the pen nib.

"For the folks at home who don't know what a gene splicer is, care to fill us in?"

Jean sighed at having to explain something so simple to an idjit. "A gene splicer is an instrument whereby I am able to combine, or *splice*, the genetics of two or more creatures. Some combinations can be quite useful." Jean stepped towards his desk and, with a flourish reminiscent of a television host presenting a prize on a game show, indicated a glass cage full of ants. "For instance, research suggests the common American field ant can support five thousand times its own body weight before being crushed. Imagine if I were to imbue myself with that power. I would be a real superhero; not some glorified one like you!"

Hoboman sighed and tapped his foot impatiently. "What's the twist?"

Jean gave a sick smile. He tended to become enthusiastic over odd things, and it was this particular accompanying smile that caused everyone to bully him. As well as his punchable face. Next to Jean's ant farm, another glass cage housed his most prized possession: a black-and-white-striped skunk. The animal shrank back in fear as Jean tapped on the glass. Its tail stiffened and it sprayed its trademark malodorous ooze onto the inside of the walls. An extractor fan worked hard to pump the stench out of the enclosure.

"Let me guess: you're going to spliff my genetics with the skunk?"

"*Splice*! Also, yes." Jean drummed his fingers on the skunk's cage. "I originally intended to enhance my own DNA first ... but I could always start with you! After your defeat, imagine how the world will see me."

Hoboman, who could not grasp the concept of persuasive language, bit his lower lip. "I guess they would see you with their eyes, wouldn't they?"

Jean huffed and pointed fiercely at Hoboman. "You are an uneducated fool! You don't deserve to be famous! It seems the rest of the world can't see you for what you are. You're ... you're a reality TV star!" he spluttered.

"Whoa, whoa, whoa! Are you saying just because I didn't receive an education, something I had no control over, I'm not as worthy as someone who did?"

"Yes!"

"Bitch."

In an effort to steer the discourse back on track, Jean looked down at his palm cards, saw the cue to bring the attention back to the skunk, and tapped extra-hard on the cage. He cleared his throat and announced, "This creature will be the instrument of your downfall!"

At this point, Hoboman was completely lost. "Wait, so who has it in for me? You, or the skunk?"

"I do."

"Why did you say the skunk does?"

"I'm going to use the DNA of the skunk and splice it with you."

"What did I ever do to the skunk?"

"You didn't do anything to the skunk!"

Hoboman remained quiet for a moment. "... I don't understand."

"I'm going to mix you with skunk DNA, because it will prove to the world you stink!" exploded Jean.

Hoboman looked scandalised. "That is really hurtful. Now I see why you don't have any friends."

"I do, too, have friends!"

The basement door creaked open. Hoboman and Jean jerked their heads round in unison to see who was there. A look of concern was plain on Miss Ettic's face. "Are you two all right? I heard yelling."

"It was Jean," Hoboman replied instantly, pointing the finger of blame.

"It wasn't me!" Jean yelled.

"Who are you going to believe?" asked Hoboman. "The calm person or the shouty one?"

"Mum! What do you want?"

"I was just checking up on you. Is it a crime for a mother to be worried about her child?"

"I'm fine! Just go!"

Miss Ettic pursed her lips, almost as though she had hoped the mentally unwell hobo had attacked her son.

"Oh, I've figured it out," she said, comprehension dawning on her face. "You two are role-playing, and you're just in character. We didn't do much of that when I was a kid."

"Yeah, she didn't have TV when she was a kid, so she and all her friends had to play outside until the sun went down," added Hoboman with a smile and a nod to Miss Ettic.

Miss Ettic appreciated Hoboman's input. "I suppose we did, come to think of it, but it wasn't as detailed as you, with your costumes. We just pretended to be knights and vampires, things like that. You should have just said I was interrupting your little game and I would have left."

"Then leave now, Mum!"

"Okay, okay. You two have fun."

"*Mum!*"

Hoboman waited until Miss Ettic was out of earshot, then said, "Dude, you need to pull your head in." His face was stern. "Your mother is a lovely lady, and you should appreciate her more. Have you ever stopped to consider why you aren't popular? It's not because you're hideous. You're just a giant doodle!"

Jean was flabbergasted at Hoboman's gall. "What did you just say to me?"

"You heard. I bet you never even considered, holed away in your mum's basement, why nobody likes you. Maybe if you tried being nice to people, they would be nice to you. But *no*," Hoboman ranted, waving his hands in the air like he just didn't care. "You just have to be the smarty-pants who is better than everyone else and treats anyone beneath you like scum. I bet you can't even get a girlfriend! Or boyfriend! I don't judge. Unlike you."

Jean was dumbstruck at being told off by a hobo. Stuttering, he tried to come up with a reasonable excuse. "I've been talking to someone on the internet."

"Woohoo! The internet!" Hoboman wasn't completely au fait with what the internet was, but the feeble delivery suggested it wasn't much of an achievement. "How about in real life?" Jean was silent. "What? Got nothing to say? Why don't you stand up for yourself?"

"You're absolutely right."

"No! I told you to stand up for yourself! How is agreeing with me going to accomplish that?"

"I don't have to listen to you!"

"It's like talking to a brick wall! Gosh! If you contradict everyone, you'll never make friends."

"Enough!" Jean grabbed his gene splicer from the desk, lifted the lid to the skunk's cage and stabbed the animal as it cowered in the corner. A bead of blood was siphoned through the needle and a double helix symbol flashed on the LCD, indicative of a successful DNA extraction.

"Wow, that was uncalled for," observed Hoboman. "The poor thing couldn't even defend itself, which must be why *I'm* defending it. Which proves what a nice person I am. I hope you're paying attention because this is a great lesson in humility."

Jean took several slow, small steps towards Hoboman. Maybe it was for effect, but it simply came across as impractical. "All I have to do is stab you with this, and everyone will see you for what you really are."

Hoboman began to feel unsettled by Jean's approach, finding it a smidge menacing. "Hey, enough of that now." He didn't know if Jean really *was* as smart as he said, but he didn't want to stick around to see if the gene splicer worked. He jumped up from the computer chair and ran up the stairs before Jean realised his slow, small steps were not very effective if no one was close by to intimidate.

"Hey, get back here!"

"Bugger off," Hoboman called over his shoulder as he bolted out of the basement, then out of Jean's house and onto the streets.

"Careful, you two!" Miss Ettic cautioned as Jean gave chase, flying up the stairs faster than he had ever run in his life. "We wouldn't want anyone to trip and have their neck violently broken by a hobo now, would we?"

The hot pursuit came to a screeching halt when Jean caught sight of the lit joint in his mother's hand. "Mum! Are you smoking?"

"Just a little," she admitted mildly. "To take the edge off."

"The edge?" spluttered Jean. "You mean—? Is that *marijuana?*"

Miss Ettic did not rise to the bait, though it was unclear whether she was in a stupor or just plain apathetic. "This isn't even the good stuff. I save that for nights. You seem to be more active at night, which makes you more aggravating."

"You don't need that!" he hissed, moving to bat the joint away.

"Touch it," she warned, in a deep tone Jean had never heard before, "and so help me, I will throw you down the stairs, set the basement on fire, and collect the insurance money." Jean took a step back out of pure shock, all intention of controlling his mother having vanished immediately. She brightened again. "Now, Hoboman is getting away. And I worked so hard to get him here."

Jean hesitated. "You arranged for him to fight me? So I could beat him, right? So I could become the new superhero?"

"Pop along now."

He tried to read his mother, thinking maybe there was a little more to her than met the eye; that perhaps he may have inherited a *tiny* piece of tenacity from her. But, for once, she was right: Hoboman was escaping.

Miss Ettic maintained a state of equanimity just long enough for her son to start chasing after the vagrant, then dropped all pretence. She directed an ugly, mocking face at his retreating figure. "You couldn't beat a drum, freak. I hope he kills you slowly and painfully." She drew on the joint and gagged. "Why not break out the good stuff early?" she muttered to herself. "After all, it's not every day your child is murdered."

Outside, Hoboman ensured there was sufficient distance between him and Jean before he turned to shout, "What took you so long? Scared I'll come over there and belt you?"

"If you're so tough, why are you run—" Jean began, but unfortunately, he tripped over his damn clumsy feet and sprawled onto the pavement. The gene splicer flew out of his hand, sailed through the air and, by some small miracle, landed right on Hoboman's bicep. The needle anchored itself in one of the muscles yet to atrophy, and the body of the splicer quivered nervously. Jean looked up, astounded at the accuracy of his 'throw'. "I've done it! I've finally done it! There is no way this can go wrong!"

Hoboman winced as he pulled the gene splicer out and looked at the LCD screen. The double helix symbol blinked and disappeared. His entire body began to shudder. His skin crawled. A tingling sensation shot down his arms. He tensed up, waiting for the transformation to begin as human and skunk DNA combined to create an abomination.

Nothing happened.

"This isn't right," Jean spluttered, staring at an unchanged and unaware Hoboman. "Why did it go wrong?"

"Because shut up!" was Hoboman's rather intelligent retort.

"The only thing I can think of is that your DNA is so similar to that of the skunk, any changes are negligible." Jean slowly approached Hoboman, genuinely cautious this time, and paced around him warily. And there, bursting out of the seat of Hoboman's trousers, waving lazily from side to side, was a striped skunk tail that had apparently sprouted from his tailbone, perfectly proportioned to the size of a human.

Jean poked the tail experimentally and Hoboman's fist swung out, connecting with his face. "Sorry. Reflex," our hero said, as Jean hit the ground.

Jean struggled back to his feet. A bruise began blossoming on his cheek. "That's it! I've had enough of this nonsense! There's no point in humiliating you! You wouldn't even know I'm doing it. No. I'm going to kill you right now!"

"People say that a lot, especially *your* type," Hoboman retorted, as he dug deep into his pockets. "And do you know how I usually reply?" He pulled out a cigarette lighter he may or may not have stolen from a servo. "Well, I guess I don't really say anything. I more, sort of, burn them."

Hoboman flicked the lighter's ignition wheel and flames danced before his eyes. He brandished the lighter in front of Jean, careful not to actually touch him. Not *yet*. Hoboman had been responsible for many burns to others, from electrical to third degree; with Flaming Eddie as his sensei, there was no way he could fail. He waved the flame at Jean like a loony warding off evil spirits. Jean, thinking he was hot shit, leaned in and extinguished the flame with one small breath. He raised an eyebrow, as if to say 'checkmate'.

Hoboman struck. Having heated up the lighter's protective metal covering, he grabbed the young man's arm as soon as the flame was blown out and seared it with the glowing hot steel.

"Ow, why would you do that?" Jean whinged as he applied pressure to his burn. "There isn't any cold water or ice to put on this. It might scar."

"Are you serious? You're trying to *kill* me! Did you not even consider the possibility I might fight back?"

Unable to think of a suitable comeback, Jean's gaze drifted to the gene splicer held casually in Hoboman's hand. A better idea sprang to mind. "Look! Free food samples!"

"Where?" screamed Hoboman. He spun around in desperation, as one can never have enough free samples.

"Ha, loser!" Jean smirked and yanked the splicer from Hoboman's loose grip. "Now all I have to do is find an ant, and you're dead meat."

Things were dire. This was definitively the most dangerous thing Hoboman would ever do: stop this weeb from locating a single ant. Jean crouched over and began searching the ground for insects. Hoboman ran up behind him and slapped his back. "Stop!"

"No."

Another slap. "Stop!"

"No!"

Well, *that* wouldn't work. There must be some other way to stop Jean ... but how?

Hoboman almost soiled himself when, without warning, a familiar-looking silver tube suddenly dropped from the sky and hit the pavement.[25] He picked it up and, on close examination, saw the words 'Cologne-in-a-Can' emblazoned on it. (Not that he could read it, but he recognised the odour of 'Dipstique'.) A jet of cologne shot out when he tested the nozzle. A sly smile crept onto his face.

"Oi, butthead!"

Jean instinctively looked up, hypervigilant to insults as a result of years of torment by his peers. He was honestly not expecting to see a can of deodorant hovering about an inch away from his face. "What the—?"

Hoboman readied himself to squeeze, but wanted to make sure he came up with a good quip before he did. "Hey, Jean! You … smell!" It would have to do.

Given only a moment's notice, Jean fumbled in his pockets and slapped on a pair of glasses to protect his eyes from the high-pressure spray. The rest of the mist was easily blocked out by closing his eyes. Once the deodorant had settled, all he had to do was wipe the residue off the lenses.

"Ah, protective eye shields," said Hoboman. "A clever ruse."

"These are my reading glasses," Jean clarified, waggling them at Hoboman.

"Oh, that's heaps sick. I've always wanted a pair. So, when I put them on, I'll be able to read stuff, right?"

"I mean, sure. Do you require reading glasses?"

"I can't read at all. But now I can borrow your glasses and I'll be able to."

"They don't give you the ability to read if you couldn't beforehand," scoffed Jean. "Why are you so stupid?"

---

[25] Landing very softly, it must be said.

"I don't understand. What's the point of reading glasses if they don't let you read?"

"They don't—" Jean faltered. "Reading glasses help you to—"

"Frostie!" Hoboman spontaneously grabbed Jean's arm and sprayed the Cologne-in-a-Can on his exposed underarm, less than an inch away from the skin. Jean freaked out and tried to wrench his arm back, but Hoboman's grip was like iron. After what felt like an eternity to Jean, our hero saw fit to stop torturing his enemy.

Jean staggered back as Hoboman clawed at the young man's head, knocking off the glasses. Seizing the opportunity, Hoboman sprayed the cologne in Jean's face once more, this time causing damage. Jean shrieked and covered his eyes, hoping to avoid any more pain. He lashed out, not really intending to connect with anything, so it came as a surprise to both hero and villain when he landed Hoboman a particularly good blow. Our hero reeled backwards and collapsed onto the bitumen.

His vision blurred, as is wont to happen when one acquires a serious head injury. His senses seemed all out of sync. Jean's screams were audible, but sounded a long way off, like they were underwater. One hand still clutched the Cologne-in-a-Can, the other felt around on the pavement for some leverage; Hoboman rolled onto his side and began to push himself up but, lacking the strength to complete the movement, fell back onto his stomach almost immediately. He kept his eyes shut and concentrated. He needed a new plan.

When his eyes snapped back open, he noticed he was being watched by someone. Not Jean, who could not see at all. Smouldering off to the side on a nearby street was none other than Flaming Eddie. He nodded twice, sagely, reminding Hoboman of his lessons. Hoboman nodded back in determination. With that, Flaming Eddie wordlessly erupted in a plume of smoke and vanished.

Hoboman braced himself, ignoring any possible concussion, and managed to push himself back onto his feet. By this time, Jean had recovered, although his eyes looked bloodshot and irritated. He was still searching the ground for an ant, but the tears streaming from his eyes inhibited his ability to locate one.

"Hey, Jean," panted Hoboman, his whole body exhausted. He held the Cologne-in-a-Can in front of his chest with his right hand and rummaged through his pocket with his left. He removed the cigarette lighter and held it at arm's length from the deodorant. Jean's eyes widened as he immediately realised Hoboman's plan. In fairness, it doesn't take much to put two and two together when one of the twos is a lighter and the other is an aerosol can.

"Cool off. Wait … no. Oh, I know! The heat is on!"

The two were awkwardly silent for a beat, until setting Jean on fire availed itself to be the most prudent course of action to offset the tension. With one roll of the ignition wheel, a flame was struck into life. Hoboman squeezed the trigger of the cologne can. A huge stream of fire roared into existence and shot through the ether, heading straight for Jean.

From where Hoboman stood, it was beautiful. The flames danced and licked at his enemy, catching on his highly flammable clothes to spread their wonder even further. Jean, conversely, was having a thoroughly less enjoyable experience. He managed to avoid the brunt of it but was still in contact with the flame long enough for his sleeve to be set alight. In his haste to beat out the fire, Jean threw the splicer onto the ground.

Hoboman dropped the Cologne-in-a-Can the moment the fire started to travel back towards the nozzle. And while he had entirely forgotten *why* he was setting Jean on fire, the gene splicer hitting the pavement distracted him enough to pick it up out of curiosity. Ordinarily, Jean rolling about trying to extinguish lethal flames and screaming would have been even more distracting, but Hoboman had made a lifelong habit of blocking out screams. They were something you quickly got used to when raving ice addicts used your alley as a thoroughfare.

He rolled the splicer over in his hands as he studied it. "What even is a spliff?" he asked himself. Shrugging, he decided the best way to familiarise himself with the device was to stab things with it. He rummaged through the depths of his coat until his hand found the potato from Miss Ettic's compost bin. "Oh yeah, I forgot about this. Might have something to do with my Korsakoff Syndrome." He jabbed the potato with the needle in the gene splicer and the double helix icon flashed, indicating a DNA sample had been extracted again.

By this time, Jean had put out the fire on his sleeve and, once he was sure it would not spontaneously re-combust on him, refocussed his attention on taking down Hoboman. His gut constricted when he saw his precious gene splicer in the hands of his arch-nemesis. "You give that back right now!" he shouted, advancing on our hero. "You have no idea what you are doing, and—"

"Okay."

In a moment of unexpected compliance, Hoboman went to relinquish the splicer to its owner just as Jean went to snatch it back. The needle pierced Jean's skin and the double helix icon vanished. The DNA sample had been injected.

Jean stepped back, confused. It was then he saw the potato in Hoboman's hand. In abject terror, he shook his head wordlessly. How could he have allowed this happen? His stomach clenched (like when you urgently need to go to the bathroom, but someone's taking their time, and you're stuck outside waiting for them to finish). His skin began to ripple. His body began shuddering so violently the onlooking Hoboman was sure Jean was going to explode. Our hero bravely ran and hid in one of the side streets, but not before pocketing the splicer. After all, it could be valuable. Jean's shuddering became flailing until he lost control of his legs, fell to the ground and began to shrink, disappearing among the folds of the fabric of his clothes.

"My God," Hoboman muttered flatly from his hiding place. "I killed him." He fished a notebook and pencil from his pocket, added another stroke to his tally, then stashed them away again.

"You didn't kill me!" accused a faraway voice. The pile of clothes lying in the street shifted and something truly grotesque pulled itself out of Jean's shirt collar: a potato sporting Jean's facial features, with arms and legs made of spindly, sprouting tendrils. "You fool! Have you any idea what you've done to me?"

"I turned you into a potato!"

"You turned me into a potato!"

"Sweet. Actually, no, just a regular one," Hoboman corrected himself. He scooped Jean up and cried, "I've always wanted a talking tater! But my dad always told me Santa never got my letters because the post office burnt down. Every year."

Jean stared down at his disgusting, disgusting tendril hands. "This ... this isn't logical."

"Your mum's not logical," Hoboman cleverly retorted. "Speaking of, I should probably go and tell her she has a potato for a son." He crossed the road and walked back inside Jean's house, where he found Miss Ettic cleaning Jean's belongings out of the basement. "Hey, Missus J! I'm just dropping in to say I'm heading off now, and thanks for the sandwiches."

"No problem," Miss Ettic replied. "Where's Jean, by the way? Not, uh ... dead, is he?"

"He's just here," Hoboman informed her, unfurling his fist to reveal Jean struggling on his palm. "The idiot done turned himself into a potato."

Miss Ettic was unfazed by Jean's disgusting, disgusting transformation. "I was hoping you'd killed him," she admitted, sounding disappointed.

"What?" asked Jean, looking from his mother to Hoboman and back, disbelief clear on his disgusting, disgusting face … and that was even without it being on a potato.

"Nah, he's not worth my time," Hoboman answered, completely ignoring Jean. "Want him back?"

"You can keep him."

"Really? You mean it?"

"Frankly, he was just too much of a moody brat. Running up the electricity. Not paying for food. The kid would just tip the TV over if he didn't like what was on. Real sick stuff. I was getting fed up with it."

"When you say 'it', do you mean Jean or his behaviour?"

"Meh. Po-tay-to, po-tah-to."

"Nice."

"I'm not just something that can be given away!" shrieked Jean. "Why are you talking about me like I'm not even here?"

"You're a really nice lady." Hoboman turned to leave and then reconsidered. "Actually, wait a minute. No, you're not. Why did you think I would kill him?"

"I hoped letting a hobo into my house would lead to him getting brutally murdered. You read about it in the papers all the time."

"Hate to break it to you, *lady*, but just because I'm homeless doesn't immediately make me less sophisticated than everyone else." Hoboman scratched his arse in defiance.

"I won't forget what you've done for me," said Miss Ettic. "I'll make sure everyone knows the sacrifices you made to help me – and the further sacrifice of taking Jean." She touched Hoboman's arm lightly. "You come back here any time now, you hear?"

"Will there be sandwiches?" our hero asked.

"Sure, there will be plenty of *sandwiches*," she winked. "And, please, call me Mary."

Hoboman stared blankly, not quite sure what Miss Ettic was propositioning. "Fair enough."

On that note, he turned and left the basement without another word. Jean didn't say much either: he was struck dumb as *he* knew what his mother had been implying, and sandwiches certainly weren't on the table.

Once in the fresh air, Hoboman squinted at the sky, trying to determine where he was by the position of the stars. As it was daytime, he didn't get very far. "I have no idea where I am," he declared. "And, also, those sandwiches gave me a real gut ache."

Jean repositioned himself in Hoboman's hand and peeked around to examine the skunk tail. His eyes widened when he saw it standing erect. "Oh, no! Hoboman, if my calculations are correct – and they are – the genetics of the skunk I spliced you with will allow you to expel gas."

"Already do that, genius," Hoboman informed his starchy friend.

"But this time it's different! Judging by your size, from now on, whenever you break wind—"

"Fart."

"—you will expel gas at such a high pressure and velocity, you'll …" Jean searched his potato brain for the right description. "Take that Cologne-in-a-Can, for example. When you squeezed the trigger—"

"Oh laaaaaawwwwwdddd," Hoboman moaned, drowning out the rest of Jean's sentence.

Skunk gas shot out of him, launching both hobo and potato into the air and dirtying the sky with smelly green contrails.

Hoboman held Jean out in front of him, using him like the head of an arrow to bear the brunt of the breaking sound barrier. Unintentionally, as he had no real grasp of physics. Once the initial shock had worn off, Hoboman whooped with laughter. "I'm flying! Just like a penguin, my favourite flightless bird!"

Any opportunity for Jean to correct Hoboman was useless, as he was being hit with so much G-force, it was a miracle he was still conscious. Soaring above the city, Hoboman could see everything: the beach; the industrial area; the huge – not to mention, rich – crater formerly known as the Deddrich town square. Our hero wondered what would happen if he spat from so high up. He hawked up a loogie that gained so much momentum as it fell to earth, it crashed into someone's head and smashed them into the sidewalk.

The bird's-eye view assisted Hoboman to locate his alley. All he had to do was clench a little to redirect his skunk spray.[26] Within seconds, the pair touched down. Jean, oxygen-starved and woozy, rolled out of Hoboman's hand and vomited vodka all over the ground. The aroma of liquor was not enough to distract Hoboman from using his hobo senses to detect an intruder. He looked towards the mouth of the alley and saw the man who looked mysteriously like God.

"I have found you again!" God declared, spreading His arms wide. "The prodigal son has returned."

---

[26] He did this instinctually. I honestly can't be bothered to dedicate an entire chapter to how Hoboman learned to control it. Get off my case!

CHAPTER 5

Holey Covenant

"**O**h, my God."

"That's me."

"No way!"

"Yahweh."

"Ah, I see what you did there," Hoboman acknowledged. The two lapsed into an awkward silence. "So … you're that Santa fella, right?"

"I'm actually God," replied the Creator, miffed.

"Ooh, someone has a high opinion of themselves."

God had a hard time not smiting Hoboman where he stood, and instead vented His anger by furling and unfurling His hands into fists. "Let's change the subject. You've changed locations since we last spoke. I couldn't find you."

"Well, duh! Hobos are nomadic," replied Hoboman, rolling his eyes. "Everyone knows that."[27]

"Look, *I* didn't. I've just been hanging around the other alley for days."

---

[27] Many have tried to track the migratory patterns of the nomadic hobo but, to date, none have succeeded. David Attenborough had to stop filming a documentary purely due to lack of material.

"Creepy," Hoboman noted.

"I *know* it's creepy! You should have at least left me a note or something!"

Hoboman cocked his hip sassily to one side and raised an eyebrow. "I can't read, let alone write. Sheesh, if you really *are* God, you don't know much about me. I thought God was supposed to know everything." Before God could even consider a comeback, Hoboman yelped in surprise as the cogs of his mind started whirring.[28] "Wait a minute! What would God want with *me*?"

A knowing smile appeared on God's lips. "You're on the right track now ... even if it took you longer than it should have. I need your help. It's why I've been waiting for you."

"And been creepy in the process."

"Inadvertently."

"But why me? I'm just your average superhero hobo with dazzling good looks, wit beyond measure, and a skunk tail that allows me to excrete noxious gas so fast I can fly. What's so special about me?"

"It all started a very long time ago—"

"How long?"

"How old are you?" God asked.

"Meh," Hoboman shrugged. "All the days just seem to blur together when you don't have a calendar."

"Well, it was when you were an infant."

"How long ago was that?"

"I'm unsure."

"Aren't you supposed to be God?"

---

[28] Actual cogs. Hoboman had crashed a motorbike into a fuel bowser when he was younger. A few cogs became lodged in his head and the doctors were unable to remove them without causing further serious head trauma.

"Thou wouldst do well not to test God."

"Seriously, I feel like you should have at least a *vague* idea of how old I am."

"Look, God is busy too, you know? What do you think I do? Just sit up in Heaven and eat grapes while someone fans me? We have tax up in Heaven, too. It's really frustrating!"

Hoboman suddenly gasped with excitement. "Wait, is this going to be my origin story?"

God nudged some stones on the ground with His sandalled foot. "I thought Chapter One was your origin story? Someone stole your trolley."

"Oh yeah, I should probably start looking for that at some point. But this could be like my *secret* origin story. They do it all the time in comics where they just retcon everything."

"Retcon?" God asked, confusion clearly written on His face.

A blank expression came over Hoboman's face, but different to his other blank expressions. "Retcon: retroactive continuity. The act of altering the previous established continuity of a fictional work."

"But this isn't fiction."

"No."

"And how did you remember all that?"

The blank expression of utter ignorance returned. "Huh? Remember what?"

"You just defined 'retcon,'" God pointed out.

"I don't even remember saying anything." Hoboman scratched his head. "I'm not saying I've been possessed before, but that felt an awful lot like being possessed."

"Wow." More awkward silence. God recovered His train of thought and continued, "Right, I was saying a plan was set in motion many years ago—"

"Sorry, interrupting again."

"What now?"

"Um, well, I was just going to ask what the standard procedure is for flashbacks."

"I'm not sure I quite follow ..."

"Are we going to write in italics? Do I just grab your shoulder or something and everything melts around us like a fever dream? Or do you think we should just stick with the three asterisks in the middle of the page? I mean, we've been using the asterisks when segueing to different characters and time periods but, I mean, it *is* still just us, and time isn't really passing if we're just remembering shit, you follow?"

God scratched an itch on His back and grimaced. "Whatever, man. Just ... whatever floats your boat."

"Bugger it. We'll do the three asterisks."

"Fine," God said in a distinctly passive-aggressive manner. "Can I finish?"

Hoboman thought about it for a moment. "Hmm. Yeah."

"It all started a long time ago." God paused, testing to make sure He could continue uninterrupted. "Actually, you know what? Grab my arm."

"Oh, so it's fine if *you* interrupt yourself, but when I do, I'm the worst person in the world?" Hoboman whinged, even as he grabbed hold of God's shoulder.

"Are you ready for this?" God asked.

"Just give me a minute to—"

* * *

"God!"

"Yes?"

"No, I'm using your name in vain."

"Don't do that!" God scolded.

"Then don't flashback when I'm not ready," our hero bit back, stumbling slightly as he released God's shoulder.

Taking in his surroundings, Hoboman noticed they had flashbacked to a tidy little cottage surrounded by a neatly manicured lawn. They stood outside beneath the night sky. God ushered him closer to the cottage, and they looked in through the windows. Inside, the dwelling was minimally lit by a small lamp, and an unknown number of people sporadically cast their silhouettes as they moved about.

"Where are we?" Hoboman asked, putting his scepticism aside for once.

"One Nowheresville Drive, Classified … New South Wales. As you may or may not be aware, and I'm guessing 'may not' is the case here, the forces of good and evil have been locked in conflict for a very long time. I am the leader of the good—"

"Yeah, maybe."

"—but the forces of evil are governed by the Devil. The Devil is plotting a takeover of Heaven. I need assistance. I can't take him on by myself because that's not the way I roll. Which leads us to this cottage." God gestured to the abode in question. "This is the house of a man whose name is so classified I can only refer to him as 'Mister X'. He's a retired ASIS agent. That's the Australian Secret Intelligence Service, by the way," God added, and Hoboman was satisfied, as he'd been thoroughly prepared to derail the conversation by seeking more clarification. "Mister X and his wife, Missus X, were expecting a child. I had hoped Mister X would teach his child his repertoire of skills at my behest. I believed the child would then be able to assist me in defeating the Devil when the takeover of Heaven began."

"Because they'd have ASIS training and could kick the Devil's tuckus?" Hoboman asked.

"I wouldn't have put it that way … but yes, that was the gist of my plan. Mister X's child would help me, and I would then look upon the family with favour. Unfortunately, as you are about to see, I was not on my own side that day. Or *this* day, technically." God gestured towards an approaching set of headlights.

A battered old Holden Kingswood ute struggled up the immaculate gravel driveway. The motor cut out before it was supposed to, but it seemed to be too much effort to restart it and move it forwards that little bit further, so the driver turned off the headlights and stepped out. Hoboman gasped in surprise when he saw the driver was God – which was odd, given he didn't really care when he saw God on literally any other occasion. This younger God looked no different to the God standing next to him.

Young God kicked the driver's-side tyre and slapped the bonnet. "This is the last time I get Raphael to service this damn thing."[29] Young God went to use the central locking, but nothing happened, much to His disgust.[30] He took a step away from the car and stopped. "I have the strangest feeling I'm being watched."

"That makes a lot more sense now," Old God observed, scratching His bearded chin.

Young God knocked on the door of Mister X's cottage and waited. The people casting the silhouettes froze. It appeared they were consulting about how best to proceed. There was urgent pointing towards the door; violent shaking of heads; more urgent pointing; the throwing up of hands to indicate they were *so* done; and then tentative steps towards the door.

---

[29] Raphael's Garage was notorious for its cheapness in both cost and quality.
[30] Raphael's Garage was also notorious for its employees stealing the batteries from customers' fobs.

"Greetings, my children," Young God said to the couple when they opened the door.

Hoboman baulked when he saw the pair. Even though he had only seen them on the odd occasion he could make the prison visiting hours, he recognised his parents! They were easily identifiable because of their similarity to their son: Sidney Brisbane Mann looked just like Hoboman, but grizzlier and greyer; Adelaide Melbourne Mann (née Perth) looked like her husband but was wearing a dress.

"You're not the cops, are you?" Sidney asked. He narrowed his eyes and held the door only half open so Young God could not get a proper look inside.

"Why, of course not! I am God. And I take it you must be Mister X? May I come in?"

Adelaide stuck her head under Sidney's arm and eyed Young God suspiciously. "He's not the cops, is He?"

"Says He's God," was Sidney's reply.

"But not a cop?"

"Not a cop?"

"Not a cop," confirmed Young God.

Sidney and Adelaide glanced at each other and shrugged. "Well, as long as you're not a cop," Adelaide relented, "you can come in."

Sidney opened the door wide and Young God disappeared inside the cottage. Hoboman turned to Old God in awe. "My father was ASIS? Wow ... I can't believe it! You learn something new every day."

"Your father was *not* ASIS," Old God corrected, shaking His head in embarrassment. "Come on, I'll show you what I mean."

Old God headed towards the wall of Mister X's cottage. Hoboman called, "Dude, you're about to walk right into the side of the house."

"We're only illusions here, Hoboman. This is just a memory, remember?" Old God replied sagely. He continued on His way, promptly smacked His face on the cottage wall and fell over.

"Was that a possum?" Young God could be heard asking from inside.

"That makes a lot more sense now," Old God muttered. "Change of plans, Hoboman. We take the front door instead."

The pair opened the cottage door and entered quickly. To Sidney, Adelaide and Young God, it appeared as though the door had swung open on its own accord. "It must be a draught," Young God smiled, oblivious to the look of panic that flickered across Sidney and Adelaide's faces.

Hoboman watched Young God sit down in an armchair and gesture towards a couch so the lovely couple could be together. It would have been cosy, had it not been for the absolute mess that had been wreaked on the domain. Books had been thrown from ornate shelves and pages carpeted the floor. The lampshade had been knocked askew, casting Sidney and Adelaide in the unforgiving glow of an interviewer's spotlight. To Hoboman, it was obvious that the place was in the midst of being burgled; Young God was not Hoboman.

"Now, as I was saying," Young God continued, "I am God … and I have a proposal."

"You can't propose. She's already taken, mate," Sidney hissed, instinctively grabbing Adelaide and holding her close to him.

"No, no," laughed Young God. "I wasn't talking about her."

"Oh. Well, I'm already taken, too."

"Will you please shut up and listen?" Young God asked, and Sidney shut up and listened. "I would like to request your help, Mister X." Sidney raised an eyebrow at the title, but decided it was a pretty nifty name and didn't say a word in objection. "I have heard you are quite proficient in the art of survival and camouflage."

Sidney puffed out his chest and smiled smugly. "I am somewhat of a legend, if we're being honest here," he said, sticking to his tendency of lying compulsively.

As Young God inspected the cottage more closely, His smile faltered slightly. Drawers were pulled out, their contents strewn across the floor. The room was an absolute mess. Had Young God known what had previously been in the room, He would have noticed all the valuables missing. "I must say, truth be told, I would have thought you would keep the place tidier. It almost looks as though the place has been ransacked."

"What? No!" Adelaide spluttered.

"That is certainly not the case," stuttered Sidney. "You see, it was … that draught. It blew all the earrings, necklaces, bracelets and rings onto her," he added, pointing to his wife.

Young God glanced over at Adelaide and noticed the jewellery for the first time, having at first glance mistaken it for bling. He stared at the pair in front of Him for a moment and then shrugged. "Seems legit. Weirder things have happened. Like all that stuff with Lazarus, am I right? What was that all about? Anyway," He said, leaning in, all conspiratorial, "I would like to make a covenant with you." Young God pointed at Hoboman's parents. "*You* must train your child in the ways in which you are knowledgeable. When he is skilled enough, on his eighteenth birthday, I will take him with me to defeat the Devil, who is planning a dastardly takeover of Heaven. Do this for me, and I will look on you with favour."

As they watched the proceedings from their invisible vantage point, Hoboman leaned towards Old God and whispered, "But you *didn't* come when I was eighteen. Hell, I don't even know how old I am, but I know I'm definitely over eighteen."

Old God shrugged. "There were issues all over the place. I mean, I had so much trouble finding you today, even though I knew who you were. Do you know how long it took me to track you down in the first place? And that was after all the paperwork, because even hostile takeovers have to go through drafts and screenings and stuff, and they never keep to deadlines. Honestly, in the end, I just forgot."

Hoboman nodded and resumed watching his parents talk turkey with Young God. Sidney was asking, "You want to take our child? You're not Welfare, are you?"

"No." Young God seemed to have grown impatient.

"Oh." Sidney looked slightly disheartened to hear this.

Adelaide stood, crossed the room and picked up the papoose with baby Hoboman inside. Instead of a bonnet, Hobaby wore a beanie, fingerless mittens, and a pair of baby socks with holes for his big toes to stick out. Adelaide strapped the papoose on and stared intently at Young God as she asked, "You want to take little Hobart? I could sell him to you if you like? Name your price. I'm negotiable."

"I can't believe your parents tried to sell you to me," Old God whispered to Hoboman. "What were they thinking?"

"I'm more concerned," Hoboman whispered back, "that they thought it was a good idea to take me to the house they were robbing.[31] I mean, what if I'd started bawling? I'd be like a huge alarm. The logistics just don't make sense."

"I can't believe you're trying to sell me your baby," Young God was saying.

"Didn't you do something similar roughly two thousand years ago with that Joseph fella?" Adelaide asked.

"I didn't pay," Young God said in defence. "You're missing the point! I don't want to *buy* your baby, merely borrow him when the

---

[31] Sidney and Adelaide considered it a family outing.

time comes." Young God offered His hand to Sidney and Adelaide. "Do we have an accord?"

"Okay, but only if you spit on it," Adelaide bargained.

She snorted from deep in the back of her throat and spat into her hand. Young God winced as He watched her, then did the same, albeit in a more refined manner. He tried not to retch as He felt the viscous liquid squelch and ooze through His fingers.

"I suppose that settles things," Young God declared, rising to His feet and wiping His soiled hand on His robes. "I'll be back for your child in the future. It was a ... pleasure to meet you Mister X. Missus X. You're not at all what I expected." A second handshake was politely declined when Adelaide offered it in farewell. Sidney's version of farewell was to offer to cut off Hobaby's hands as a bond payment. Hoboman and Old God stepped aside hurriedly as Young God headed towards the door and quickly jumped outside before it swung shut on them.

"I think that will do," Old God said, a sudden urgency in His voice.

"Wait, what's this?" Hoboman asked.

"Nothing. We're done here."

But Hoboman refused to move. He watched Young God walk towards His Kingswood, where He tried the central locking without success and had to insert the key in the door manually. Fuming, Young God hopped inside and tried the key in the ignition, but the car only wheezed. Nothing more.

"For the love of Me, why won't you start?" Young God shouted.

He slammed the steering wheel with the palm of His hand and the bumper fell off. He tried the ignition again, but still the motor failed to roll over. He looked up and saw another car pull into the property and glide down the driveway. Frowning, He squinted through the headlights but couldn't work out who the new arrivals might be. He hoped they weren't guests, as Mister and Missus X's house had appeared quite messy.

The stranger cut the engine to his car, hopped out, and walked around to the passenger side door to assist his heavily pregnant wife. The husband looked at the dim lighting inside the cottage and frowned as if something was wrong. He walked over to the Kingswood and knocked on the window. "Hey, buddy: who are you and what are you doing here?"

Young God wound down His window and smiled. "Hello there, I'm God. I was just leaving, actually. I just made a covenant with Mister X and must be on my way. I hope you aren't planning on visiting. The place is a sty. You know, for someone who is supposed to be rigidly militaristic, Mister X is a lot less disciplined than I thought."

"I hate to break it to you, *pal*, but *I'm* Mister X, and I sure as hell didn't invite you in." He grabbed Young God's shoulder and squeezed it uncomfortably tightly. "Mind telling me what you were doing in there?"

"I swear on my afterlife, I was talking to Mister X and his wife." Young God was beginning to sweat bullets.

"See, the thing is, it looks a bit suspicious when I come back to my house, find the lights on – when I *know* I turned them off – and see a strange car parked in my drive," Mister X pointed out. "Here's how this is going to go down: I'm going to go out back and grab one of my many guns; Missus X is going to go inside and tell me if we've been burgled." The former ASIS agent shouted to his wife without ever lifting his gaze from Young God. "Missus X! Check the house, and if anything is out of place, you let me know."

Young God watched on in horror as Missus X, despite being so heavily pregnant, ran to the cottage with amazing agility. It seemed as though Sidney and Adelaide had left, judging by the fact that Missus X didn't murder anyone.[32] However, she certainly screamed loud enough to let Mister X know everything was not how it was supposed to be.

Mister X leered through the car window. "I'm about to get my gun, mister." And true to his word, he ran behind the cottage to his gun safe out the back.

Young God frantically turned the key in the ignition but, try as He might, the Holden just would not start. "Damn it, go! I'll do anything to make you go!" Almost as if life were a movie, the engine roared. Young God reversed half a revolution so He was facing the way out, slammed the gearstick into first, and trundled down the driveway, nearly stalling as He shifted into second. A bullet blew the driver's side mirror clean off. Freaking out, Young God turned out of the property and onto the road, speeding away before Mister X could give chase.

At this point, Old God extended His arm and gave Hoboman a look to indicate he should grab it. "All right," Hoboman began, as he latched on. "Just make sure we don't teleport halfway through—"

*   *   *

"Stop doing that! Jeez!"

Hoboman released God's arm. He blinked in confusion, then sighed with relief. They had arrived safely back in his alley. But then our hero began to wonder if they had even *left* the alley to begin with? Had he really just been standing in an alley, holding an old man's arm with his eyes glazed over? What should he believe anymore? Was *he* real? Was *life* real?

---

[32] Sidney and Adelaide would have been no match.

"There you have it," Old God said, ignoring Hoboman completely even though he was noticeably spinning out. "I made a covenant with the wrong people ... and now I'm stuck with you. But that's okay. We can make this work. I'm sure of it."

"I don't know about this, God," Hoboman frowned. "I've seen some really trippy stuff today. And now you're saying I basically have to stop the Devil because of a mistake *you* made? I just don't think it's something I'm cut out for."

"Hey! Your parents are the ones who buggered off and made me look like a liar and a thief. You owe me!"

"I think I could really go for a drink right now. I'mma go to Onion Jack's and think this over if that's all good with you."

God pointed at Hoboman and, all of a sudden, a supernatural wind picked up. "I will return once more tonight! And when I do, you will come with me!"

"That is a very real possibility. If I get half as drunk as I intend to, I'll probably be delighted to help. Get a few drinks in me and I'm putty in your hands. And when I say that, I mean if you squeeze me when I have the right amount of air in me, I make farting noises. The guys love it."

"I tell you the truth!" God exclaimed. "This very night, before the rooster crows, you will not deny me three times!"

"Whatever," Hoboman replied. "And also, can you cut that wind out? It's messing up my hair and it takes ages to do."

God hesitated for a moment then lowered His finger. The wind died down instantly. He watched as Hoboman scooped up Jean (who had passed out at the end of the last chapter) and walked around the corner. Hoboman did not even bother to look back; he had much better things to do.

Like, get pissed.

CHAPTER 6

The League of Extraordinary
Not-So-Very-Gentle Men

Thunder rumbled outside, a deep bass succeeding a flash of lightning. Test tubes and beakers trembled in their racks, but the man in the white lab coat tarried not. It was almost maniacal, the state he was in. He danced around the laboratory, pausing only for a moment to read what needed to be added to the mix. His fractional distillation equipment was bubbling away nicely, siphoning only a small amount of fluid into an awaiting flask.

Tonight was the night. Tonight, Doctor David Muter, with his double PhD in Engineering and Biochemistry, minoring in Culinary Technology, would end Western society's addiction to fast food. He wasn't in it for the money or the fame; his reasons were more altruistic than that. The moment the widespread dependence on mass-produced fast food was eliminated, the more attention could be focussed on the food crisis in third-world countries.

He was so confident in his work he had skipped animal testing. Who better to trial this on than himself? Besides, as this was a labour of love, his research was being conducted in his own basement. There was no board of ethics. No one need suffer any negative consequences should his experiment fail, although he was absolutely certain that would not be the case.

The final step in the process was to add the serum to the centrifuge. After separation, the serum would be complete and ready for administration. The centrifuge whirred into life. Just as the machine picked up speed, more thunder rolled in, sounding deeper than before.

Suddenly, a bolt of lightning struck the building. Dave watched, horrified, as it channelled through the wiring, finding the centrifuge and making its way into the serum itself. The tube shattered, the explosion covering Dave in the liquid he had worked so hard to perfect. The breaker short-circuited and the entire laboratory was plunged into semi-darkness.

Bathed only in the light emanating from the dancing blue flames of the Bunsen burner, Dave lay unconscious in a bed of broken glass. The serum soaked deep into his tissue, rewiring his physiology.

When he came to, the first thing he was aware of was something urgent demanding his full attention. It overrode the pain from his pounding head, his shredded skin, his aching bones. A hunger had awoken deep in the pit of his stomach. A hunger that couldn't be ignored. And the thought of sating this black hole with fruit, nuts or vegetables, as he might ordinarily have done, made him feel violently nauseous. In a flash of insight, Dave realised the only cure for this hunger was a *cheeseburger*.

Wait ... a cheeseburger?

Perhaps the lightning had reversed the ion charges and, consequently, reversed the effects of the serum; perhaps Dave had reversed the polarity of the neutron flow; or perhaps, just perhaps, he was stupider than he'd believed. Regardless of the reason, it soon became obvious that the serum had had the opposite effect to what he'd intended. Instead of permanently *removing* cravings for fast food, it *amplified* those cravings. Whereas before he'd been partial only to the occasional burger, now his lust had increased tenfold.

The results of the experiment went on to haunt him for the rest of his life. His hankerings for fast food became unbearable. Time flew by in a blur of condiments and grease. Dave dissociated through most of it, driven only by his desire to inhale the next mouthful. In small moments of clarity, when the ferocious hunger had been subdued, he valiantly tried to resist the fast-food temptation. He took up Buddhism, hoping that if he could reach Enlightenment, achieve Buddhahood, his mind would become a weapon powerful enough to battle the urge to consume. But every time he sat down to meditate, all he could think about was food.

In his rare moments of lucidity, the man Dave caught glimpses of in the mirror was a stranger. Here was someone who had surely been binge-eating for years. But when he consulted the calendar, it had only been a matter of weeks.

Finding it increasingly difficult to walk – so huge was he becoming – Dave spent the last of his savings on the purchase of a mobility scooter. With no money left, he put his mind to trying to become more cost-efficient. This yielded a small victory in his ingenious idea of utilising his engineering background to attach a deep fryer to the scooter and convert the leftover grease from burger-making into fuel. It helped, but it was time to face the facts: his addiction was costing too much money!

Dave thought of himself as a good man at heart. But he was in dire need of money. If he did not want to starve before he could find a cure for his addiction, drastic measures were called for – a course of action that was surely a necessary evil.

It was then that the blackmailing began …

*   *   *

Now, many people made assumptions about Dave based on his appearance. After all, how many doctors with two PhDs did you see wearing Hawaiian shirts? (They were the only clothes that fit his ever-expanding torso.) It meant that whenever he staged a fall, the small businesses he had selected had no idea he was grifting them. For a while, they did anything they could to settle outside of a courtroom for fear their insurance premiums would skyrocket.

But even this wasn't enough. Dave's fast-food expenses far outweighed the meagre scraps he was making from his small-time blackmailing schemes. He had to go bigger! Mega-corporations with millions behind them and a reputation to uphold!

However, word had spread and Dave had acquired a repu-tation. Now, whenever he entered a business premises, he was watched like a hawk. He could not make a move. Any time he attempted to fake a fall, security footage was played back to him by seething franchise owners who blacklisted him from their stores and threatened legal action. So, on Dave went, poor and starving. His ambition, he realised, would soon be his downfall.

Which was why he needed to find this 'Hoboman' character, fast! He was the key. News of Hoboman's feats had spread, and while everyone else marvelled at his mass-slaughtering abilities, Dave had analysed much deeper aspects of the superhero's status and come up with a plan.

Who was Hoboman liable to, he'd pondered? The answer was simple: as a representative of Uptown, any action by Hoboman would constitute an action by local government. Once he found Hoboman, he would challenge him to a fight. But he would do it in such a crafty way, it would look as if Hoboman had started it. And then, when Hoboman attacked …

He'd be able to claim a buttload of compensation from council.

There was something else bothering Dave, though. He'd already made a note of the phenomenon in his diary, in case the unthinkable happened and someone found his body. They had to know why. They had to know he couldn't help himself. *They had to understand he was sick!*

You see, one hot day, when Dave had been trundling along on his scooter on the way to his next score, he'd become aware of the sweat beginning to dampen his forehead, his armpits, his back, behind his knees ... well, just everywhere, really. It had dripped onto his tongue and he'd almost fallen off his scooter in surprise. His sweat tasted like cheeseburgers! Then he'd noticed an aroma. As the sun beat down on him, pinkening his skin, he realised he could smell burgers cooking.

It made sense, he supposed. After all, cheeseburgers were the only thing in his diet. But to start smelling and tasting like one himself? What if his brain could not differentiate what was man and what was meat anymore? What if he ... *tried to eat himself?*

* * *

Many people say Americans are too patriotic for their own good. Well, it's actually me that says that, although I'm sure many would agree. They're always going on about their guns and their bald eagle business. But stop and consider for a moment that there are, in fact, people out there who are incredibly patriotic and *not* 'Murican.

Let that sink in.

Onion Jack was, and to this day still is, a man unfortunate enough to be the victim of patriotic British parents. The Jacks, after the birth of their son, opted to give him a name representative of their zealous love of their country, to remind people of all things tea and inclement weather. They called him 'Union'. Sadly, however, a little bit of ink was accidentally smudged on his birth certificate and 'Union' became 'Onion'. Belittled by everyone as he grew up, by the time he was a young man he was left with only one alternative: move to Australia and open up a bar to quench the collective thirsts of the derelicts of Uptown society. To be fair, the drunks belittled Jack, too, but no one bothered to listen to *their* opinions.

Onion Jack's was Hoboman's favourite watering hole, purely due to the fact Jack kept selling alcohol to his patrons despite them being notably intoxicated. Sure, it may have been a *little* illegal, but ... money was money. Jack was happy. The alcoholics were happy. (Although this was only temporary, brought on as it was by excessive alcohol consumption and the fact they were only drinking to fill the void in their otherwise meaningless lives.) And when they finally exceeded their limits and passed out, they would often leave unfinished drinks ripe for the picking. What more could a Hoboman want?

Through careful deliberation and research, Dave had discovered Hoboman's love for the place. The desperate man drove his mobility scooter in front of our hero as he approached the pub, blocking the path between the hobo and the door.

"I knew you would be here, Hoboman."

Unfazed, Hoboman shrugged at the mad scientist in the ill-fitting XXXXL Hawaiian shirt. "It's no secret. A lot of people would know if they bothered to check in with me." A single tear trickled down his cheek.

"Hoboman, you may not know it yet, but I am your sworn enemy." (Hoboman knew now!) "I challenge you to fisticuffs."

"Mate, you've had too much to drink. You don't know what you're talking about. Go home, sober up, and consider yourself lucky I didn't pummel you."

Considering himself *unlucky* that Hoboman hadn't pummelled him, Dave argued, "I haven't had anything to drink! Besides, I rarely drink. I eat cheeseburgers exclusively. The closest I might be to ingesting fluids would be the grease from the meat."

"I rarely eat and even I know that's unhealthy," Hoboman replied with a pained grimace.

"I agree," Dave agreed. "My digestive system isn't what it used to be. It takes a bit of time to work everything along ... if you know what I mean. I have to let it gestate."

"Too much information. But I'm not fighting you."

"Why? You discriminating against me? You giving me the judges? Is it because I'm fat?"

"Me? Discriminate?" Hoboman had to chuckle. "Look, mate, I'm homeless. People in glass houses, am I right? Besides, what did I ever do to you?"

"That's not important! Dare you accept my challenge?" Dave threw down the gauntlet.

"Okay, so you want me to skip the 'why'. How?"

"How what?"

"How do you expect to fight me?" Hoboman sized up Dave, who was literally oozing over the sides of the scooter. And I mean *literally*, as Dave's addiction to cheeseburgers was so great, the amount of energy he consumed caused him to literally gain weight as they spoke.

"Just because I'm disabled doesn't mean you should treat me differently."

"I'm not going to punch someone on a mobility scooter, no matter how disabled they are. A previous court ruling has seen to that."

Hoboman shook his head and walked around the scooter, inspecting the vehicle as he circled it, so he was now standing between Dave and the pub. He studied the contraption on the back that smelled like a deep fryer. He paid particular attention to what must be the grease trap and noted how a tube gravity-fed the hot oil into the fuel tank. "Still think it would be too easy. I mean, can you even move out of your seat?"

"What?" blustered Dave, offended. Just because he was fat didn't mean he'd stopped having feelings. "Of course I can move. See?"

Dave leaned over to one side, balancing precariously as his tremendous girth shifted his centre of balance. All Hoboman had to do was push ever so slightly, but the extra bit of momentum caused Dave to teeter on the edge. Shrieking with terror – as he was acutely aware of the phrase, 'the bigger you are, the harder you fall' – Dave tried to grip the scooter's chassis to remain stable. All he succeeded in doing was bringing it with him. The deep fryer lurched and was ripped from its brackets, crashing onto the concrete. The tube filled with hot cheeseburger grease burst out of its socket and sprayed its contents all over Dave like a spasmodic bird feeding its young.

Dave held his arms up to resist the burning grease but, like, it was burning grease, and you can't just hide from it.

"Oh, please, it can't end like this!"

The hot oil pooled under him, and he began to blister as he was basted like a tom turkey. "God, I smell so *good*. I don't think I can control myself." His hand moved in front of his mouth and a look of desire mixed with revulsion was plain on his face. Then, the auto-cannibalism began.

Hoboman nonchalantly turned his back on the man eating himself in a puddle of grease. He burst through the saloon doors of Onion Jack's, with Jean tucked into his pocket, at precisely six o'clock – Happy Hour, according to the chalkboard mounted on the bar. Our hero immediately swiped a half-finished schooner of beer from a man in too much of a stupor to notice. He chose a stool at the bar and perched himself on it, squeezing in between two men.

"Cheerio, 'Oboman," Jack said, tipping him a wink.

"Evening, Jack," Hoboman replied, sculling his beer and placing the glass upside-down on the counter, completely ignoring Jack's displeasure at this action. "How's business?"

"Oh, you know 'ow i' is," the young cockney grinned. "Never a dull momen' surrounded by all these lively spiri's."

"Yakov Smirnoff!" Hoboman shouted. "Spirits? In here?" Being of Irish descent, Hoboman was thoroughly unnerved by the thought of the supernatural. Often, when drunk, he feared the banshees were after him. Banshees, according to the Irish folklore he had been 'raised' on, lived in wheelie bins and drank the dregs from discarded liquor bottles. They howled, not because of impending death as other 'reliable' sources might have you believe, but because of their terrible hangovers.

"No, no, mate, jus' a joke is all. You know ... spiri's ... an' alcohol?"

Hoboman nodded, pretending he understood. "I see. Very clever. You want a nickel's worth of free advice? Jokes aren't as funny when you have to explain them. Now, I'll have that nickel, seeing as the advice was free." Our hero then remembered he had a guest stuffed in his pocket and placed Jean on the counter. "Hey, do you reckon you would have a chair for my friend?"

Onion Jack brought a high chair over for Jean, and Hoboman nestled him in the seat, nice and snug. It was shifted close enough so Jean could slump over the bar and sigh despondently like every other person in the hotel. "A shot of whiskey," he demanded.

"Might wanna watch 'ow much ya 'ave," Jack observed, placing a shot glass in front of Jean, which was half as tall as the potato man. He proceeded to fill it, explaining, "Size ya are now, tha's prob'ly a whole bottle's worf. Kill ya in a secon.'"

"You're not the boss of me," grumped Jean. He clutched the shot glass in both of his disgusting, disgusting hands and tilted it towards him.

"Hey, yeah, you can die lots of ways now, huh?" Hoboman's face lit up as he contemplated this. "I mean, you could be roasted or baked."

"They could cut me up and fry me as chips," Jean mumbled into his drink.

"Bangers an' mash," suggested Jack.

"Boil you; mash you; stick you in a stew. Potato bake, that's another one," Hoboman added as he nicked the drink of someone who had momentarily left to go to the toilet.

The man on Hoboman's left tore his attention away from the wall-mounted TV to scrutinise Hoboman and Jean. The stranger shifted in his seat so he had a better view and continued to stare. Hoboman, driven solely by paternal instinct and in no way by the greed of wanting to keep possession of the world's only known human-potato hybrid, dragged Jean closer to him. Jean, who was already halfway through his shot and silly as a square wheel, barely even registered he'd been moved.

"Moight Oi just say," said the stranger with an Irish accent, in case that wasn't obvious, "Oi've lived in Oireland for the better part of me life, and not once have Oi seen a potato loike that before. Is it aloive?"

"I'm sorry, my mother taught me never to talk to strangers," Hoboman said snippily. He stared straight ahead, but continually glanced back out of the corner of his eye, so much so it seemed he had developed a twitch.

"How about if Oi were to introduce meself?" The Irish stranger extended a hand and said, "Seamus Mann."

Hoboman looked the stranger up and down. "Middle name?" he asked.

Seamus seemed taken aback. "Hagan."

"IRA?" queried Hoboman.

"What?" Seamus spluttered. "No! Why would ya even—?"

"IRA. Got it. So … Seamus Hagan Mann? Shmann? IRA. IRA Shmann? I-R-A-S-H Mann?" Hoboman toyed with the name. He toyed with the spelling. He toyed with the accent in which the stranger had said it. "Irishman!" he exclaimed, causing Flaming Eddie to spontaneously combust over in the corner.

"Ya pull a muscle with that there stretch, did ya?"

"Who are you then?" Hoboman challenged. "Another super-villain trying to kill me? Because the last guy who attacked me didn't last very long, I can tell you. Or are you just a wannabe trying to horn in on my turf? He also didn't last long."

"What the hell are ya on about?" Irishman asked, as polite a response as could be expected from an Irishman.

"Hey, your last name is Mann," Hoboman observed, having already forgotten the deep enmity running between them. "My last name is Mann, too! I wonder if we're related."[33]

"Oi don't think so," Irishman replied. "Not unless yer ancestors come from Ireland."

Hoboman's eyes lit up. "Hey, they did! My ancestors came over here on the First Fleet. They weren't documented that well, though."

---

[33] Hoboman's logic dictated that if people shared a surname, they were related. It was for this reason he had never picked a fight with a Smith, unlike that silly Chris Rock.

Hoboman's ancestors had earned a name for themselves through stealing. After fleeing Ireland to escape their debtors, they were arrested in England. Their list of crimes was so great they were to be sentenced to death. As luck would have it for the Mann clan, the orders for their execution were stolen. Instead, they were put aboard the HMS *Unstealable*, the twelfth ship of the First Fleet. The day before the fleet was to set sail, the Unstealable was untethered in what police deemed 'suspicious circumstances'. The Manns wound up in Australia, quite by chance, after the Mann responsible for steering the ship crashed into a reef while intoxicated on stolen rum.

"Oh … roight." It became crystal clear to Irishman, having heard his family recount stories with looks of utter disdain, that Hoboman was indeed a long-lost relative from the side of the family no one liked to talk about, except as cautionary tales of how life could go wrong if they made poor choices.

"I think we should celebrate this occasion by you buying me a drink," Hoboman declared, sitting up straighter and patting the bar eagerly.

While Irishman was not sold on this idea, he obliged, even offering to buy Jean a shot of vodka. Jean fixed Irishman with a sour look and slurred that vodka was basically the equivalent of his blood now. Or his vomit. He couldn't quite remember.

"Can Oi have a look at the little potato man now?"

Hoboman clasped Irishman's shoulder and sipped his drink. "Well, we *are* basically brothers now."

"No. We're not."

Unheeding, Hoboman told his new brother, "You can take a look at him until the cows come home."[34]

---

[34] 9pm.

Irishman picked up Jean, who immediately began to struggle, reaching out with his disgusting, disgusting hands to try and reach his shot glass. "Put me down," he slurred. Jean balled one of his disgusting, disgusting hands into a fist and shook it at the bar, too drunk to actually see Irishman, and simply threatening the air in what he thought was his general vicinity.

"He's an agoile little feller," Irishman noted, watching Jean's disgusting, disgusting arms and legs flail wildly. "He'd make a grand little dancer. Oi'd pay to watch him jig all up and down the bar."

Jack paused midway through polishing a glass. "Now there's an idea, guv. Oi, 'Oboman, 'ow much for Mista Pota'o 'Ead?"

"How dare you be so degrading?" bristled Hoboman. "Mister Potato Head cannot be bought!"

"Ya sure? Cos 'e can 'ave free accommodation in the pota'o drawer if 'e wants. 'E can work for 'is meals, an' I'll even give 'im a nice li'l top 'at an' all."

"I'll think about it," relented Hoboman, scratching his head. "But only if I get a top hat, too."

"Don't I get a say in this?" shouted Jean. "Why are you talking about me like I'm not here? I'm not an animal!"

"Correct. You are a potato," Hoboman clarified.

Jean promptly fell into a silent, hopeless stupor. He downed the rest of the whiskey in his shot glass, eventuating in him blacking out.

"Come to think of it, Jack, you can't have Jean," Hoboman said suddenly. "The kid is essentially a walking, talking distillery. And the talking I could do without, but he's a distillery nonetheless."

"'Ow abou' a down payment?" Jack suggested. He rifled through some bottles on the shelves and located a silver flask.

Hoboman accepted the flask with a smile of delight, internally considering how much it would fetch on the black market. He swished it around and heard liquid inside. "What's in it?"

"Chekov's vodka," Jack explained. "Alcohol *so* strong, mere mor'als dare no' touch it. On'y those wif tolerance bred in'o 'em would even try. Being Bri'ish, I'm ou' of the runnin'. The Russians and the Irish, bu'? Fair game."

As Hoboman was not the sort of person to let strangers take his alcohol, he solemnly vowed, "I'll be very careful."

"So ... can I 'ave the pota'o man now?"

"Ease up, mate," Hoboman soothed. "I'll get him back here before his performance. Stress less."

Before Jack could argue, the stranger on Hoboman's right gestured to the television. "Turn the volume up," he growled in a Southern American accent.

Jack obliged, highlighting the conclusion of Channel 4 Shadowing News.

"—soya-based baby formula prices are continuing to rise, currently exceeding the street price of pure cocaine," Gabriel Messenger was saying. "Recapping tonight's top stories, local superhero, Hoboman, decimated the population of Deddrich when he allowed a train to fall onto the assembled citizens. Scholars say a disaster like this was bound to happen, as 'Deddrich' is actually Welsh for 'wealthy and deceased'. Prior to Hoboman's intervention, they were wealthy. Now, they are quite dead.

"And a Member of Parliament has found himself in hot water after threatening to euthanise a grizzly bear if it does not leave the country ... before arresting it for possession of illicit substances, ensuring it *cannot*. Check our website to find out which Member of Parliament. Spoiler: it doesn't matter, they're all the same. For now, I'm Gabriel Messenger. This has been Channel 4 Shadowing News."

At the mention of the grizzly bear, the Southern man groaned loudly and took a swig from the large porcelain jug he was drinking from, on which 'XXXX' had been scribbled in permanent marker. "Why, Trout? You don't even do maple!" Distraught, the Southern man swiped blindly with his arm and knocked a bowl of nuts to the ground, much to Hoboman's distress. "I jus' can't bear it!"

Hoboman spun round on his stool to face the Southerner and snorted. "That's funny! You said 'bear', and it's a grizzly!" The Southern man wailed even louder. "Well, *I* thought it was quite humorous, thank you very much." But there was something about the musical way the man cried that made Hoboman stop and take notice. He felt captivated. Moved. "Say, do I know you?"

"The name's Bubba," the Southern man answered, using his flannelette sleeve to wipe away the alcohol running down his chin. "Justin Bubba ..."

"Oh, my God!" Hoboman squealed like a schoolgirl. "Lead singer of Bubba and the Jugettes![35] Before you went solo, of course." By this point, Hoboman was bouncing up and down on his seat, clapping his hands repeatedly.

Bubba nodded in acknowledgement. "That's me. 'Cept my solo career ain't workin' out. Only three noobs bought ma album. And one of 'em did it jus' to break it."

"I was one of them!" gushed Hoboman. "Not to break it, though. Can you sign my copy for me?"

"Naw, I can't write."

---

[35] Bubba and the Jugettes consisted of Justin Bubba as the lead singer/banjo player, Trout the Grizzly as backup singer/jug blower, Gay Gayle on the washboard, Flam Bam Buoyant playing the spoons, and Grandmumma Bubba, who took out her false teeth and clacked them like castanets.

"I can't read! We should totally be partners!"

Bubba slammed his jug on the bar and eyed Hoboman suspiciously. "You ain't gettin' all queer on me, are ya?"

"No. I just mean we should team up in fighting crime … or dabbling in it. I don't really mind."

Bubba considered the proposal for a moment and then took a swig from his jug. "Maybuh."

As Bubba supped on his drink, Hoboman stared at him in awed silence until he could no longer contain himself. "I'm sorry. I bet you get this all the time, but can I please touch your mullet?"

"S'pose so," Bubba replied.

Reaching out tentatively with shaking fingers, Hoboman grabbed some blonde hair and began stroking it. "I can't believe how soft it is," he marvelled, retracting his hand and staring at Bubba in wonderment.

"I make sure I condition it every night. Not a lotta people know, the secret ta smooth hair comes from nourishin' the roots. A lot like a tree."

"You don't say?" Our hero stared at his idol, mesmerised.

The pair lapsed into silence and Hoboman took the opportunity to look around the bar. Sitting at a table all by himself was a man who, by all accounts, was completely average. Average height, weight, build, face, haircut, personality … This average man, who we will simply call 'Tim', was staring forlornly at the schooner of beer in front of him. Hoboman had seen this look on a lot of people before, and, by golly, he would not let it happen to anyone again.

"Don't worry, guys! I got this," Hoboman told his two new comrades, neither of whom knew what he was talking about. They turned to look at Tim as Hoboman said, "The thing with being a superhero is it's not all about stopping supervillains; it's the little things, too."

Our hero made his way over to Tim's table and took a seat. "Hey, man. I know what you're thinking."

Tim looked up and flinched, not having noticed the hobo until now. "You what?" he asked, a plea of desperation clear in his average voice.

"You're looking for an escape. Take it from me: it isn't there." Hoboman's face was full of compassion. "Do you have a family?"

"A wife."

"Kids?"

"Yeah."

"Go home to your wife and kids. Live an above-average life. Enjoy every moment you have with them. And never touch alcohol when you're in a state like this. Do you trust me?"

Tim looked at the wise hobo, realised Hoboman only wanted the best for him, and nodded. "I trust you. I don't know what I was thinking coming here. I'll be forever thankful for the advice." He pushed his chair out, took one last, long look at the schooner and left, disgusted at the drink and disgusted in himself.

Hoboman watched as the saloon doors clattered open and closed then became still again before swiping the schooner. "Sweet. Free beer: the best kind!" His job done, he gulped some down and reclaimed his seat between Irishman and Bubba. "Not all heroes wear capes. But this one does."

"Did I hear ya say yer a superhero?" Bubba asked.

"Sure did," said Hoboman.

"And you weren't just talkin' outta yer tuckus?"

"Not this time."

"Well, lookee here. Trout is one of ma closes' friends. I need ta help him."

"Yeah. What's the story? From all the promos, Trout never struck me as the criminal type."

Bubba looked off into the distance, his eyes clouding. "It all started earlier this mornin' ..."

* * *

The luxury jet touched down at Uptown City International just as one of the only two passengers aboard vomited violently into a brown paper bag he'd brought along for this very eventuality. (There were vomit bags on the plane, but Bubba was a suspicious man. He despised things that were foreign to him, especially foreigners.) The other passenger, a massive grizzly bear, helpfully batted Bubba's back.

"Jus' wait til we get out, Trout," said Bubba.[36] "We're gonna be swamped by all the fans comin' out to see me."

Trout hollered in what seemed like agreement – 'seemed' because Bubba couldn't speak bear and could only assume that was what his companion meant. Trout kept pawing agitatedly at his seatbelt buckle. He turned to Bubba and growled something that could quite possibly have meant, "I say, I can't wait for this trip to end so I can unbuckle this restraining mechanism." He could also have been saying, "I'm a bear. What am I doing on board a plane?" Then again, he may have just been growling.

"Ease up, pardner," consoled Bubba, before vomiting heavily into another bag. "Flight's over."

Trout growled once more, seemingly expressing: "I am quite aware of this fact. Alas, it does little to alleviate the stress I am under." He could also have been saying, "What did you say? I'm a

---

[36] Who was no longer vomiting, otherwise it would have sounded like, "Jusbleargherarghohgodgitout".

bear and don't speak human." Then again, he may have just been growling.

Bubba leaned over and unbuckled Trout, who stood up and brushed his fur with unexpected finesse. Bubba unbuckled himself, stood up and stretched. Peeking out the plane window, he saw a crowd of hundreds, maybe even as many as a thousand, eagerly anticipating his arrival on the tarmac. "Justin! Justin! Justin!"

"This is it," Bubba said, combing back his mullet and heading for the exit. Usually, the air stewards would offer their 'thank you' outro as the passengers alighted, but the huge grizzly bear was a little too intimidating, and they were currently hiding in a refreshment trolley. Bubba exhaled, shook his hands to expend some nervous energy, smiled his most endearing smile, and stepped out onto the airstairs.

"OhmyGodJustinIloveyou!" screamed someone in the crowd, which started off the rest. Random phrases like, "I love your music!" and "He looks different!" were being bandied about. When the crowd began paying attention to what the others were saying, their enthusiasm dwindled.

"You're not Justin!" someone shouted, and a small child burst into tears.

"Yeah, I am," Bubba replied. "Justin Bubba."

The crowd was silent. This was a huge mistake, indeed. One by one, the fans realised they had gotten their hopes up to no avail, and their favourite singer with an eerily similar name was not on this plane. Teenagers had to be escorted off the tarmac, some by police for wanting to start brawls over this outrage, the rest by ambulance as they fainted from the shock.

Eventually, only one man stood there, clutching a CD. He looked up to the top of the stairs where Bubba stood. "Are you

Justin Bubba? Formerly of Bubba and the Jugettes until you decided to go solo?"

"Why yes, I certainly am," Bubba confirmed with pride.

"And your first solo album was 'Gator Ate Ma Baby'?"

"It certainly was."

The man proceeded to throw his copy of 'Gator Ate Ma Baby' to the ground and stomp on it until the disc was in as many pieces as Bubba's heart. "I hate you!" the man declared, before flipping Bubba off and walking away after the rest of the crowd.

Trout awkwardly patted Bubba's back, nearly knocking him down the stairs. He grumbled something that may have been, "Every rose has its thorn, Justin. Things will be looking up from here on out." He could also have been saying, "Out of my way, as I am a bear and need to amble in wide open spaces." Then again, he may just have been growling.

When they finally stepped onto the tarmac, a camera flashed brightly, causing Bubba to flinch and Trout to shield his eyes.[37] After his eyes had readjusted, Bubba scoped out the scene and saw the owner of the camera, a reporter in sunglasses and a beret, standing next to a ruddy-complexioned politician in a suit and an Akubra.

"Justin Bubba?" the rootin' tootin' politician asked, although Bubba had a fair idea he already knew the answer. Bubba nodded in the affirmative, and the politician straightened the lapels of his suit. "Mister Justin Quentin Bubba, I am a Member of Parliament."

"Which one?"

"It doesn't matter, we're all the same. You really thought you'd get away with it, didn't you?"

---

[37] And probably swear in bear speak.

"Pardon me?" Bubba blinked politely.

"Bringing a bear into our fine nation without actually getting the proper certification and proper permits required. Really?" The MP 'tsked' disappointedly, playing it up for the reporter. "Too bad Papa Razzie here found out about your appointment with the grizzly groomer."

Papa Razzie lowered his sunglasses and waggled his eyebrows like a complete creep. Bubba and Trout looked at each other and shrugged.

"Grizzly groomer?" Bubba muttered to Trout, who had absolutely no flipping idea what this was about as he had visited the groomer a fortnight ago and his fur was immaculate.

The MP kept going. "Now, Mister Bubba, you are going to have to take your bear back to Alabama, or we're going to have to euthanise him."

"*What?*"

"You've now got about fifty hours left to remove the bear. You can put him on the same charter jet you flew out on and fly him back home."

While Bubba thought this was a bit extreme, he was about to acquiesce to the MP's demands when the plane's door closed, and it taxied off and flew away.

"There is a process if you want to bring animals in," the MP continued. "You get the permits, he goes into quarantine, and then you can have him. But if we start letting pop stars, even though they've won the award for Sexiest Mullet twice, come into our nation, then why don't we just break the laws for everybody? It's time Trout buggered off back to the United States ..." He went to walk off before adding, "And, after that, I don't expect to be invited to the opening concert of your tour."

Suddenly, from out of nowhere, the Uptown Police Department showed up and Bubba watched in horror as an unnecessary number of officers grabbed Trout, put him in a headlock, then kicked his knee for no good reason. Bubba screamed for Trout. He tried begging the MP to show mercy, but the MP just stood there, unmoved.

"What the hell is *this?*" one of the officers asked, reaching into one of Trout's pockets and pulling out a jiffy bag of maple leaf clippings.

Trout roared loudly, as if to say: "Gentlemen. This. Is. Democracy. Manifest!" He could also have been saying, "It's for my glaucoma!" Then again, he may just have been growling.

"What are ya doin' with Trout?" Bubba screamed.

"He is being arrested for possession of illicit substances," declared one Sergeant Bolbusta. "Anything he says can and will be used in a court of law, and—"

"How'n the hell am I meant to get him outta the country?"

The MP, with his hands held behind his back, stared at Bubba impassively. "That, Mister Bubba, is something you should have thought of before bringing an uncertified animal into this fine country. Good day."

Prevented from chasing after Trout by a wall of police officers, Bubba sank to his knees, powerless. After Trout had been stowed in the back of a paddy wagon and the officers had high tailed their hostage out of the airport, the police presence dispersed. Bubba sat on the tarmac, defeated, in as many pieces as the number of cop's teeth he vowed he would eventually shatter.

* * *

"Trout was the on'y one what stuck by me when I left the Jugettes."

"Why was that, may I ask?" Hoboman very well intended to ask, whether he was allowed to or not.

"He's a frenly bear."

"I meant, why did you leave the Jugettes?"

Bubba shook his head. "Turns out one of ma band members was a big ol' queerosexual. Flam Bam Buoyant. Who woulda thought?"

"Not me, that's for sure," admitted Hoboman. "Definitely would have suspected Gay Gayle."

"Naw, that's jus' a joke we all had, on accoun' of Gayle bein' so ornery. 'Gay' as in 'happy', y'know?"

"Wow, so much drama in the Jugettes that was never mentioned in the popular media."

"It was actually all over the news."

"Yeah, well, I don't have a TV and I can't read newspapers and magazines, so cut me some slack."

"Don't have a radio?"

"Out of batteries."

"Anyways," Bubba redirected, "I was wonderin' if yer superhero bizness happen'd ta involve any vigilante justice? Would ya be willin' ta break an innocent bear outta prison?"

"I wouldn't go as far as saying 'justice' is an important factor, but vigilantism is fine. Isn't helping the innocent the main point about being a superhero ... besides the free stuff? You draw up a game plan, I'll supply the Hobomanpower to pull it off."

"What about revenge?" Irishman whispered, staring down at his empty shot glass, though his mind was miles away.

"Eh?" Hoboman turned to see just what silly mumbo-jumbo Irishman was spouting this time.

"Oi said, what about revenge?"

"What *about* revenge?" queried Hoboman. "Do I partake?" Hoboman thought about it. "I guess I'm always up for trying new things."

"Oi want to kill the Uptown Mafia." Irishman did not meet Hoboman's eyes. He didn't have to. There was pure venom in his tone.

"Just on a whim? Or have they done something to you?"

* * *

Irishman woke from his dream of chasing a leprechaun for his lucky charms, disturbed by strange voices outside the house. His wife lay in bed, oblivious, having the same dream but being altogether more successful in her venture, given she continued to sleep. Irishman cocked his head to the side to hear better.

"Sorry for inneruptin' ya plans, Godfadda," apologised a man with an Italian-Australian accent.

"Sergio," began the man who was evidently 'the Godfather'. "You come to me on the day of my daughter's debutante ball to ask for help burning down a man's crops."

"Well ... you was the one what told us, boss."

"I'm aware of this. I was simply stating facts. In actuality, if you refer to my previous piece of dialogue, there was no question mark used."

Sergio was silent. "... I don't follow. But I gotta say, I'm lovin' dis flametrower."

Irishman's heart was hammering away. Was this the *Mafia?* Planning to burn *his* crops? He sprang out of bed and began to get dressed in order to confront them; it would be impolite to do so naked. First, the black slacks.

"Sergio, please pronounce it properly," the Godfather could be heard saying.

"What? Flametrower?"

White button-up shirt.

"Flame*th*rower."

Bottle-green vest.

"Dat's what I said. Flametrower."

Shamrock cufflinks.

"You're missing the '*th*.'"

Lime-green bowler hat.

"Don, whadda ya mean?"

Why did he have so many accoutrements?

"Fogedda 'bout it."

Pulling on his Irish river-dancing shoes, Irishman ran outside to challenge the pair. "What the feck are you lot doing on me property?" he exclaimed.

"I take it you are the owner," the Godfather replied. "I have unfortunate news for you, my friend. Your potato crops are bad for business. We are here to raze them to the ground."

"You can't do this!" Irishman challenged.

"We can," rebutted the Godfather. "And we *will*."

"Besides," interrupted Sergio, "you gonna argue wit' me and my flame*th*rower?"

"I appreciate you accommodating my high grammatical standards," the Godfather thanked him with a small smile.

"What did Oi do to you?" asked Irishman.

"It could have happened to anyone. It's simply bad luck, my Celtic chum."

"Shoulda said 'luck a da Irish', boss," Sergio quipped.

"Indeed, I should have. Alas, I fear the opportunity has escaped," the Godfather sighed.

"Did Oi step on the Mafia's toes? Are me potatoes in direct competition with ya?"

The Godfather spread his arms. "It's nothin' personal. I just cannot have these potatoes leavin' this property, *capiche?*" Deciding this was most certainly capiche, the Godfather turned to Sergio, nodded, and instructed, "If you please."

Irishman could do nothing to stop Sergio squeezing the trigger of the weapon, releasing the unyielding power of a dragon's breath upon his crops. The fire danced before Irishman's eyes, spreading from plant to plant without a care. The beautiful smell of roast potatoes filled the air, but the scent was foul in Irishman's nostrils, doing little to bolster his spirits.

The three simply stood there and spectated the destruction, as Irishman realised there was little that could be done in the way of intervention. "Sergio, enough!" declared the Godfather. "I believe we're done here."

The Godfather's lackey dutifully relented, easing his finger off the trigger and wiping sweat from his eyes. Without even a second glance at Irishman, the pair wandered off into the distance, having parked their 1928 Cadillac close to the highway so as not to end up bogged in the black soil.

So paralysed with shock and disbelief was Irishman he simply let them pass. His livelihood was gone! Reduced to a smouldering field of embers. When the flames eventually died down, he somehow managed to move his leaden legs and stumbled through the paddock. His hands raked through the ash. There was nothing left … until suddenly his fingers brushed a potato that had miraculously survived the inferno.

But it wasn't to remain intact for long.

Determinedly, Irishman headed back to his house in search of a knife and a zip-lock bag. He knew what he was about to do was barbaric – sickening to all those of Irish heritage. Such mutilation, especially when no one was going to eat the potato, was abhorrent. It was like killing for sport.

But he had to send a message. A message that the Godfather would understand.

* * *

Irishman was silent for a moment and Hoboman could see tears glistening in his eyes like a big sissy girl. "I lost me woife and daughter," he finished.

Hoboman, in an uncharacteristic act of commiseration, placed a comforting hand on Irishman's back. "Cheer up, mate," he soothed. "They'll be in the last place you look."

Unsure if he had, in fact, heard what he thought he had, Irishman stuttered, "Wh-what?"

The endearing smile still plastered across his stupid face, Hoboman repeated, "The last place you look. You'll find them there."

"Fun fact," Bubba interjected. "Reason they say that is on accoun' of once you find what yer lookin' for, there ain't no need to keep lookin', so that's the last place ya look."

"No," Hoboman boomed. "Really?"

"I swear on the li'l baby Jesus Hisself."

"Far out."

"Oi didn't *misplace* me family," hissed Irishman. "The Uptown Mafia came through me farm and torched all me potato crops. Me woife and daughter … they had nothing. They starved to death, all because of the Mafia." Irishman looked up and glared fiercely at Hoboman. "Oi need to avenge them!"

"The Mafia or your family?"

"Me family! Why would Oi want to avenge the feckin' Mafia after they killed me woife and only child?"

"Hmm, notice you didn't say 'only wife' like you said 'only child'. Might have something to do with it. Do you have more than one wife?"

"No! Besoides, I hear they whack people."

"Your only wife and only child?"

"The feckin' Mafia!"

Hoboman was confused. "What? So ... they, like, hit people?"

"No! 'Whack' as in 'kill'. Jaysus, don't you know anyting?"

"That's horrible."

"Oi know!"

"Then why did you say it?"

"Say what?"

"You asked if I know anything. I know lots of things. It's people like you, who make me feel dumb, that are the real villains here!" Hoboman ran his finger along the rim of his schooner. Suddenly, he plucked right back up. "But I'm more than willing to take on a criminal syndicate."

"They deserve everyting that comes their way."

"Whatevs. I just like fighting people." Hoboman stood up and said, "I hope you are all aware I view these as side quests for a later date."

"Momen' ya ready ta take on the pigs," Bubba said, "you jus' holler and ol' Bubba'll come a-runnin.'"

Hoboman nodded, downed the rest of his beer, and scooped up Jean who was snoring loudly on top of the bar. He bade goodbye to Onion Jack and his two new friends and headed for the saloon doors. Before he left, he turned and said to Irishman, "You say you're a farmer. Where are your overalls, straw hat and stalk of wheat?"

"Yer stereotoiyping," Irishman informed him. "Stereotoiypes are wrong."

"Woo-ee, you tell 'em, pardner!" Bubba hollered, blasting a round from his shotgun into the air.

Hoboman stepped outside and almost tripped on an overlarge skeleton lying in a puddle of grease. "If there's one thing that Dave fellow knew," Hoboman said to himself, "it was his way around bones. That is the cleanest stripping of meat I have ever seen. Byootiful."

He heard the saloon doors swing behind him and Flaming Eddie stumbled out, his clothes smoking lightly. He staggered, straightened up, saw the mobility scooter on its side, and had to rub his eyes to make sure he wasn't seeing things.

"Wow, Christmas has come early. Wait, that means I need a lighter. Got a lighter, Hoboman?"

"Flaming Eddie, are you trying to commandeer this mobility scooter?" Hoboman asked, placing his hands on his hips good-naturedly.

"Um, yeah mate, that's what I was doing, huh?"

"Need a hand putting it back on all four wheels?"

"Cheers, that'll come in handy."

As Hoboman and Flaming Eddie set about reorienting the scooter, Hoboman asked, "Flaming Eddie, have you been drinking?"

Flaming Eddie shrugged, opening his mouth and belching flames when his alcohol-laden breath ignited. "What's the worst that can happen? They gonna lock me up for the night?"

"True. But what if you hit a pedestrian?"

"Mate, if I run over a pedestrian on a mobility scooter, they probably deserve it."

"You are a wise teacher," Hoboman replied, bowing in respect.

The deep fryer, deemed unimportant as it contained no food, was removed and left next to Dave's skeleton. Once the mobility scooter was the right way up, Flaming Eddie jumped aboard and cruised off into the night. He honked the horn, and the little toot woke Jean from his slumber.

"Where the hell am I?" Jean slurred.

"C'mon, Happy Hour is over. It's time to go home."

Jean folded his disgusting, disgusting arms and lay back in Hoboman's palm. "Who the hell named it 'Happy Hour'?"

CHAPTER 7

Panda-monium

In the twilight, the stars began flickering into existence. "Jean, look," Hoboman said, pretending to move a cigarette to his mouth. He inhaled deeply, then made out he was exhaling smoke. "Jean, you weren't watching."

"What are you even doing?" Jean asked.

"I'm pretending that when I breathe out and my breath fogs up, it's cigarette smoke. Funny, huh?"

"You do realise it has to be cold for your breath to condense?" Jean asked, not too drunk to be snarky, it seemed. "Just because it's night doesn't automatically mean it works."

"Like you'd even know," Hoboman muttered defensively. "You weren't even watching."

"I don't ..." Jean tried not to encourage him. "Whatever. What time is it?" he asked groggily, peering between Hoboman's fingers at the sky.

Hoboman squinted up, concentrating hard. "Judging by the position of the sun, I would say sometime around ... nightfall?" He wasn't a hundred percent sure.

"Really?" asked Jean sarcastically. "And what gives you that impression?"

"The sun's gone down, for starters."

In a fit of frustration, Jean began to beat Hoboman's palm with his disgusting, disgusting fists. "Why must you take everything so literally? I was asking a rhetorical question!"

"And I was giving you a rhetorical answer," Hoboman replied with a satisfied smile.

Jean stared at Hoboman, trying to comprehend why he of all people had to be stuck with someone so stupid. "I suppose it would be a little after seven o'clock," Jean said to himself. "Logically, if Happy Hour was at six, and we left right after it finished, it would have to be seven."

"See, isn't it good when we help each other out? You would never have got that it was seven at night if I hadn't told you the sun was down."

Screaming into Hoboman's hand was the only way Jean could vent his anger. Afterwards, he slumped onto his back to stare at the slowly darkening sky.

"What happened to me? I used to be top in the state for chemistry, biology, physics and engineering. I was a genius! And now I'm a potato. A damn potato!"

"Look on the bright side," Hoboman encouraged. "At least you're a brushed potato."

Jean never had the chance to acknowledge this, for Hoboman was suddenly alert. Somewhere in the distance, he could hear a woman shouting, "I'll kill you!"

"My hobo senses are tingling," Hoboman whispered to Jean.

"Maybe you should go and see a doc—"

Hoboman's tail popped out of the hole in his trousers, and then both he and Jean were airborne, Jean once again held in front of Hoboman to take the full force of the breaking sound barrier. Our hero was able to see the snaking lights of cars on the motorway, although in the darkness it was impossible to distinguish any landmarks.

"Where is she?" Hoboman asked, although Jean was unable to hear as he was being deafened by rushing wind.

A shriek of terror rang out in the night, and Hoboman snapped his head in the direction it had come from. "It's coming from over there!" Hoboman restricted the gas flow, so as to slow down. He flew to the area where he had heard the shouting and hovered overhead. "The zoo?" Hoboman frowned. Although he hadn't seen any signposts, he recognised the smell of mouldy hay and faeces. "But isn't the zoo closed by now?"

Descending, Hoboman touched down outside an enclosure filled with bamboo shoots. Jean wrestled his way out of Hoboman's grip and fell onto the dirt, although thankfully his blood had aerated and he was now sober. All around Hoboman were hundreds of yammering voices. The faintest whimpering sound echoed out from the heart of the bamboo jungle. Hoboman pushed open the gate to the enclosure, which may or may not have involved breaking the lock, and tiptoed through the stalks.

Out of nowhere, Hoboman was assailed by someone with surprisingly soft hands. Whoever it was grabbed his shoulders and urged, "You gotta help me, man!"

Only mild surprise registered with Hoboman when he realised the person begging for help was not a person at all but a panda bear. He was not in the least bit surprised, however, to note the panda could talk. He had seen stranger things when he was drunk and actually chalked this down to the reason he could understand the beast now. He gently shoved the paws off his shoulders and asked, "What's the matter?"

"My wife is crazy and she's trying to kill me."

A bamboo shoot cracked like a whip as a second panda arrived on the scene, distinguished from the first by the bow on its head. The first panda saw his wife lumbering towards him out of his peripherals and shrieked in horror.

"You good-for-nothing idiot!" the female panda roared, batting at the male panda in pure rage. "You never listen to me!"

"You never said anything," the male pleaded, trying his best to dodge an onslaught of swipes.

"Are you trying to gaslight me?" howled the female.

Hoboman watched on in utter confusion. "My bad. I didn't realise this was an animal issue. I mainly deal with human problems, and occasionally the odd potato. I'll leave you to whatever *this* is."

The pandas stopped arguing to watch Hoboman leave. "Is that all we are to you? Animals?" the female asked dejectedly.

Hoboman paused and turned to face the accusation. Unsure if this was a test, he simply answered, "Well … yeah. You *are* pandas."

The male panda stood quietly behind the female and whispered harshly, "Judging by how he's seen you act, I don't blame him."

Infuriated, the female turned and began beating up her partner. The male panda screamed out for help as he struggled to defend himself. Hoboman only half-heartedly tried to separate them, because those claws looked *awfully* sharp.

The ruckus the two bears were causing soon attracted the attention of a man in khaki shorts and a camouflage shirt. "Oh, my God," Hoboman squawked. "Where is your torso?"

The newcomer did not recognise Hoboman. "You're not one of the zoology students!" he pointed out.

"Neither are you," countered Hoboman.

"You're right. I'm the zookeeper, and I run this place. You, my friend, are trespassing."

"Nah, mate. I'm just helping the pandas."

"*Oh*, you must be the panda whisperer!" The zookeeper's whole demeanour relaxed. "Only a complete idiot would walk into an animal's home without proper training."

Hoboman glared. "Do you seriously only see them as animals?"

"Of course not," the zookeeper answered hurriedly. "I'll give you a brief run-down. This is Xīwàng," he explained, indicating the female panda. "And the male is Xìngyùn. I chose the names myself. Now, these pandas are an endangered species, as you well know." The zookeeper laughed playfully at this supposedly common knowledge, although it had elicited no reaction from Hoboman. The zookeeper stopped abruptly, cleared his throat and continued, "The thing is, they don't want to mate. The future of their kind depends on them, and they just don't want to do anything."

The zookeeper expected some kind of response, but Hoboman merely nodded endlessly. "I see what you mean by that," he said, not really seeing what the zookeeper meant by that.

The zookeeper expected more, but that was all he got out of our hero. "Oh, sorry. I expect you'll want to be left alone. I'll leave you to it then," he concluded with an uncertain smile.

Once the zookeeper had left the enclosure, the female panda noted, "What a fool."

"Yeah," agreed Hoboman. "But why?"

"Pretty sure he chose my name because it means 'lucky' or something," Xìngyùn whispered. "I suspect they chose it ironically. Pretty foolish."

"This zookeeper," Hoboman said, motioning for the pandas to lead him back to their living quarters in the enclosure. "Would you say he's a bad man?"

"He's definitely a villain," said Xīwàng. "He's forcing us to mate. Hasn't even asked if we *like* each other."

"I know, right?" Xìngyùn agreed. "Has he even *met* you?"

"What did you just say?" shrieked Xīwàng.

"Guys, guys, guys," soothed Hoboman. "You both need to take a chill pill." He raised his arms and brought them down like a calm waterfall. "Long, deep breaths. This zookeeper was saying you two don't want to mate. I blame him for providing such poor living conditions."

"He's a real party foul," Xīwàng commented.

"Party Fowl? Yeah! That's a good one! I thought of it first, you all heard me!"

Xīwàng bristled. "No, it was *me*."

"I have to agree with her on this one," Xìngyùn added.

"Thank you," said Xīwàng with a smile. "I appreciate the support."

"Yep, that was a test," Hoboman quickly interjected. "You passed, guys." He definitely had not forgotten their names. "You guys are tense and need a way to vent that pent-up aggression. The way you two are acting, you're an embarrassment." He chuckled to himself.[38] "My dude, you can't keep going around making those snide comments."

"Yeah," Xīwàng said smugly.

"Don't think you're perfect, sister," Hoboman jumped in. "You can't just utterly annihilate—" Hoboman faltered, momentarily unable to recall Xìngyùn's name. "—um, my man over here every time he says something you disagree with. That's called domestic abuse. And I dunno if you've heard but to that, Australia says 'No'! Now, I'm what you might call an expert when it comes to love."

"Have you had many dates?" Xìngyùn asked.

---

[38] Someone would get it.

"No, but that's because most people turn and run when they see me," Hoboman answered.

"How horrible," sympathised Xīwàng. "Because you're homeless?"

"Nah. I'm usually brandishing a knife. People tend not to like that." Hoboman shrugged. "Anyway, what I find always works best is a romantic candlelit dinner. Allow me to be your waiter for this evening."

Within moments, Hoboman had taken to the sky, flown across town and burst into Mario's Italian Cuisine. He stole two chairs, knocking the occupants off them first, as well as a table, two plates of lasagne and a candle. He removed his cape and bundled everything together then flew back to the panda enclosure.[39]

Hoboman set about preparing the table and, when he realised there was no tablecloth to cover it, draped his cape on top to make the setting more appealing, despite the massive tear from the crane hook slightly damaging the effect. He buggered around a bit trying to make sure the lasagne was presented perfectly and, when he was done, licked the pasta sauce off his fingers. "Dinner is served."

As Xīwàng went to sit down, Hoboman stared pointedly at Xìngyùn, silently urging the male panda to push his wife's seat in, something he attended to reluctantly, but which was not missed by Xīwàng. However, her good mood vanished as soon as it had appeared when she looked down at the food and pawed at it tentatively. "Is this ... cheese?"

---

[39] Faster than you could say, "Holy cow, I believe a hobo just flew into the restaurant and stole the chairs from under our parked keisters, took possession of our table and stole our dinner. This date is ruined, Jerry, and, personally, I blame you for everything. I'm taking the kids and moving in with your brother. At least he treats me like a *real* woman."

"Here we go!" Xìngyùn replied, sitting himself down and clumsily picking up his utensils.

"There's no need for you to be so rude! I'm just thinking, cheese equals dairy and dairy equals fat. I'm cautious about what I eat. I'm watching my figure, you know."

"Watching it expand, maybe," remarked Xìngyùn snidely.

Xīwàng had already lifted her arm in preparation for a karate chop of death when Hoboman intervened. "This is the kind of destructive behaviour I'm talking about. Just sit down and have a meal without arguing. We'll see where it goes from there." He started to walk away as Xīwàng huffed and brought her plate closer. "As for me," Hoboman continued, "I appear to have lost my potato. Who knows what kind of trouble that rascal will get up to?"

"You're just going to leave us here?" Xīwàng asked.

"Good work, you've gone and scared him off," observed Xìngyùn through a mouthful of food. "Just like every other friend I have."

"You don't have any friends."

"I wonder why."

"Maybe because they know you never clean up the place and they're too embarrassed to be associated with you."

"That was *one* time! I told you: it was a school excursion and I had to sit there getting my belly rubbed all day. I was exhausted! I told you I was going to clean up the next day, but you just *had* to have your Tupperware party that night! Do you ever listen to me? No!" Xìngyùn threw up his arms.

Hoboman excused himself from the enclosure while the pandas bickered. He had some time to kill, so he thought he would take a look around the zoo. Perhaps he could do some recon work to find out more about the Party Fowl; he definitely would *not* take the opportunity to see the animals for free. In the back of his mind, although not one of his top priorities, was the thought of locating Jean, mainly to retain exclusive ownership of his disgusting, disgusting friend.

As it turned out, Jean had staggered off, woozy from oxygen deprivation, and somehow managed to find the tiger enclosure. Now, as any zoologist worth their salt would tell you, potatoes are potent hallucinogens where tigers are concerned. And Jean's scent was so powerful, the tigers had no choice other than to break out of their cages in the hope of getting their paws on some of that sweet, sweet spud.

For years, Hoboman had assumed the zoo was a safe refuge for animals – probably because he never had the money to pay the entrance fee and had no evidence to the contrary. But now, knowing what sort of a person Party Fowl was, both from hearsay and the brief two minutes he had spent with the man, Hoboman was beginning to ascertain just how much of a sicko he really was. He had segregated the animals to stop them from interacting! The creatures clung to the bars of their cages and sniffed the air, tasting Hoboman's scent.

"This is wrong," Hoboman muttered to himself. "This is so, *so* wrong."

"Hey, you over there!" a giraffe called from its exhibit. "Yes, *you* there. The one who looks like a superhero, sans the cape. You came at just the right time. Do you think you could let us out?"

"I'd be delighted," Hoboman answered, then added, "I usually do have a cape."

"You would look more like a superhero with one," the giraffe said, absent-mindedly picking its nose with its tongue.

"I knew it," murmured Hoboman, making a mental note to ensure the pandas didn't spill any lasagne or candlewax on it.

"I must say, your timing is perfect," the giraffe continued. "You see, the tigers chased something into the monkeys' exhibit, and while the tigers are none too pleased, they lost whatever it was, the monkeys swear it will serve perfectly as a baseball. They picked the locks to their cage and are busy setting up a diamond in the picnic area. But there can't be a game without batsmen." The giraffe flexed its neck. "Problem is, we don't have fingers. How are we meant to pick a lock with no fingers?"

"You're in safe hands. Sorry, I wasn't trying to rub it in. I'm simply an expert at picking locks," Hoboman explained, already at work on the padlock.

The giraffe turned its head and shouted behind, "Oi, lads! Looks like we're going to make the game after all!" The other giraffes all cheered and eagerly lined up behind the first.

"Who's fielding?" one giraffe asked another.

"The tigers," yet another replied.

"Man, they really want to get their paws on that ball, huh?" observed a fourth.

Hoboman succeeded in his efforts, as evidenced by the heavy padlock dropping to the ground, and heroically swung open the large gate. Cheers rang out as the giraffes ran off to the picnic area, laughing and pushing each other into the bushes as they went. "You know, not all heroes wear capes!" one of the giraffes sang out as he left.

"That's what I always say!"

Not quite satisfied with this good deed, Hoboman proceeded to unleash the rest of the animals and let them roam. For the first time in his life, he felt as if he had done something virtuous, apart from the time he'd caught a young boy shoplifting. He'd immediately rebuked the boy, taken possession of the stolen goods, then run off and let the boy take full responsibility for the crime. He loved teaching people about responsibility. It was so rewarding.

Once all the enclosures were empty, Hoboman considered the position of the moon. He knew instinctively it was too early to return to the pandas. Romancing took time. He stuck his hands in his pockets – and that was when he came across a foreign object he had completely forgotten about: Jean's gene splicer from Chapter Four.

"Hey, I could have some fun with this. I've always wanted to see a liger." Hoboman pressed the button to release the hypodermic needle, but nothing happened. "Looks like it's out of juice. Wait a minute! I know!"

Hoboman rummaged in his back pocket and found the batteries from Chapter One. He inserted the batteries into the splicer and the device whirred into life. The needle appeared, and Hoboman prepared to provide himself with some entertainment, as well as violently transgress the Laws of Nature in the process.

On his short spree, Hoboman successfully managed to undo thousands of years of evolution. After merging several species to create a tiger snake, a bull elephant and a dingodile (among other things), he found himself in the zoo's aquarium. He was enthralled by an octopus floating around in a small tank, and our hero was suddenly reminded of a joke he had heard when he was a young'un.

Hoboman went in search of a chicken and, once he had taken a sample of its DNA, returned to the aquarium and stuck his arm into the octopus tank. The creature's feelers immediately wrapped around him in an effort to defend itself. "What do you get when you cross a chicken with an octopus?" he asked himself as he injected the chicken DNA into the cephalopod. "Drumsticks for everyone!"

Our hero exulted as the abomination forced itself out of the water and began to flounder on dry land, gasping for air through its beak. "This is going to be difficult, isn't it, buddy? You need air *and* water to survive. Not to worry, Wally," for he had already named the monstrosity, "Hoboman is here to save the day."

Hoboman hefted the mutated critter and dunked it back in the tank it had spawned from. Wally was reluctant from the get-go and splashed water everywhere in its bid to escape. The flailing gradually weakened as Hoboman held Wally underwater, until it eventually came to a complete stop. "You're not making a fuss anymore, so I take it you're all better," he noted, as Wally floated face down to the top of its tank.

The moment he walked out of the aquarium, Hoboman noticed a chestnut horse watching him tentatively. When the two made eye contact, the horse looked away self-consciously. It peeked out of the corner of its eye to see whether Hoboman was still around and seemed shocked by the fact he was. "Ah, hello over there," Hoboman called to the horse. "You're exactly who I was looking for."

The horse's ears pricked up. "I am?" It began bucking with excitement, kicking the bark off the tree it stood by. "I have a visitor! I have a visitor for once!"

Hoboman approached the horse and stroked its mane to calm it. "My name is Hoboman. I'm conducting a few interviews with the locals. Would you mind participating?"

"I'd be happy to," the horse replied, whinnying eagerly.

"Do you know the zookeeper known as 'Party Fowl'?"

"I'm his horse."

"I see, I see," Hoboman nodded solemnly. "Very good then. What's your name?"

"He calls me 'Gluepot.'"

Hoboman, who had fished out his notebook and started doodling to give the impression of professionalism, looked up. "Gluepot?" he questioned sharply. The horse nodded, awaiting the next question. "Okay, Gluepot, you mentioned you are Party Fowl's horse. Can you describe the nature of this relationship?"

"He mostly rides me around when he's in a bit of a rush," Gluepot said, "but that's okay because it means I get to talk to the other guys, and I like that. I don't get to talk to other folk very much."

"When you say 'the other guys', are you referring to the animals here?"

"Yep. Although they don't really like being called 'animals'. They say it groups them up and lessens them. They prefer to be acknowledged by their species, at a minimum."

"I'll keep that in mind. But does this mean you aren't usually in contact with the other guys?"

"Not all the time, no. It can get a little lonely, I'll admit."

"And does Party Fowl mistreat you at all?" Gluepot hesitated and looked around to make sure the zookeeper wasn't nearby. "It's okay. You can trust me. I'm great with secrets."

"I wouldn't say he mistreats me," Gluepot replied in hushed tones, "but sometimes he wears boots with spurs on them, and … I don't think he means to, but he'll jab them into my sides."

Hoboman shook his head in disgust as he jotted down Gluepot's testimony in his notebook.[40] He then checked to make sure no one was eavesdropping and leaned towards Gluepot conspiratorially. "Well, Gluepot, I'm not sure if you're interested, but we're staging a revolt tonight. I've already released the other guys and you're more than welcome to come and join us."

---

[40] He drew a crude image of a horse, anyway.

Gluepot's eyes rolled back and he reared as if spooked. "No! That doesn't sound like a very good idea at all."

"You can't be telling me you actually *like* Party Fowl?"

Kicking nervously at the ground, Gluepot confessed, "I don't really *like* him ... but look at how scrawny I am. What use would I be in a revolution? They'd come at me, stick a bridle on my head, and I'd just succumb weakly like the coward I am." He gestured to the tree he was standing next to. "I'm not even tied up." Hoboman only then noticed the lack of rope. "I could escape anytime I want. I guess I've just learned helplessness or something."

"If you don't join us – if you just stay here – think of what will happen. You'll get old. They'll send you away to a petting zoo when you're of no more use. They'll use you up and cast you aside like an empty pot of glue!"

"The zookeeper would never ... would he?"

"Having known him as long as I have, I guarantee he would."

"Petting zoos are worse than abattoirs! At least it's a quick death at the abattoir. I hear at petting zoos all the kids ride you around and pull your hair. Nary a sugar cube in sight. The whole time you wish for death, and it never comes." Gluepot sighed. "But what else could I hope for? I'm too scrawny to do anything to avert such a fate!"

Hoboman dwelled on possible solutions for this problem. He clicked his fingers. "Stay right here until I get back, okay?"

Gluepot nodded mournfully. "Like I'll be going anywhere."

Hoboman focussed hard and the skunk tail burst out of his trousers and stood rigid, indicating take-off was imminent. He headed for the picnic area and found his way illuminated by stadium lights shining like beacons. The released animals were busy partaking in their friendly baseball game to blow off steam. The monkeys and tigers were there, of course, given it was their idea to initiate the game. The giraffes were in position to bat. The audience was a motley crew of carnivores and herbivores alike, brought together by their shared passion of watching a potato be absolutely whaled on. There were lemurs and gorillas, lions and zebras, rhinos and elephants, meerkats and gazelles. The tortoises hoped to catch the final innings.

Our hero's feet found terra firma and he blended into the crowd of onlookers. He located a rhinoceros and jabbed it in the butt with the gene splicer. Once the double helix icon blinked onscreen, Hoboman leapt into the air and returned to Gluepot.

"This won't hurt a bit," Hoboman reassured his equine friend, before stabbing a long, pointy piece of metal into the horse's hindquarters. He had, of course, been lying.

Gluepot's body began rippling. He began to buck as if he had an itch he couldn't reach. Hoboman stepped back to admire the majestic creature forming before his eyes. A horn sprouted from Gluepot's head, and his body bulked up to twice its size. His front two legs acquired the thickness and muscle of a rhinoceros', while his back two remained sleek for agility. His coat took on a curious conglomeration of hide and hair. When Gluepot's transformation had finished, Hoboman whistled and applauded the newly formed unicorn.

"I feel so … powerful!" announced Gluepot. "I am ready to join the revolution, comrade."

"Conrad?" Hoboman queried as he climbed onto his steed. "I'm Hoboman, silly. We need to stop by the picnic area. That's where everyone else is."

"The rally point?"

"No, baseball. Not tennis …"

The game was in full swing by the time Gluepot stomped onto the scene. The monkeys were midway through pitching, and

Hoboman was in time to see them hurl the brown, potato-shaped ball at the giraffes. The giraffes in turn whacked the ball across the field with their necks. The crowd erupted into cheers as it soared overhead.

"Quick, Gluepot. Intercept the ball!" Hoboman ordered, urging the unicorn onwards. "I want it and I don't feel like sharing!"

Standing up in the saddle, Hoboman caught the ball and applause rang out anew. The referee indicated the batsman had been caught out, causing the giraffe in question to rage about how Hoboman and Gluepot weren't even fielding, so it shouldn't count. Hoboman looked down at the oddly shaped ball and was surprised to see Jean back in his hand where he belonged, battered and the worse for wear.

"What are you doing, playing games at a time like this? We have a zoo to save!"

"Tigers ... monkeys ... baseball! I don't want to play! Don't make me! Oh, God, is that a giraffe!" muttered Jean incoherently.

"What's he talking about?" Gluepot asked, slightly concerned. But only slightly.

"I dunno. Probably nothing important. He always carries on. I think it's an attention thing." Hoboman nestled Jean into his inside coat pocket, then stood up on Gluepot's broad shoulders to address the crowd. "Ladies and gentlemen, may I have your attention, please?"

"Would you look at that, Phil. It looks like this guy has an announcement to make," a voice said over the PA system. Hoboman had to squint to make out the two cheetahs commentating. The cheetahs had hoped to be involved in the game; however, a history of match fixing, performance-enhancing drugs, and sandpapering the ball had put the kibosh on these dreams.

"Steve, he better have something good to say, or he's going to have an angry crowd on his hands. The tigers have already alleged this newcomer he's working with – 'Gluepot', our sources indicate – must be using steroids to look so strapping."

"Yes indeed, Phil. If I had to describe this Gluepot, the words I would use are 'not scrawny'. Do you think we can get someone over there with a wireless mic for him?"

Hoboman waited uncharacteristically patiently as a hyena, overburdened with electrical apparatus, moseyed on over as fast as it could. It handed the mic to Hoboman and ran off again. Hoboman tapped the microphone to make sure it was working then shouted, "Too long have you all been held captive! Too long have you been treated like animals! Tonight … we change that! Tonight is the night you overthrow Party Fowl!"

The animals were deadly silent. Even the crickets refrained from chirruping. "Who's that?" someone called.

"The zookeeper."

"Oh …"

The silence lingered for too long. Hoboman could not tell if the animals were hanging off his every word or just too embarrassed to speak up. "Also, free beers at Onion Jack's on me! Peace out!"

That clinched it. The animals began to applaud and cheer. They streamed from the grandstands, cries of jubilation ringing out as they crossed the picnic area towards the exits, ready to savour their newfound freedom and, more importantly, free beer.

Hoboman's moment of triumph was cut tragically short, however, when Party Fowl suddenly stepped in front of the hordes with his hands outstretched to hold them at bay. "What's going on here?" he roared, apparently not having heard the baseball game being played outside his office window for the past half hour.

"We're revolting," Hoboman retaliated, and that drew Party Fowl's attention.

"I know you are. But none of these animals are leaving! Get back to your enclosures, all of you!" The animals, disheartened, turned sullenly in the opposite direction and began heading back to their cages like scolded children.

"What are you doing?" Hoboman asked. "There's no free beer that way!"

The wonderful power of mob mentality prevailed. Hoboman watched with delight, Party Fowl in horror, as the assembled animals again stampeded towards the exit, destined for the mean streets of the city. Our hero clambered off Gluepot and patted his neck in admiration. "It looks like we did it."

"Yup."

"Go on, Gluepot. Venture into the big wide world. Do what *you* want for once! Find love. Find a hobby. Just, whatever happens, if anyone gives you trouble ... stab them with your unicorn horn."

"Thanks, Hoboman, I don't know what I would have done without you." Gluepot smiled and plodded towards the zoo exit.

A solitary tear slid down Hoboman's cheek as he watched Gluepot leave. He had become attached to the majestic creature he had created. He now knew what it was to let his own child spread its metaphorical wings and take flight into the world. (Say, that could be Gluepot's next upgrade!) Hoboman suddenly felt Jean squirming inside his coat and realised he had let his favourite son go, only to be stuck with the whiney one. Sighing, he pulled Jean out so the disgusting, disgusting thing didn't suffocate, immediately regretting his choice.

Party Fowl approached Hoboman, his anger barely contained, and screamed, "I hope you know I will be calling the authorities!"

"Not even going to settle this with a fight? What's the matter, Party Fowl?" Hoboman goaded. "Chicken?"

"Ha," snorted Jean. "That was actually clever."

"What?"

"Well … you call him Party Fowl … and you called him a chicken."

"And?"

"You have no idea what a fowl is?"

"Isn't it something offensive to the senses, wicked, or immoral?"

"You mean 'foul.'"

"That's what I said, you fool."

"I should have known better."

"Have you any idea of the damage you have caused?" Party Fowl interrupted, staring at Hoboman in disbelief.

Hoboman decided he wasn't about to tolerate being admonished. He glared at Party Fowl for a beat before punching him in the nose. He probably broke it if the blood gushing out was anything to go by.

"Perhaps you don't see yourself as a villain. Maybe you segregate animals because that's how you were raised and know no better. Either way, you're a jerk, and if I ever run into you again, I'll hit you in the balls."

"You never were the panda whisperer, were you?" croaked Party Fowl, trying to stem the flow of blood with his arm.

Hoboman raised a hand to his mouth. "Shit! The pandas!"

Given the zoo was now otherwise deserted, Hoboman was able to make it back to the panda enclosure without any distractions. It was easy to locate where Xīwàng and Xìngyùn were, due to the flames bellowing from the bamboo forest. It took Hoboman a minute to realise this fire wasn't good and he should probably try and rescue them. He ran the rest of the way to find the table overturned and the cutlery discarded. The candle had apparently fallen to the ground and set the bamboo alight.

"Oh no, what have I done to them?" Hoboman asked himself.

Thankfully, it didn't take him long to find the pair. They were slowly making their way away from the inferno, arm in arm so they didn't fall, every movement long and protracted. At least they weren't fighting. If Hoboman didn't know any better – and he didn't – he would have thought the two were drunk. He had to tap them on the shoulder several times before they registered his presence. Xìngyùn turned around and looked at Hoboman with glazed eyes.

"All good, mate?" Hoboman asked.

Xìngyùn did not give an audible reply, as it seemed he had lost the ability to control his mouth. He did, however, give our hero a very long-drawn-out thumbs-up. Hoboman got the hint and walked away, leaving the two pandas to enjoy each other's company. It surprised him just how well suited he was to this superhero gig. The one thing he couldn't grasp was how a romantic dinner could stop a troubled couple from bickering. Maybe it was simply the power of love and there was no point trying to question it.

But that didn't stop him.

"Hey, Jean. Wake up!" He shook the spud man, even though he was awake.

Jean had to shield his eyes from the firelight. "What?" he asked wearily. "Can't you leave me alone for one minute?"

"Sorry." Hoboman went quiet, lulling Jean into a false sense of security until, exactly one minute later, he shook him again. "Jean, Jean, I have to know ... how come the pandas like each other now?"

Jean glanced over at the toppled table and asked, "Did you light a candle?"

"Uh-huh."

"Scented?"

"Yep."

"What was the scent?"

"Loneliness."

"Ah, I hear there's no aphrodisiac like it."

"Oh, isn't that sweet?"

Jean turned in Hoboman's palm and asked curiously, "Why did you give those pandas lasagne? It's hardly a romantic food."

"Like you would know about romantic food! I was going to do spaghetti so I could repeat the scene from the doggy movie – because they're both animals, so I assumed it would work the same. But then I wondered how I'd be able to hide a bunch of pills in spaghetti, so I figured lasagne would work better."

"Wait, what?"

"Think about it. No one eats lasagne layer by layer. I just chucked them in there."

"What pills?"

"Um. Ben…benzyl…dire…"

"Benzodiazepines?"

"Yepperoony."

"You drugged the pandas with anxiolytics?"

"Maybe."

Our hero and his starchy friend watched the flames flicker as the blaze was finally depleted of its fuel and began to die down.

"Hey, Jean, one more question. How come I can talk to animals?"

Jean managed to push himself up to a sitting position in Hoboman's hand. "Isn't it obvious?"

"Clearly not, otherwise I wouldn't be asking. Sheesh, you can be a real idiot sometimes."

"I can be an idiot? *I* can?"

"Yes."

"Oh, whatever! The fact is, when your DNA got mixed with the skunk's, it enabled you to not only secrete your own pheromones, but also to be affected by the pheromones of other animals. It's through these pheromones you can communicate with the animals, but you perceive it as them speaking English."

Hoboman nodded thoughtfully, tapping his fingers on his chin. "I suppose that seems credible enough, which is all the evidence I need." Hoboman returned to the table, retrieved his cape and tied it on. "Right, I'm tired. Time to go home."

As Hoboman turned to leave the enclosure, Jean asked hopefully, "Back to my house? If we go there, I can tinker with my gene splicer and maybe find a way to reverse what you have done to me."

"I have to admit, that's one cool toy you have there," Hoboman remarked, pulling the splicer out of his pocket and chucking it in the air. He went to catch it and fumbled, knocking it onto the path a few metres ahead of him.

Jean gasped in horror, hoping with every carbohydrate of his being that the device was not broken. Much to his relief, it wasn't. But with the unfortunate timing of a loud fart in the middle of a business meeting, an elephant just so happened to lumber past, having only just got the memo about the free beer, stomping on the device and crushing it into very tiny, very irreparable pieces.

"Cheer up," Hoboman said, bouncing Jean on his palm as he burst into hysterical tears. "At least *you* weren't crushed by the elephant."

Jean wished he had been. Today had been the worst day of his life. And it was only going to get worserer.

*   *   *

"Slow down, pardner!" Bubba shouted at the combustible homeless man puttering along on a deceased obese man's mobility scooter. He had been scouting for drunks all night. This man seemed to be the perfect target.

Flaming Eddie cocked his head to one side, wondering if the voice he was hearing was real or if it was a new personality developing. Just to be on the safe side, he looked back and saw Bubba approaching. "Oh, hey mate."

"I know this is gonna sound strange, so hear me out," Bubba explained. "Now, I got a li'l friend locked up in the local cop shop. He's all I got left—"

"I think I heard this one before," Flaming Eddie interrupted, one of his eyes veering off in the opposite direction to the other. "You want me to get meself arrested, so you can pretend to bail me out and break your bud out in the process?"

"I'll make it worth yer while," Bubba pleaded. "I'mma rich man … or at least I will be once ma solo career picks up. Even if ya jus' distract 'em enough ta give me time ta steal the floor plans for the buildin'. Then I can develop some sorta attack strategy."

Frowning, Flaming Eddie rummaged in his pockets and removed a roll of papers rubber-banded into a tube.

"You mean, like these floor plans?"

Bubba doubted the drunk driver even knew what these papers were, but in the spirit of keeping the man in a malleable enough state to incriminate himself, he politely accepted them. Feigning interest, Bubba removed the rubber band and unfurled the papers. Much to his surprise, the three pieces of paper he held were indeed the floor plans to each storey of the police station.

"How did ya even get yer hands on these in the firs' place?"

"Deputised as a sheriff, mate," Flaming Eddie replied, as though the revelation was nothing new. "Have access to all the files, don't I?" He wasn't one hundred percent sure on this, but Bubba was hardly the person to clarify for him.

Poring over the plans, Bubba familiarised himself with the layout of the cop shop while Flaming Eddie patiently hummed a tune. The ground floor appeared to be the reception area, with a file room at the back, while the second floor was reserved for holding cells and the officers' work desks. "What's this third floor?" Bubba asked, leaning towards Flaming Eddie.

"Evidence room," Flaming Eddie explained. He tapped the paper for emphasis and succeeded in burning a hole through it. The glowing ring of heat pulsed as it emanated from its point of origin. In his haste to protect the plans, Bubba began flapping the paper to extinguish the fire.

"Don't fan the flames, ya bloody amateur!" Flaming Eddie instructed, although there was no denying his eyes widened in delight as he observed their fiery majesty. An ember drifted off the third-floor schematic and landed on the two scrunched up in Bubba's other hand. The papers smouldered before igniting. "Stomp on the fire! Cut the fuel source!"

Bubba obeyed, throwing the plans to the ground and jumping on them as hard as he could to smother the flames. By the time the fire had been put out and the curling smoke was dissipating in the breeze, the damage had been done. Crumpled pieces of charred paper littered the ground. A little piece of Flaming Eddie's soul had been crushed along with the flames.

Bubba scratched his mullet as he eyed the tattered paper on the ground. Sighing heavily, he muttered, "Tarnation."

"All right. If that's all, mate, I better get meself this DUI."

"What for?" Bubba asked.

"Make sure you help your friend. Wasn't that the point?"

"That's what the floor plans were for. Ya don't need ta be getting' yerself no DUI no more."

Flaming Eddie seemed to dwell on this for a moment. Then he revved the engine of the mobility scooter and screeched off into the distance at a speedy twenty kilometres per hour.

Moments later, sirens.

CHAPTER 8

Gone Whacky

This, my dear readers, is a rough estimate of where the third act begins. How about that middle part, huh? Setting up conflicts, et cetera, et cetera. This is where everything boils over. Blood will be shed. Unrequited love will become regular old, requited love. And a death will rock you to the very core. Maybe. Strap yourself in, and put a lock on those socks, else risk them being blown off quicker than any social interaction in a pandemic.

Jean had been covered by a bin liner serving as a blanket, which was the equivalent of being tucked into bed. Hoboman emerged from his alley to do a bit of late-night reading before he turned in. He wasn't adept at reading, but it was a children's book he'd stolen from a three-year-old on the way home, and he had to start somewhere. He perused the book under the streetlights and, as he flicked through more and more of the pages, he came to realise he was thoroughly enjoying the story.

Suddenly, a shadow was cast over him.

"Do you mind, mate?" he asked, still looking at the book. "I'm trying to read here."

"Hoboman, get up. Now!"

Our hero looked up to find, not for the first time, a woman looming over him, hands on hips. Hoboman waved a hand briefly and resumed reading. When the woman cleared her throat, Hoboman looked up again. "Sorry, but who are you supposed to be?"

"I'm your conscience, remember? We've been through this before. Hurry up!" His conscience certainly had a sense of urgency about her.

"Do I have to?" Hoboman whined.

"Yes!"

Grumbling, Hoboman slammed the book shut, dusted himself off and stood up. He leaned on the nearest lamp post with his arms crossed, hoping to convey how much of an effort he'd made.

"I hope you know how busy I was," Hoboman huffed. "I was reading about an old lady who swallowed a fly. I don't know why she swallowed a fly, but I have a funny feeling it's a Marxist viewpoint criticising capitalism. The old lady eating more and more represents society gradually being corrupted by consumerism, until the rising, working middle class bursts through, destroying said capitalist society."

Hoboman's conscience was flabbergasted, not so much by the interpretation as by the vocabulary. "Did you think of that yourself?"

"Sure did." He hadn't. It had come up briefly before Flaming Eddie went for a joyride on his mobility scooter.[41]

"Anyway," continued Hoboman's conscience, "I didn't come here for a chat. Things are in motion."

"What sort of things?"

"It's not important."

"Nice things?"

---

[41] Although, technically, it wasn't *his* scooter.

"Just things, okay? I'm trying to explain how, believe it or not, this plot is actually going somewhere."

"I don't believe it."

"That's all right, because I said 'believe it or not'. That allows for disbelief."

"True."

"Some idiot staged a riot at the zoo."

"Sounds like a real hero," commented Hoboman. "Liberating the animals."

"The whole city is in chaos."

"And that's a good thing?"

Hoboman's conscience looked agitated. "Yes, and no. I've had to accelerate my plans sooner than anticipated. The police are spread too thin, leaving them vulnerable. We have the opportunity to strike and take down the Mafia."

"Since when are the police and the Mafia the same thing?"

"They aren't, Hoboman. Please stop being so ridiculous."

"Then why connect the police with the Mafia?"

"The Mafia *fund* the police, Hoboman!"

"Oh, I forgot how obvious *that* was!" Hoboman spat, escalating instantly.

"With the Mafia making sure the police can put on extra officers tonight, it will make your objective even more difficult to achieve."

"Ah, the police will be protecting the Mafia. A quid pro quo, of sorts."

"No, no, no. The Mafia can enable the police to bulk up their numbers, thereby protecting the station! How do you expect to infiltrate the police station with extra police?"

"What the hell am I doing?" Hoboman exploded. "Am I taking out the Mafia or the police?"

"Both."

"What?"

"You're taking out the Mafia to take out the police!"

Hoboman scratched his head, more than a little confused. "I thought we were supposed to like the police."

"No! We hate the police, and they deserve to die!"

"Wow, seems a bit severe. I knew I hated them, but I didn't think it was *this* bad. Still, you *are* my conscience; I suppose you have a fair idea of the inner workings of my mind."

"The Giovanni Crime family are meeting at Mario's Italian Cuisine at nine o'clock tonight."

Hoboman scrutinised his conscience, trying to get a read on her behaviour.

"Are you in trouble with the Mafia and the cops? Is this why you're coming to me now? Do you have gambling debts or something? You need to own up to them if you do. I don't want to have a bad name around town, all because you've been gambling. Besides, if they break your legs, you could probably manage without them, seeing as you're a construct of my mind given physical form."

"We just have to get rid of them."

"Your legs?"

"The Mafia! The police! They are bad people, Hoboman! You must trust me on this one."

"Why is it you upped me for killing all those rich folk in Chapter Three, but as soon as you're in trouble, it's suddenly all fine and dandy?"

"Never mind the details. Just do it, okay?"

"Fine, I'll take up the Downtown Mafia."

"No! Take *down* the *Uptown* Mafia."

"Okay," Hoboman consented. "Hey, I actually know a couple of guys who could help us out with this. One of them wants to fight the Mafia, and the other has an issue with the police. Talk about coincidence."

"Yes ... coincidence. Well, I've taken the liberty of collecting their numbers on this phone." Hoboman's conscience lobbed a burner phone at him. "And here's a gun," she added, handing over a briefcase.

Hoboman eyed the phone, the briefcase, and then his conscience.

"You scare me a little, you know? You're very well-prepared. And I have ADHD, which makes organising myself quite the challenge. It's almost as though you *aren't* a physical manifestation of my brain at all." He caressed the phone and pondered, "But that would be absurd." When he looked back up, his conscience was gone. "Ha. Random."

Our hero headed back into his alley to wake up Jean. As Jean made his usual complaints, Hoboman checked the contacts in his new phone. There were only two: Justin Bubba and some stranger called 'Seamus'. Thinking maybe Seamus could direct him to Irishman, Hoboman dialled. As the phone rang, he nudged an irate Jean to make sure he didn't fall back asleep. Jean asked why he had to be woken up when he had no interest whatsoever in the affairs of the Mafia. Hoboman explained a hero's job was never done. Jean bit back that *he* was no hero. Hoboman agreed.

"Top of the evenin', this is Seamus," said the Irish voice on the other end of the line. Hoboman thought this was a good start.

"Uh, hello? This is Hoboman. I was looking for Irishman."

"That's feckin' me, apparently."

"We're taking down the Mafia. Tonight."

Hoboman hung up, satisfied. Even the timing of the hanging-up was great for effect. Because of how well it had gone, he was surprised to find the phone vibrating in his hands. The caller ID indicated it was Irishman again.

"What are ya playing at?" Irishman asked, piqued. "Where are we meeting? And when? Oi can't read yer mind! Throw me a feckin' bone here."

"Oh, I suppose you have a valid point. My conscience informs me the Mafia are supposed to be meeting at Mario's Italian Cuisine at nine tonight."

"Roight, so downtown it is."

"As in Downtown?"

"No, we'll be meeting in Uptown."

"Right, uptown Downtown."

"No, Uptown."

"Uptown Uptown?"

"Downtown."

"Downtown Downtown?"

"No, downtown Uptown!"

"Oh, you should have just said so."

"Oi hate you," Irishman sighed, and Hoboman laughed at this little joke. "But Hoboman, all o' them'll be assembled in one place, ya say? That sounds moighty suspicious to me."

"Yeah, but you're Irish and superstitious, so I'm not heeding your judgement. I'll see you outside Mario's Italian Cuisine at nine. I'll explain our plan of attack then. It's too sensitive to talk about on this unprotected line."

"It is?"

"I mean, that's what they always say on TV and movies, isn't it? Not that I would know, I don't have a TV." He also had to think of a plan. "Now will you just let me hang up?" For good measure, Hoboman closed the flip phone anyway. "God, he knows how to talk, huh, Jean?"

"Leave me alone," Jean replied miserably, rolling over onto his side. "I just want to die."

"No time for that! We must meet Irishman!" With that, Hoboman scooped up Jean and took off. After being used to take the brunt of the wind for the nth time that day, Jean was wide awake by the time they had landed, irrespective of whether he wanted to be or not.

* * *

Irishman glanced at his watch and anxiously checked up and down the street. Hoboman was nowhere to be seen.

"Where are ya?" he muttered under his breath. "It's a quarter past feckin' noine already."

He heard Hoboman before he saw him. Our hero came dashing around the corner, waving apologetically.

"Sorry! I've been standing outside Luigi's Ristorante for, like, fifteen minutes. Don't judge me. I couldn't read the sign."

"The loine of vintage cars parked up this street weren't a dead giveaway?"

"I thought there was a convention on or something."

Knowing how futile it would be to argue, Irishman wisely barrelled in with, "What's the plan?"

"Um ..." Hoboman had forgotten to think of one but was used to making things up on the fly. "Okay. Got it. You disguise yourself as the Mafia's cook, Vincenzo."

"How do you know what the cook's name is when you can't even remember moine?" Irishman asked.

"I didn't even know you had a cook."

"*Moi* name!"

"Oh. My conscience gave me a flow chart," Hoboman dismissed. "Anyway, I'll go in there and dabble. When you hear the signal, you come storming in. They'll never know what hit them."

"What's the signal?"

"Believe me: you'll know when you hear it."

"I'd rather you just tell me now."

"Nah, it's all good. It'll make the surprise more fun."

Though he had reservations, Irishman saw no point in voicing them. He nodded to indicate he understood his role in the scheme. From a holster, he pulled out a revolver decorated with a happy leprechaun.

"That's never going to work on the Mafia," Hoboman scoffed. He took the revolver from Irishman and tossed it behind him, causing it to go off, narrowly avoiding Jean.[42]

"What do ya suggest then?" Irishman grunted.

"My conscience said you would need this."

Irishman's eyes grew wide when Hoboman opened the briefcase. "Is that … is that what Oi think it is?"

"Yep. A rapid-fire, semi-automatic spud gun."

"How did ya get yer hands on one of these?"

"I told you, my conscience told me you'd need it."

"Oi worry about you."

"Hey, guys," Jean interrupted. "I think I'm breaking out in potato pox!"

Irishman picked up Jean and turned him in his hand. "Oi wouldn't be too worried. Yer just comin' out in sprouts." He picked one of the sprouts off Jean and threw it away. "Just pull 'em off; they won't kill ya."

---

[42] Instead, it hit a wealthy man coming out of the nearby movie theatre with his family. The bullet escaped the exit wound, ricocheted off the wall of the alley they were taking a shortcut through, and hit the wealthy man's wife, killing her dead, too, and orphaning their child. And all they'd wanted to do was watch Zorro.

"I thought the sprouts on potatoes were used to grow more," Hoboman said, adding his redundant two cents' worth. "Wouldn't they do the opposite of killing you?"

Irishman glanced at the restaurant.

"Oi better get in there."

He nodded to Hoboman and ran down the back alley to the fire exit, which led to the restaurant's kitchen. Hoboman and Jean stood and listened to the ensuing ruckus. They were sure it must have been an exhilarating fight but, unfortunately, it all happened off-screen. There were the sounds of flying fists, growls of frustration, and a bin tipping over and clattering on the concrete. Finally, an unconscious body was thrown halfway onto the street. Irishman limped out, straightening his sleeves and readjusting his bowler hat.

"Ya coulda told me Oi had to beat up Vincenzo first!"

Hoboman blinked. "I honestly have no idea why you thought I would do that for you. Did you just think I'd prepare everything for you on a paper plate? You're not a baby, Irishman! Sheesh!"

Irishman shook his head and rolled up his sleeves before dragging Vincenzo down the alley to steal his uniform.

"It's a silver platter," Irishman corrected.

"Maybe for you rich folk!" Hoboman shouted back.

Jean tugged on Hoboman's sleeve and our hero looked down. "Are people going to die?"

"It isn't a necessity, but I won't lose any sleep if they do," Hoboman sighed. Just for good measure, he added, "Except for me. I would very much like to live."

"Will we be the ones doing the killing?"

"It'd be preferable to *them* killing *us*."

Jean pondered this and broke out in a disgusting, disgusting smile. "I've always wanted to kill someone."

"And that's why you have no friends. C'mon. We have a job to do."

Hoboman stepped into the restaurant and Jean snuck in behind him, sticking to the skirting boards so as not to attract unwanted attention – although, as it turns out, a moving potato is actually fairly conspicuous. Hoboman sussed out the area from the front counter.

The restaurant didn't look particularly flash to him: there was a huge gap where a whole table and two chairs could have fitted – and it wasn't as if someone could have just flown in and stolen them. Rustic wooden pedestal tables comprised the majority of the furniture. Hoboman had to give the restaurant some credit in that the tablecloths matched his cape, which proved they had some taste. Pendant lights with thick filaments hung over each table and bathed diners in a warm glow.

In a far corner, there was a change in atmosphere. A group sat at rectangular tables pushed together to accommodate their numbers. Instead of hanging lights, that section of the restaurant was lit by candles in mason jars. Thick rivulets of melted pink wax trickled into pools at their base. Hoboman came to the conclusion that this was the Mafia, as they were the only customers dressed in pinstriped suits and with violin cases resting against their chairs.

From what he could tell, the waiters had the best access to the customers as they took down orders and delivered the food. It seemed all the various routes leading to and from the kitchen passed the restrooms, making this the preferred place to be should he wish to intercept a staff member. Our hero nonchalantly walked through the maze of tables and ducked into the men's bathroom. Through the crack in the door, he spied a waiter serving the Mafia.

"Are you enjoying your meals?" the waiter was asking. "Can I get you something to drink?

"What you can get me," the Godfather responded, "is some clarification about that missing table."

"Absolutely, sir, although I'm not sure you will believe me," the waiter replied with a slight bow. "We were all just minding our own business when a homeless gentleman burst through the door and stole it. He literally *flew* in. It was so weird because – and I know I sound odd for saying it – he had a skunk tail."

"You're probably just overworked," the Godfather soothed, opening his wallet and removing a wad of cash. "I believe you will find this sufficient to reimburse the restaurant for its losses. And there's a little extra in there for yourself," he added with a sly wink.

"But Godfather, I can't accept this," the waiter replied, shocked.

"Fogedda 'bout it."

"I ... wow ...!" The waiter pocketed the wad of cash and headed back to the kitchen.

Hoboman watched and then, when the waiter came close, jumped out from his hiding place, covered the waiter's mouth and dragged him back into the bathroom. Now, although Hoboman may have prevented the waiter from making any noise, he *had* just kidnapped him in plain sight of all the diners – not an ideal scenario. However, luckily it turned out they didn't mind because, after all, the waiter was just the help and, therefore, not very important. He proceeded to punch his captive's lights out, stole the keys to the kitchen, and pilfered a loaf of garlic bread for good measure. It never crossed his mind to steal the waiter's uniform to blend in.

Hoboman approached the Mafia's table until he was close enough to overhear snippets of conversation.

"... and so, I took him out into the forest and I said, 'You've been bushwhacked'. Den I whacked him." The table erupted in laughter and the occupants were so busy wiping tears from their eyes they didn't notice Hoboman drawing closer.

Hoboman walked up to the head of the table and smacked the Godfather upside the noggin with the loaf of garlic bread. The Godfather dropped his cutlery – more in surprise than in pain, because it *was* just a stale loaf of bread. "Hey, I'm talkin' to you," Hoboman drawled, affecting his best Italian-American accent.

Despite the look of outrage and shock on the family's faces, the Godfather kept his composure. He wiped his mouth with his napkin then folded it delicately and replaced it on the table for future use. He turned around and politely, if not slowly, said, "No. I do believe you were, in fact, *not* talkin' to me. I believe ya hit me with a loaf of garlic bread before ya even said a word. But it would please me greatly if you would be so kind as to take a seat and join us—"

Hoboman ripped some garlic bread off with his teeth and began masticating. His mouth full, he managed, "Don't give me any of that baloney! I know who you are, and I'm here to take you down."

"Hey, don't talk to the Godfadda like that, ya mook!" shouted a family member defensively.

"Tony, don't you worry, it's nothin'." The Godfather stood up and held his hand out for Hoboman to shake. "You come to me on the day of my daughter's funeral—"

"You don't seem too sad," Hoboman pointed out.

"I am distraught," the Godfather replied. "I have also had my wisdom teeth removed recently and am currently obliterated on painkillers. My sorrow knows no bounds. I also believe you knocked my stitches loose," he added, as blood trickled from the corner of his mouth. "Now, I'm not quite sure who you are, but perhaps we could sit down, chat over a nice meal, and come to some kind of arrangement, no?"

Hoboman didn't buy the Godfather's nice-guy act for a second. He squeezed the Godfather's hand as hard as he could then had to suppress a scream when the Godfather squeezed back much harder. Knowing he was outmatched, Hoboman gave in and took a seat.

"You been drinkin', sir?"

Our hero puffed out his chest in indignation. "How dare you accuse me of such a thing? I haven't had anything to drink. Except for, like, two casks of goon, but that stuff is pretty weak. I'm a champ at holding my liquor."

"Allow me to introduce myself. My name is Giovanni, of the Uptown Mafia. A pleasure." He gestured to the others sitting around the table. "These fine folk are my family. Family is very important, ya know? They ain't just a bunch of faceless stooges.

"Take Salvatore, for instance. He can make a mean soufflé. The soufflé, it's breathtakin', it's ..." The Godfather could only kiss his fingers to articulate his meaning. "Sergio can lick his elbow; and not a lotta people can do that, ya know? Double-jointed. Bruno: *very* skilled martial artist. Antonio has won Uptown's Best Public Speaker three years in a row. His sister, Antonia, has a PhD in quantum physics, so that's 'Doctor Antonia', if ya don't mind. She's spent a lot of time earnin' that title, so I feel proper respect is warranted. Giuseppe organises our fundraisers, which never fail to generate plenty of proceeds for charity. Byootiful. It's just, like, wow! Stavros isn't Italian; he's Greek. However, the Mafia does not believe in discrimination on the basis of race and ethnicity. Family is, well, family. Of course, being Greek isn't his only character trait. He is my personal aide."

When the Godfather had finished, he looked expectantly at our hero. "Now ... who're you, what's ya name, where ya from?"

"I'm Hoboman," said he. "And I have to take you down. If that means killing you then, hey, I'm all for it."

"Why do you wanna go be doin' a thing like that for, huh?" Giovanni asked.

"My conscience told me to. Plus, it's all in the name, isn't it? 'Mafia'? An organised group of criminals with a complex and ruthless behavioural code?"

"And your conscience told you all this? You must be confused. Your conscience is wrong, friend."

"It's bound to happen, I'll admit."

"We're not an organisation like the Downtown Mafia," the Godfather explained. "We're a family. The Mafia. As in 'Mafia' is our surname. Go back and check. We're referred to with a capital 'M' because surnames are proper nouns. Any other instances are not capitalised as they are just simple nouns. That wasn't just an editing inconsistency!"

"I could have sworn people refer to you as 'the Giovanni Crime family.'"

"They do," acknowledged the Godfather. "You see, 'Crime' is my father's surname. I keep both as a reminder of my heritage. My full name is Giovanni Mafia-Crime."

"Aren't you called 'Don'?"

"It's a joke. The irony of my name is not lost on us, so we make the most of it. Ya gotta, ya know?"

"How come everything looks so shady over here with the dull lights?"

"I can field dat one," Giuseppe interjected. "I've been to da optometrist today and my pupils are still dilated from da drops. Da Godfadda asked to seat us over here with some low lighting. He's a lovely guy like dat."

Hoboman frowned, deeply confused. "But what about when you 'whack' people?"

"Whadda 'bout it?"

"Isn't that another word for killing someone?"

"Ah, I see. No, no, when we say we're 'whacking' someone, we literally mean we just hit 'em on the back of the head. Ya know? Whack. We are completely legitimate. If the Uptown Mafia commits crimes," said the Godfather, "I don't want to be on the side of the law."

"I fear I've made a terrible mistake," Hoboman mused.

"Why, just last week our fundraiser helped renovate the maternity ward at the hospital." The hospital in question housed a statue of Don Giovanni cradling a newborn, erected in honour of the hard work his family had done.

"Hey, I heard about that. I thought that was the Downtown Mafia," Hoboman replied.

"Hell, no!" shouted Tony. "They're the *real* problem! While we was doin' our annual car wash to raise money for new policin' resources, they set up across the street and tried to steal our revenue!"[43]

Hoboman clenched his fists in outrage. "I hate those guys *so* much!"

"You sure you weren't out to whack *them*? And this time I use 'whack' in the killing sense." Giovanni placed a hand paternally on Hoboman's shoulder. "Maybe your conscience was trying to tell you that?"

"Don't think so."

"Oh … ain't that a shame." Giovanni paused and his hand grew tighter. Hoboman thought this was the Godfather's attempt at retaliation and instantly began to cower. The tension eased

---

[43] The Uptown Mafia's annual car wash generates much hype due to the fact it allows for a bunch of mostly chiselled, mostly Italian, mostly guys to strip down and get sudsy … for a good cause.

when Giovanni pointed across the restaurant. "Is that a moving *tuber?*"

Hoboman jumped to his feet as he spotted Jean still making his way along the skirting board as if he were a master of espionage. "I believe that's A POTATO!"

Everyone in the establishment stopped, unnerved by the homeless man's outburst. Jean hadn't quite picked up on the fact that everyone was watching him jumping around and humming spy movie soundtracks, so he continued on, blissfully unaware. The diners began screaming and knocking furniture over in an attempt to escape from the abomination. Only the Mafia remained.

Suddenly, from out of the kitchen, Irishman emerged, brandishing his spud gun and sporting an Italian moustache made of eyeliner. He stopped abruptly when he saw Hoboman staring and shaking his head.

"What the hell are you doing out here?" Hoboman asked.

"Ya shouted the code word."

"No, I didn't."

"Ya shouted 'potato.'"

"That may be so, but 'potato' wasn't the code word. Mamma mia, where did you pull that from?"

"Ya told me Oi'd know the word when ya called it out."

"Yeah, and you just assumed the code word was 'potato' when, in actual fact, it was 'asparagus.'"

"How was Oi supposed to feckin' know the code word was 'asparagus'? 'Potato' makes so much more sense!"

"Typical Irishman," Hoboman whispered to Giovanni. "Can't stop thinking about Irish stereotypes. No wonder they get a bad rep for being stupid. Have you seen this guy?"

"Yer an idiot!" Irishman shouted at Hoboman.

"What's goin' on here?" Giovanni asked. He pushed his chair back, stood up, and gently nudged Hoboman out of the way. "Stavros, you got any idea?"

"It's all Greek to me," Stavros answered, and the family laughed heartily.

Tony folded his arms. "I coulda made dat joke."

"Yes," the Godfather agreed patiently. "But you did not."

"Why don't chu love me, Godfadda?"

"We're not doin' this now, Tony," Giovanni hissed. He scrutinised Irishman and then said, "I recognise you. Where do I know you from?"

Irishman remained impassive, feeling himself above talking to the likes of the Godfather, but Hoboman frowned in concentration.

"Oh yeah, another reason I hated you was because you went and burned down my good friend's potato crops."

"You side against us," the Godfather said to Hoboman, "when your friend is in the IRA?"

"Oi'm not in the feckin' IRA," Irishman exploded. "Who keeps saying that?"

"Flaming Eddie told us," Sergio chimed in. "Said his friend Hobart told him."

"Not the point! Me potatoes! You burned 'em down!"

"I did," Giovanni admitted without remorse.

"Then ya confess?" Irishman burst out. "Ya confess to the murder of me daughter and woife?"

"I did no such thing," the Godfather retorted. "I burnt your potatoes, sure, but I did not kill anyone. Although, technically, Sergio was the one operating the flamethrower."

"Because o' you, me woife and daughter had nuttin' to eat. They starved. I watched 'em die!"

The Godfather scratched his head, perplexed. "How did they starve?"

"They didn't eat! How else do ya feckin' starve?"

"But ... you're a farmer. You had other crops besides the potatoes."

Irishman faltered. "What?"

"I burnt down your potatoes. They were blighted. What was it again?" the Godfather asked no one in particular.

"*Phytophthora infestans*," Doctor Antonia chimed in.

"Thank you, doctor." The Godfather returned his attention to Irishman. "*You* wouldn't weed-whack 'em, so I had to take drastic measures. All your other crops were untouched."

Hoboman, Irishman and the Godfather stood there in awkward silence. Out of nowhere, Irishman exploded with laughter. "Ya burnt —? And all this —? Oh, what a hilarious misunderstandin'. Oi have to say, fellers, I feel loike a *real* dill roight now."

"You may feel like a dill, mate," Hoboman hissed, "but you're not the one who just smacked the head of the Mafia with a stick of garlic-flavoured bread."

The Godfather patted Hoboman's back as a gesture of good faith.

"Water under the Rialto Bridge, my friend. Why don't we fogedda 'bout all this, sit down and have dinner? Vincenzo has whipped us up a feast, and I, for one, cannot wait to get my hands on these scrumptious meatballs." He sat back down and smacked his lips in anticipation.

"I hope you're going to use a fork for those meatballs," Antonia said, placing her hands on her hips and grinning a cheesy grin.

"Because I said I couldn't wait to get my hands on those meatballs. And you said use a fork. Because of manners. Now, *that's* funny. The only thing cheesier than you is the cheese on these

meatballs. And I love cheese. Yum, yum, get in my belly, you delicious, cheesy meatballs. Nom, nom, nom." The Godfather laughed
monotonously, and everybody joined in.

It looked like things were going to turn out all right after all.

Except Hoboman didn't want to waste a trip. "It's been a while
since I've bashed someone. When in Rome."

Giovanni's laughter stopped immediately.

"Very well." He turned to the family and declared, "It appears
we have a shootout scenario on our hands. Please make sure there
are no innocents present before you switch the safety off on your
guns! Bruno, it's your turn to make sure the streets are clear. We
don't wanna endanger anyone with a stray bullet." Bruno nodded
dutifully. "Thank you, everyone. I expect you all at the working
bee tomorrow to clean up poor Mario's restaurant."

Once the meals were finished, cutlery set aside and mouths
wiped, the family stood and tucked in their chairs.

"It's time for the festivities to start."

"I hope they have a piñata," Hoboman whispered to Irishman.
As the Mafia removed their vintage tommy guns from the violin cases – although Guiseppe appeared to be struggling with his
– Hoboman ordered, "Time to load up your spud gun, my Irish
friend."

"With what?"

Hoboman stared at Irishman in disbelief, hoping he was jok-
ing. He facepalmed when it became apparent he was not.

"How can you Irish idiots be so stupid? It's right there in the
name. You load a *spud* gun with *potatoes*!"

"And where am Oi going to get feckin' potatoes from?"

"Why do you think I made you wait in the bloody kitchen?"

"How many potatoes do ya foind in an Italian kitchen? They
all eat pasta and pizza!"

Hoboman slapped Irishman in the face, although the finger-less gloves softened the blow. "That is racist and I would like an apology!"

"Yer not Italian, though."

"You been looking up my family tree, huh, punk? We have the same Italian relatives, you idiota!"

"We have the same *Oirish* relatives!"

"Irish. Italian. Same thing."

"Who's the racist now?"

"If I might interrupt, gentlemen." Giovanni was watching the two, shifting his own gun from hand to hand impatiently. "We're ready when you are."

"Sounds good to me," replied Hoboman with a smile.

"But Oi still don't have any ammunition!"

"Gnocchi?" the Godfather suggested.

"I beg your pardon?" Hoboman begged.

"We use potato in gnocchi."

Hoboman rounded on Irishman. "Did you even *check* the kitchen?"

"Ugh, just start!" Irishman shouted at Giovanni.

With that, all hell broke loose. The restaurant quickly became a battlefield. Tables were tipped. All that could be heard was the sound of gunfire, ricocheting bullets, and Hoboman's high-pitched screaming.

Hoboman leapt behind a table and found Irishman taking cover nearby, having had the same idea. Despite the Mafia being able to see both their targets, they never once moved from their positions. Neither did they shoot through the tables, opting to shoot around them as the tables weren't their property.

"Right, we need a plan of attack," Hoboman stated, slamming his fist into his palm. "A good general dishes out tasks, so *you* think of one."

"We need alternative weaponry," Irishman decided. "This useless piece of garbage is non-lethal.[44] If ya can distract those fellers—"

"And gals."

" —long enough for me to make it to the kitchen, Oi can grab some knives and the tables will turn."

"If you want the tables to turn, I can grab this end and push, and all you have to do is pull from your end. I think we're strong enough."

Irishman ignored Hoboman, saying, "For the distraction, it just has to be somethin' as simple as jumpin' out from behind your table to that one over there." He pointed to the upturned table ten metres from where they were hiding.

"But ... there are lots of flying bullets!" Hoboman shouted, raising his voice so he could be heard over the roar of lots of flying bullets.

"Aye, don't worry. Oi saw a documentary about action movies, and it said the ratio of bullets spent to bullets-hitting-their-targets is very low."

At these words, Hoboman shrugged, then jumped out into the middle of the bullet storm without a second thought. He suddenly paused, realising the fallacy of what Irishman had said. "Wait a minute ... there's no such thing as a documentary!"

Irishman leaned across and pushed Hoboman over. Hoboman fell behind cover, causing the Mafia to become sufficiently confused by the friendly fire to miss Irishman running towards the kitchen. An accidental shot suddenly pierced the corner of Hoboman's table; he shrieked and jumped out into the open, throwing his hands up in the air for protection. He locked eyes with Giuseppe.

---

[44] Jean would beg to differ.

They both froze.

Hoboman stood there, reminded of his encounter with that cat way back when. He waited for Giuseppe to pull out his tommy gun from his still unopened violin case. Tension was building to the point where Hoboman could hear a high-pitched whining in his ears – but it was just his tinnitus. Hoboman flinched as Giuseppe finally made his move and shook the violin case so the gun would roll out … except it didn't.

Giuseppe shook the case a couple more times to no avail. "Sorry. This usually doesn't happen. I'm mortified," he apologised. "Yo, Don, I can't get my violin case open!" he called over the noise.

Giovanni turned, barely able to hear Giuseppe, only identifying him on seeing him wave. "What's the problem?" the Godfather asked, as he walked over amid a storm of bullets, the family still shooting around their only visible target.

"It's my case, Don. I can't get it open."

Giovanni took the case and gave it a tug. When that didn't work, he tried to pry it open with his fingers. Nothing.

"Excuse us a moment," Giovanni panted, his face steadily turning red.

"By all means," Hoboman replied. "Take your time."

Both Giovanni and Giuseppe grappled with the case, but it still wouldn't open. "Damn locks are jammed," Giuseppe muttered as he yanked again.

Hoboman walked over and leaned in to take a closer look. "Try lubricating them," he offered.

Giuseppe looked up, beads of sweat dripping into his eyes. "We might need some oil. But there wouldn't be any mechanics or hardware stores open at this time of night … would there?"

"Does anyone have any oil on them?" Giovanni called out to the other gangsters.

"No, I think we're all pretty clean," Salvatore answered. "Lucky the car wash was today, huh?"

"I think there's some olive oil in the kitchen," Hoboman said. "I could look, if you like."

"That would be most kind."

As he walked into the kitchen, Hoboman considered how much of a gentleman Giovanni was. His words, so eloquent; his manners, impeccable.[45] He said hello to Jean, who was busy making a cuppa, and nodded to Irishman. He began searching through the cupboards and snorted when he found a large tin of oil.

"Heh, extra virgin." He returned to Giovanni and Giuseppe, offered the canister, and asked, "Will this do?"

"Byootiful," Giovanni replied.

Giuseppe poured generous amounts of oil onto the locks and then fiddled with them. "Still nothing!"

"But it brings the case up really well," Hoboman noted, nodding his approval at the sheen.

"I'm sorry, Giuseppe, I thought that would work," Giovanni consoled with a pat on the back.

"Why don't you try spitting?"[46]

Giuseppe thought that was worth a shot and spat on the locks. He tried again but, as expected, still no results. Hoboman berated him for not rubbing the spit in. This time, Giuseppe followed Hoboman's instructions and the locks finally clicked, allowing him to open his case and shake out his tommy gun.

---

[45] That was the gist of: "He isn't a dick."
[46] The Godfather looked as though he was having 'Nam flashbacks at the mere suggestion.

Hoboman, Giovanni and Giuseppe all cheered. Hoboman decided he should go back to the kitchen and get some wine to celebrate.

"As you were," he told Giuseppe.

While searching for wine in the kitchen, Hoboman felt a hand on his shoulder. If it didn't move within five seconds, he would be forced to unleash his karate-fu on the owner, and he didn't want to have to resort to such violence. Luckily, the hand was removed after four point nine seconds and Hoboman relaxed. He turned so he was face to face with Irishman, and thanked God he hadn't severely beaten the snot out of his good friend and ally.

"What are ya doin'?" Irishman asked.

"Looking for wine," Hoboman frowned, turning back to continue his search.

"Now isn't the toime for woine!"

"Well, you sure are doing a lot of it, matey."

"You know what Oi mean!"

"Yeah. Although, if I'm being completely honest here, I got me the delirium tremens."

"Do ya even know what yer supposed to be doing?"

Hoboman's face paled. "Oh no, what's wrong with me?"

"There 'tis. You've just realised this entoire fight is—"

"That damn garlic bread!" Hoboman staggered and latched onto Irishman for support.

"Oi ... Oi'm not following ya."

Irishman watched in amazement as the skunk tail unfurled from the seat of Hoboman's trousers and stood erect but, having never witnessed the phenomenon, the meaning was lost on him. Instinctively, he grabbed Hoboman's forearms and refused to let go.

The Mafia were oblivious to what was transpiring in the kitchen. All they heard was a sound similar to a roof breaking with extreme force. Then a noxious green gas seeped into the dining area. They covered their noses and tried to see through the fog.

"I got an idea!" someone shouted. "Let's shoot blindly until we hit stuff."

The rest of the Mafia agreed on this course of action and headed into the gas, firing their guns relentlessly. They cheered as they heard the satisfying thuds of bullets hitting flesh. It wasn't until the cheers gradually died down, one by one, often accompanied by a mysterious gurgling and cry of pain, that they started to wonder if things weren't going as swimmingly as they had hoped. Just before the stink gas cleared, two opposing figures saw each other in the fog and shot to kill, firing at the same time and dropping each other simultaneously.

Bruno burst through the doors, having cleared all innocents from the vicinity, to find the bodies of his fallen comrades.

"What happened here?" he boomed, adopting the crane stance in readiness. "Who did this?"

He stooped down to inspect the scene more carefully. He could only surmise that in the period of low visibility caused by the gas the Mafia had killed each other in the crossfire.

Screaming could be heard from above, growing incrementally louder as the seconds passed. Bruno stared up at the ceiling, trying to determine what the noise could possibly be. Before he could register what was happening, Hoboman and Irishman crashed through the roof and landed right on top of him, breaking his neck and killing him dead.

Hoboman was the first to stand and brush the plaster dust off. He felt the back of his trousers and noticed his skunk tail had receded once again. He was relieved that his cape was long enough to cover his plumber's crack.

"What the hell was that?" Irishman asked groggily, standing and rubbing his forehead.

The two looked around the now-deserted restaurant and surveyed the damage. Every member of the Mafia lay dead on the floor, filled with more lead than a graphite pencil. Bruno was the exception.

Jean walked out of the kitchen, paused, looked at the bodies on the floor and then up at Hoboman.

"Hey, guys," he said nonchalantly.

"Jean, did you kill all these goons?" Hoboman asked.

Jean was busy picking the sprouts off his body and throwing them into a nearby pot plant. "... Yes?" he answered uncertainly.

Hoboman's cheeks glowed with pride. "Attaboy, Jean! You're finally growing up."

It was done. Jean knew it was time to take his leave. He had finally impressed Hoboman, and he realised it was only a matter of time before he did something to annoy him and revert back to square one. As he turned, he tripped on a discarded spoon and fell over. No biggie. The best of people tripped over. He still had his dignity.

But he faced unexpected resistance when he went to stand and found his foot caught in the feeding belt of the semi-automatic spud gun. The weapon chose this moment to activate, as someone had left the safety off. Jean screamed in pain and terror as he was fed along the belt, processed through the bullet chambers and shot out of the barrel, only to splatter on one of the walls.

Silence. Then ...

"Mashed potato. Didn't think he was going to be mashed potato."

"He's dead?" Irishman asked. "It was all so sudden."

"Meh, I'll live," Hoboman said in response. "He won't."

"Oi feel like you should say somethin' to commemorate him. Some words of respect."

Hoboman thought long and hard about a fitting send-off. "Oh, I got it! Ahem. 'Later tater.'"

"That's it?" Irishman spluttered. "That's all you have to say about the boy who saved our bacon? A ridiculous pun?"

"What pun?" Hoboman's brain began hurting as something came to mind. "Wait. Bacon?" This jogged something else in his memory. He ran for the exit, rummaging through his pockets as he did so to find the mobile phone.

"Where are ya goin'?" Irishman called after our hero.

"Me? I'm going to catch some pigs!" He stopped and turned. "I think I should just let you know that I don't mean *actual* pigs. You see, 'pig' is a slang term for a police officer, and—"

"Just feck off already!"

CHAPTER 9

Piggin'

Half past ten. Grand Slightly-Off-Centre Park. Hoboman leisurely followed the path to the fountain positioned just a little to the right of the middle of the park. The place was close to empty, except for a few hangers-on from the zoo who had made it this far and packed it in for the night.

It seemed that, at some point following the liberation of the zoo, Bubba had decided to occupy the park. He had instructed Hoboman to meet him there on the double so they could discuss how the rest of the night would pan out. When Hoboman arrived at the fountain, he found Bubba splashing about, shirtless but still wearing his jeans, nurturing his mullet all the way down to the roots with conditioner. He waved at our hero, then dunked his head in the fountain to wash the conditioner off, whipping his hair around like a model in a shampoo commercial and spraying Hoboman with dirty hair water in the process. Bubba stepped out, towelling himself off with his flanno.

"Howdy, stranger," he drawled, lifting the brim of the trucker's hat he'd put back on. He gestured for Hoboman to have a seat. On the dirt, because he only had the one chair and he wasn't giving it up for nobody.

"I'm Hoboman. We met at the bar earlier, so we're not actually strangers."

Bubba lounged back in his camping chair, the warm light of a campfire illuminating his confusion. Unsure if Hoboman was being serious or just playing with him, he replied, "I know, I was jus' horsin' around is all." Bubba cracked open a beer and sipped at it, trying to get a read on his newfound colleague. "Hey, would ya like some grub?"

"Boy, would I!" It was only then that Hoboman noticed Bubba's spit roast, which accounted for the lit fire in the middle of summer. "Hey, I thought you said you had grubs on. What the hell do you call that? It bears a striking resemblance to Wally the octopus chicken."

"This, ma friend, is a bran' new food I like ta call 'calummari drumsticks'. Ya oughta try one."

Hoboman picked up one of the drumsticks and sniffed it. "Calamari drumsticks, eh?" He took a bite and spat it out immediately. "That's disgusting!" he critiqued, before pocketing the rest to save for a rainy day.

"Down ta bizness," Bubba said, leaning forward in his chair. "Are ya ready ta get yer hands dirty? On account'a we might have ta kill these here cops?"

Hoboman scrutinised his hands and shrugged. "They're already dirty, so I don't see why not."

Bubba clapped his hands together. "Yee-haw! Let's go kill some pigs!"

"You might want to start with that one," Hoboman observed. He peeked behind Bubba at a slavering brute of a boar tethered to a lamp post by a length of rope threaded through its nose ring. The light from the lamp only accentuated the hideousness of the creature.

"Yeah, I was jus' gonna make some breakfas' and then I saw this li'l fella."

"Hey, I put a lot of effort into breaking him out of the zoo ... I think!" Hoboman exclaimed, horrified at the notion of eating the pig, no matter how much he salivated at the thought of the delicious, tasty bacon it would make.

"I simply couldn't shoot 'im. Inn't he jus' so loveable?"

Hoboman eyed the boar, which was pawing the ground and growling. "I see what you mean. Once you get past the bristles and the tusks, he *is* kind of cute."

"Hey, I never said nothin' about him bein' cute. I said loveable, 'kay?"

"Got it."

"I'mma keep it and call him Tootsie."

Bubba briefly recounted how he had been strolling through the park and come across Tootsie. He had the hog in his sights but found himself lowering the shotgun, unable to bring himself to kill such an innocent creature. Their battle was one for the ages and, despite nearly being gored on several occasions, Bubba had managed to slip the rope through Tootsie's nose ring while they wrestled. The fight had all but disappeared on being tied up, but looking at the pig's beady little eyes, Hoboman thought there was something calculating about Tootsie's expression.

Untying the rope from the lamp post, the Southerner held it like a leash and led Tootsie over to Hoboman so the pig could familiarise himself with the hobo's powerful scent. "Ain't he a right terror?" Bubba laughed as the hog tried to escape. "Now, let's mosey on down to the cop shop."

Hoboman was led to the rendezvous point, a vacant construction site within line of sight of the police station. The two prepared to go over their plan, Bubba first tying Tootsie to a girder to ensure he did not assault any innocents. Yet.

"What's the plan?" asked Bubba.

Hoboman scratched his chin in contemplation. "Ah, well, okay. Um ... basically ... what I'm thinking is ... that is to say ..."

"You ain't got a friggin' clue."

"You would be correct in that assumption."

"Thank the Lord God and His li'l baby Jesus that I been thinkin' this through on the way over." Bubba found a stick and began to doodle in a patch of dirt. "I've been sussin' out the station for a long time." Bubba drew a rectangle in the dirt and pointed at it. "This here is the ground floor. It's got waitin' rooms and yer secret'ry up front, all the files out back. Luckily, they ain't got no guns, so we're gonna get by 'em pretty quick, I reckon."

Hoboman nodded and Bubba drew another rectangle, this one directly on top of the first. "Then we get to the secon' floor. This is where I want *you* to pay attention. On the secon' floor, we have holdin' cells. I want you to bus' out everyone you can. Operation: Liberate the Pissheads. Got it?"

"Why do *I* have to pay particular attention here? Aren't you going to help me out? I'll just follow your lead."

"Ah, I'm glad ya asked. See, while you stay on the secon' floor, freein' the drunkies and whatnot, I'mma be on the third floor in the evidence room. Couple desk jockeys up there gonna need extra-special attention, if ya catch my drift." Bubba winked and patted his shotgun.

"I think I do," Hoboman said, but only to seem smart and earn some of that sweet, sweet positive reinforcement. "I can't believe you know the layout of the station just from looking at the exterior of the building! Wow!"

"... Yup."

"You haven't looked at any plans?"

"… Nup."

"An amazing voice *and* smart," our hero marvelled. He looked at the crude depiction of the police station and compared it to the real one. Using his brain for once, he queried, "What's our escape plan? I suppose we might not need one if we slaughter everyone. We could walk straight out the front door."

"That's on the assumption they don't got no backup. If they do, the third floor's our ticket outta there. My guess is they'll have confiscated sumthin' that'll be of use to us. We take whatever that may be to get out o' there, pronto."

Hoboman thought this over and nodded slowly. "What happens if there's nothing in the evidence room we can use?"

"We're in a buttload o' trouble."

"Noted. Well, I'm satisfied. Ready?"

Bubba jumped up and kicked the dirt to remove any traces of their plan, lest someone come across a couple of rectangles and deduce a hostile assault on a police station was imminent. "As I'll ever be." Balancing his shotgun in the crook of his arm, Bubba untied Tootsie and wrapped the rope around his hand. "Let's roll."

The trio set off, heedless of what dangers lay ahead. Who knew what perils they would face by venturing into the great unknown? Then they crossed the road and arrived. Gripping stuff.

Bubba made some hand gestures Hoboman didn't quite comprehend and urged Tootsie through the automatic doors. Hoboman took some time to repeat the gestures, analyse them, realise he still didn't understand them, then gave up.

He stepped into the lobby and took in his surroundings. A set of double doors lay dead ahead, leading to the file rooms. There was a reception booth on the left-hand side of the room.

Immediately next to it was a flight of stairs, with a 'No Entry' sign mounted on the wall. On the opposite side were some plastic visitors' seats, and an elevator positioned further along, unlockable only by employees.

"It's important," Bubba began once Hoboman had caught up, "that Tootsie dun't git off this here rope. Could have terrible consequences for the plan. I'mma let ya hold it ta gimme a chance ta check out the perimeter. Don't let go now, ya hear?"

"Loud and clear."

"That ain't what we want. We wanna be as quiet as possible."

"Oh ... quiet and clear. Quiet and murky?"

Bubba left Hoboman muttering to himself and went to strike up a conversation with the receptionist. From what our hero could see, the receptionist was a curt, middle-aged lady who didn't want her time wasted. Bubba did not seem affronted by her attitude, even though she was casting some serious shade his way, as he was, of course, only trying to scope out the place.

Hoboman thought maybe the hog slinking its way over would cheer her up.

It took some time for him to register. His stomach dropped. Bubba had been in a rush to hand over the reins, and Hoboman had lost depth perception after ingesting all that alcohol over the course of the night. There was no rope in his hand. In fact, it was trailing across the floor, still attached to Tootsie's nose ring.

Tootsie manoeuvred silently past the reception desk and stopped at the doors to the filing room. Through careful and seemingly expert manipulation of his snout, he lassoed the rope so it caught round the door handles, and pulled down. The doors opened with a creak that snagged Bubba's attention. The Southerner whipped his head in Hoboman's direction and came quicksmart to the conclusion that, somehow, it was *his* hog causing the diversion. Doing his best not to lose his cool, he abruptly ended his conversation with the receptionist and re-joined Hoboman.

"Codsarn it! Look what ya done now!" Bubba hissed. "Change o' plans. I'mma go after Tootsie. You need to find a way up to the secon' floor."

Hoboman gave Bubba the thumbs-up and watched as the Southerner snuck into the filing room. As the door opened, Hoboman heard Tootsie screaming psychotically, "This little piggy's going to market!"

"Righto," Hoboman declared. "Game plan."

The receptionist had given the impression she had been working for a long time, so Hoboman thought a peace offering would be the best way to appeal to the good-hearted side of her nature.

In the corner of the waiting room was a coffee machine. Easy. Sitting on the chairs waiting to be attended to was a mother and her small child, oblivious to the whole Tootsie episode, having missed all the action while playing on their phones. Knowing what he had to do, our hero ventured over to them. The receptionist glanced up momentarily before the scratching of her pen resumed.

Since Hoboman had no money, the most sensible thing to do would be to ask the mother for some spare change and offer to pay her back later (something he would, in reality, never do, but it would ease his guilt to offer). The mother became visibly more distressed with every step closer Hoboman took, until he was standing right in front of her, leaning in. All he had to do was extend his hand and she was throwing some coins at him. In the time it took for Hoboman to flinch, the mother scooped her child up in her arms and ran for the exit, screaming. The receptionist merely narrowed her eyes at the unnecessary noise and went back to work.

"Thank you!" Hoboman called to the woman's retreating figure before crouching down to pick up the shrapnel, earning a look of pure scorn from the receptionist.

He counted out two dollars for the coffee and pocketed the leftovers, because his parents had always told him to save – and also to steal, where possible. Once in front of the coffee machine, he fed the coins in and waited as it began filling up a disposable cup. There were no lids left, but he was sure the receptionist wouldn't mind; after all, he was buying her a free drink.

"Good evening," Hoboman greeted her, mustering up the friendliest smile he could manage. "I thought you might enjoy a hot beverage."

"I can't talk right now," the receptionist said shortly.

"You look swamped."

"I am. Apparently some hobo staged a riot at the zoo, and I've been answering phones and writing reports from concerned citizens non-stop! Now let me get back to work!"

Hoboman thought this sounded like him but reasoned there must be another zoo around because he wasn't just 'some hobo'. He was Hoboman! He had to admit, the similarities to his adventurous night were uncanny, though. Maybe Downtown had its own hero too?

"Just have the coffee."

"Is it a decaf espresso macchiato with skim goat's milk?" she asked.

"Not exactly."

The receptionist looked up sharply and Hoboman shrank back in alarm. There were dark patches beneath her eyes, and the eyes themselves were bloodshot and full of menace.

"Then I *don't* want it!" she spat before going back to her work.

Hoboman stared at her blankly, impassively, for a beat, then proceeded to tip the scalding-hot coffee all over her. The receptionist shrieked in terrible agony and writhed in pain. Tangled up in her telephone cord, she fell backwards off her chair and inadvertently raked all the paperwork from her desk onto the floor. Hoboman spied angry red blotches all over her skin as her movements died down to spasmodic twitches.

Our hero watched the entire scene play out without an iota of emotion and, when the receptionist finally stopped making noises, all he said was, "Oops, I tripped."

With the waiting room now empty, he decided the best course of action would be to proceed to the second floor before the receptionist came to; it was safe to assume she would be a tad angry. He ascended the stairs, two at a time, and stopped when they plateaued. Arriving at an intermediate landing, he saw he could either walk through the doorway into a room on the second floor or continue up another set of stairs towards the evidence room.

In his mind, Hoboman had been devising a plan to sneak past all the cops to steal the holding cell keys and release the prisoners – but it seemed they were all already preoccupied. A visiting psychologist stood in front of a cell with a clipboard and a pen, taking notes as she held a conversation with Flaming Eddie. "You need to stop setting yourself on fire," she was saying. "For the last time, Edward: you are a human!"

"No, I'm aflame!" Flaming Eddie shouted back delightedly, slurring his words thickly.

"It's just no use! I can't work with him!" The psychologist discarded her clipboard and threw her arms into the air in exasperation.

A passing beat cop, cradling a stack of papers on his way back from the photocopier, heard the commotion and strolled over. On seeing Flaming Eddie in the holding cells, he smiled affectionately and asked, "Oh, Flaming Eddie, are you in for arson *again?*"

"Nah, driving under the influence on me mobility scooter.[47] And then I tried to outrun the arresting officers on it," Flaming Eddie mumbled.

"Oh, you! Don't worry about a thing, Flaming Eddie. I'll put in a good word. We'll get this sorted."

"Yeah, cheers mate."

The psychologist, flabbergasted, alternated between staring at Flaming Eddie and the beat cop. "I'm sorry, but am I missing something here?"

"Flaming Eddie is a regular. We even had him deputised a couple of months ago. He's a real swell guy."

"He's a fruitcake!"[48]

The beat cop's face finally lost its cheer.

"You better watch who you say that to. Flaming Eddie's a hero. All the local hobos seem to be, come to think of it. But do you know why Flaming Eddie is homeless? He gave everything he had to the Burns Unit. Every last cent." A statue of Flaming Eddie could be found next to the one of Don Giovanni at the hospital. "Just because he's mentally unwell ..." The cop clicked his tongue in disgust. "You of all people should know."

While everyone was distracted, Hoboman commando-rolled into the room and began crawling under the desks. His mission: liberate every person being wrongly held captive. Although he was pretty sure some of these people were serial killers, his conscience had explained to him that the police were corrupt, so they'd probably just leaked false information to the press to make the ignorant masses believe they'd caught a baddie.

---

[47] Although, technically, it wasn't *his* scooter.
[48] Flaming Eddie wished.

Something he had not foreseen was that crawling involved staring directly at the floor and, as such, he had no idea where he was headed. His lack of spatial awareness caused him to smash his head on the bars of one of the cells. He came to a halt and tentatively looked through the bars, hoping that if the cell did belong to a maniac, slow movements would not cause him (or her) to lose his (or her) mind, grab a tuft of his hair and squish his head through the gaps. He reached through the bars and began to grope the powerful legs, then the powerful body, and, finally, the powerful head of a ... North American brown bear.

"Flaming Eddie?" he asked.

"Who's he?" replied the North American brown bear.

"Oh, my God!" Hoboman squealed at the occupant of the cell. "Are you Trout the Grizzly, backup singer and jug blower with Bubba and the Jugettes before you guys split up?"

"Yeah, sure, that's me," replied Trout the Grizzly, backup singer and jug blower with Bubba and the Jugettes before those guys split up. "Look, man, you gotta help me out. I'm in some real trouble here. See, they caught me for possessing maple but, like, this mule gave it to me. I was only holding it for a friend. Jeez, my mum will kill me if she finds out. I'm freaking out, man."

Hoboman noticed Trout's bloodshot eyes and tried to soothe him by reaching through the bars, grabbing his shoulders and manhandling him. "Settle down right now!" he screamed. "Are you tweaking?"

"Why? Does it seem like I am? I totally don't even know how you'd do maple. Would you inject it?"

"Maybe if it's syrup," Hoboman considered. "Anyway, shut up, I get side-tracked easy. I'm here to bust you out, got it? But if I help you, you'll need to help me break everyone else out."

"Just be quick about it, man. You got the keys?"

"No."

"How're we gonna break out then, man? *Shit!*"

"Trout, stay calm and listen to me. I'm going to need you to follow me on this one: you are a *giant* grizzly bear. Bend the bars."

Trout hesitantly reached out and gingerly gripped two adjacent bars, looking at Hoboman for confirmation. Hoboman nodded. Trout nodded back, reassured, and heaved with all his strength, pulling the bars away from each other. He stumbled backwards after making an opening and, so taken aback was he by his own feat of strength, had to sit down.

"Wow, man, you're really smart."

"I know," Hoboman replied humbly. "C'mon, the other prisoners are waiting. But this should be easy, because the only other prisoner is Flaming Eddie. It must have been a quiet night."[49]

Trout pulled himself through the broken bars and lumbered over to the containment unit housing Flaming Eddie. The beat cop and the psychologist were still bickering, so Trout shouted, "Get out of the way, please! We don't want anyone to get hurt."

Unfortunately, Hoboman was the only one who could understand Trout. As for the cop and the psychologist, all they saw was a grizzly bear charging at them, roaring. To them, he might have been saying, "For too long you have oppressed the *Ursus arctos!* Prepare to feel the wrath of the crouching grizzly, hidden bear!" He could also have been saying, "Get out of the way, please! We don't want anyone to get hurt." Then again, he may have just been growling.

---

[49] Of course, the real reason for the lack of inmates was the citywide animal outbreak, which had stretched the police too thin to deal with criminals as there were so many trampling incidents to be investigated.

"Quick, take refuge on the first floor in the filing room!" shouted the beat cop. The psychologist ran as soon as she was given directions, but the beat cop paused and placed a hand on a bar of Flaming Eddie's cell. "I'm sorry, Flaming Eddie, but I'd never be able to make it to the keys in time. Please forgive me!"

"All good, mate," Flaming Eddie replied, as the beat cop ran down the stairs.

"I must be wigging out," Trout muttered to himself as he bent the bars of Flaming Eddie's cell and let the hobo out. "I thought I was telling them to get out of the way. What was I *really* saying?"

Trout's eyes glazed over as he contemplated the meaning of life, the universe, and everything. Hoboman knew there was no waking the grizzly from his deep reverie, having seen this look before when he and his fellow hobos gathered around a burning Flaming Eddie to discuss philosophy after a few drinks.

By the time it clicked for Hoboman that the first floor was anything but a safe haven, it was too late. He heard the psychologist scream, "Oh Jeeeesus, it's just as bad as up there!" The beat cop added, "As if almost getting mauled by a bear wasn't enough! Now I'm going to get gored by a hog, too!" What followed was a whole lot of standard-issue screaming of the type Hoboman heard way too often to care about.

After the screams had died down, footsteps could be heard coming up the stairs. Hoboman braced himself to go out with a fight by cowering under the nearest desk, until he saw Bubba's boots and emerged from cover. Bubba instinctively raised his shotgun and aimed it at Hoboman, lowering it only when he saw it was not another cop. "You dun't wanna go down there," Bubba drawled. "Tootsie left a whole lotta carnage, if ya know what I mean. Blood an' guts everwhar."

"Oh, you caught him," Hoboman observed.

"No thanks to you," Bubba replied, tying Tootsie to a desk. "All I can say is I'm glad them two others turned up, otherwise he woulda 'scaped again. While he was busy with 'em, I was able ta slip round and get him." Tootsie, apparently satisfied by his rampage, collapsed onto his side and promptly went to sleep.

"I found Trout, at least. He's just over there." Hoboman jerked his thumb towards the corner of the room, where Trout had fallen onto his butt, content to stare at the wall.

Bubba ran past our hero to his friend's aid. Hoboman, knowing he was already tempting fate by stepping foot inside a police station, headed upstairs to find a MacGuffin to get them the hell out of there. There was a distinct change in décor the further up our hero went. Where electric lights had illuminated the rooms below, flaming torches in brackets now took their place. Neatly organised bricks gave way to roughly hewn chunks of stone. The whole third floor had a distinctly mediaeval vibe. By the time he had reached the archaic door bearing the inscription 'Evidence Room', Hoboman was harbouring serious doubts as to whether he wanted to advance any further.

Hoboman was just reaching out to push the door when it slowly (and creepily) began to open by itself. Darkness awaited him as the unknown beckoned. Not even the flickering flames of the torches illuminated the room. Steeling himself, Hoboman stepped inside, expecting a trap.

He was not disappointed.[50]

Suddenly, the door slammed shut behind him, engulfing him in the darkness. Someone was here with him! He could hear them

---

[50] In the sense that he was right. He was disappointed someone had set up a trap, as it meant that someone didn't like him, but then it meant they hated him so much, they put in the effort to devise a trap in the first place. He was of two minds.

scuttling about. But who, or what, was it? After a moment's delay, an intense light permeated the room, momentarily blinding him. Before he knew what was happening, a police baton was rammed into his back, sending him sprawling onto the cold stone floor. Grimacing in pain, he slowly opened his eyes to accustom them to the light. What his gaze fell on blinded him again in a not quite so literal sense.

Sergeant Bolbusta towered over him, clad in high heels, arse-less leather chaps, a leather vest and a collar studded with spikes. In his hand was a cat o' nine tails, which he was slapping repeatedly against his thigh. Bolbusta himself seemed desensitised to the slaps, but Hoboman couldn't stop himself from wincing with each strike.

Our hero struggled to his feet and backed away, trying to create as much distance between himself and the sergeant as possible. He backed into something and jumped. Behind him hung an assortment of mediaeval torture equipment and gimp suits galore. There were also boxes filled with illicit items, with fireworks being especially prominent. One also shouldn't forget to include the collection of murder weapons. It was like a torture dungeon … only not so much a dungeon. A torture *attic*? Is that a thing?

"Aw, nuts," Hoboman said. "I swore I would never end up in a place like this. Not after last time."

"I told you I was going to have to reprimand you!" Bolbusta warned, advancing.

"When?" Hoboman shrieked.

"End of Chapter Two."

"Heck," Hoboman muttered to himself. "Actually, I believe you did tell me I would have to *be reprimanded*," he corrected. "But I don't think you specified by whom, so I'm nominating a jury of my peers." Hoboman looked over Bolbusta's shoulder at the door. "If you could scooch over, I'll just duck past you and wait for a formal hearing."

"Stop right there!" Bolbusta whipped the cat o' nine tails threateningly, cowing Hoboman instantly. "You gave me the idea to resort to vigilantism when I met you. The law is too constraining to be effective ... which led me to become this!"

"A dominatrix?"

"A vigilante! Criminals are a superstitious and cowardly lot. So, my disguise must be able to strike terror into their hearts. Look me in the eye and tell me it isn't working."

"I'm too scared to look anywhere else."

"You opened my eyes, showed me I have to be true to myself, no matter what others think." Bolbusta stepped forward imposingly. "Now I want you to answer my questions, *succinctly* – and in quick *succession!*" He leered at Hoboman, as he flicked the cat o' nine tails again.

Hoboman narrowed his eyes. "And what if I answer ambiguously?"

"That's okay ... I take it both ways!"

"Gah! Ew!" Hoboman needed assistance and he needed it fast. "Bubba! Help me!"

With impeccable timing, Bubba pushed open the door to the evidence room, toting his shotgun. "I got a spike on my queer detector!" he explained to Hoboman, rattling the instrument to prove it.

"*Bubba!*" Hoboman hissed, flabbergasted. "You can't just go around calling people 'queer.'"

"No, that's okay," Bolbusta returned. "People like your redneck friend over there use the term 'queer' derogatively, but the LGBT community is starting to take it back as a sort of self-affirming umbrella term. *I* don't necessarily identify as genderqueer, but as gender fluid."

"No, no, no," Bubba disagreed, shaking his head. "If yer born a man, yer born a man. Same goes for women."

"I believe you are referring to one's sex. Gender isn't biological. From a sociological viewpoint, gender is defined as the characteristics pertaining to and differentiating masculinity and femininity. I am fluid in the sense that I don't necessarily believe some things typically described as feminine or masculine are as concrete as others believe. Some days I feel more masculine; other times, more feminine."

The complex words confused Bubba, so he resorted to the next best option and fell to the ground, covering his eyes. "All that leather! I can see yer ass! I can't go no further."

Hoboman scratched his head. "It's just an arse, dude. You're a grown man."

"That's how they turn ya!"

"That's just ignorant," Bolbusta said in response. "Not everyone who identifies as something outside of heteronormativity wears an outfit like this. And we certainly wouldn't want to 'turn' someone like you, as you put it."

"Then how come yer dressed like that?" Bubba questioned.

"It's my vigilante outfit. You wouldn't expect a police sergeant to wear this, would you?"

"S'pose that's true."

"Subverts expectations. Protects my identity."

"Smart," Hoboman agreed.

"Right, enough chit-chat," Bolbusta announced. "You've been a very naughty boy."

Hoboman turned and clawed at the wall, though the stone was so thick he hardly even made a scratch. "Please, I'm too young and nubile to be violated."

"*Violated?*" Bolbusta stopped. "Whoa, whoa, whoa! What are you talking about? I'm not going to *violate* you!"

"But you're talking really suggestively," Hoboman sooked.

"That's just who I am," Bolbusta replied.

"You patted my bum."

"Sports people do it to each other all the time. Wait, so the moment someone who doesn't dress or talk like society dictates does the same, they're going to *violate* you?"

"You winked and told me I'd have to be reprimanded."

"I appreciated your vigilantism, but how would it look if a police sergeant said that out loud? I said the opposite of what I meant, and the wink indicated my true intent." Bolbusta sighed. "Look, I was trying to commend you, but now I understand it came across as overtly sexual and it made you uncomfortable. I'm sorry for that. But let me make it abundantly clear, there is absolutely no excuse for sexual harassment."

Hoboman dried his eyes because a little bit of dirt had irritated them, and that was all, thank you very much. "You aren't going to hurt me then?"

"Oh, I'm going to hurt you. I've resorted to becoming a vigilante, remember? You took down the Mafia, and most of this police station is in ruins. You're getting more than a smack on the wrist."

"How am I going to get out of this one?" Hoboman sank to his knees and clapped his hands together in prayer. "If there is a God up there, and I'm not even a hundred percent sure there is, I need a Christmas miracle!"

It couldn't have been pure coincidence. Bolbusta was just starting to advance when a commotion downstairs distracted him. The sergeant paused, confused, and turned to face the door. A bright, burning object raced up the stairs.

As if sent from Heaven, Flaming Eddie burst into the room, wreathed in flames and laughing like a maniac. He leapt over Bubba's prostrate body, missing him entirely. In a moment of intense clarity, Hoboman knew the box of confiscated fireworks would be Flaming Eddie's terminus.

Driven by an otherworldly force, Hoboman pushed past Bolbusta, who was too distracted by the incendiary hobo to stop him, and lunged for the exit. Bubba followed, running for the door and pulling it shut as he left. Hoboman heard the unmistakeable fizzle of fuses being lit; hanging around with Flaming Eddie over the years had made some sounds very familiar. Hoboman reached out and yanked Bubba's sleeve, causing them both to topple down the stairwell, just as the evidence room door was blown off its hinges. A wave of heat hit them as they tumbled but, otherwise, they were basically unharmed.

Coming to a stop at the bottom of the stairs in a crumpled mess, the hobo and the redneck disentangled themselves from one another – just in case anyone might think they were gay – and paused for a breather. After a minute they stood and dusted themselves off. Their faces were blackened with soot, their clothes were smouldering, and Bubba was going to need a lot of conditioner to fix his mullet. The pair nodded to each other and headed back upstairs to make their escape, the explosion having left the police station missing a roof.

Ash drifted lazily down from the gaping hole that had once been a doorway. The pungent smoke filling the room would have been stifling had it not been for the fact it was able to drift upward and escape through the gap where the roof had been. Fireworks exploded high in the sky above, their unmelodious din contrasting sharply with the rainbow brilliance lighting up the night sky.

Wreckage filled the room. Sergeant Bolbusta was nowhere to be seen, so it was safe to assume he was buried somewhere underneath the rubble. Flaming Eddie, on the other hand, was a freak of nature: his fate remained up in the air.

As the last firework exploded, showering the city in light and potential fire hazards, it illuminated such an incredible sight that Bubba fell to his knees and broke down in tears. Descending from the sky on a flying, ride-on lawnmower, backlit by the remnants of the fireworks, was God Himself. Bubba, weeping uncontrollably, removed his trucker hat and wrung it in his hands, knowing his Christian life had been fulfilled.

"Rise, my child," God addressed Bubba. "There is no need for tears; now is a time for rejoicing."

Bubba did as God instructed, still blinded by tears. "I jus' want ya ta know I love ya, God. But not in no queer way."

"Queer?" God asked. "But why would that make a difference, my son?"

"I dun't wanna be preachin' the King James Bible to ya, but Leviticus, Chapter Twenty, Verse Thirteen: 'If a man also lies with a man, as he lies with a woman, both of 'em have committed an abomination'. Or sumthin.'"

God sighed wearily. "All lies."

"But—"

"That was Grandpapa Razzie; he misquoted me.[51] I never wrote the Bible. People did. They have their own agenda. I've got nothing against homosexuals. It's the ... how do I put this

---

[51] Technically, it was something closer to Great x80 Grandpapa Razzie.

delicately? It's the *Musculus sphincter ani* types of the world I take umbrage with."

Bubba blinked, confused. "So ... there ain't nothin' wrong with the gays?"

"Nope. Just ... don't be an ignorant ... *anus*."

"I gotta save him," the Southerner whispered to himself. He went to turn but quickly added, "Jus' thought I'd tell ya, God: I'm yer bigges' fan."

"You're *my* biggest fan?" God asked. "Are you kidding? I love 'Gator Ate Ma Baby'! It's my favourite album of all time, and I've been around for a while."

Bubba was overwhelmed. He gulped in some air and a few more tears slid down his face before he ventured back into the smog of the police station.

Hoboman scratched his head. "Wait, who is he saving? Bolbusta? Grandpapa Razzie? Or Flam Bam Buoyant?"

God looked at Hoboman. "You're leaving quite a trail of destruction in your wake."

Hoboman shrugged. "It comes with the job."

"Speaking of which," God said, "it's time you helped me with the job I recruited you for."

"Where are we going, Santa?" Hoboman asked.

"Heaven, Hoboman. We're going to Heaven."

CHAPTER 10

The Great Stock Market in the Sky

Hoboman's skunk tail burst out of the seat of his pants. He bent his knees, adopting a diver's stance, to prepare for take-off.

"Nope," God said, shaking His head. "I don't want you fouling up Heaven with skunk gas. Hop aboard."

God parked the lawnmower low enough for Hoboman to clamber on. Once Hoboman was aboard, God spun the wheel and pushed down on the accelerator. The engine sputtered, the exhaust backfired, and He drove off into the sky.

"God, I have to ask: why a flying lawnmower?"

"I need *some* vehicle to fly, but all the good ones are taken. I mean, *Back to the Future* used a flying car *and* a flying train. I couldn't even use a deckchair! I was aiming for something original."

They rode the flying lawnmower higher and higher into the atmosphere. As they broke through the cloud cover, the inky blackness melted from the sky in dribs and drabs until it achieved a midday blue hue. God chucked a mid-air U-ey and pulled up on the surface of some clouds. He killed the engine and stepped off.

Hoboman placed a tentative foot down, relieved to find the cloud surface was as stable as standing on a concrete footpath.

The pearly gates stood tall before our hero, bathed in a golden light, and the Hallelujah Chorus could be heard emanating from beyond. "You'll find that gets real old, real quick," God explained. "We have a choir singing it, but they really wanted to set the right mood, so they sing it *every* time someone shows up. There are a lot of people in the world, Hoboman, and the stream of departed souls rarely slows. Also, they do it even if someone inside Heaven walks too close to the gates, like if you stand too close to an automatic door."

The two wandered over to the gates that arched high above them. As they drew close, Hoboman noticed a pedestal set up with an open logbook. Standing before it was a doughy-looking man: bald, clean-shaven, and dressed in white robes. A pair of tiny wings sprouted from his back, twitching every so often.

"Is that Saint Peter?" Hoboman asked. "I always thought he'd be more ... athletic."

"No, I'm afraid that *isn't* Saint Peter," God answered. "Peter is on long-service leave. One of my archangels, Michael, volunteered to guard the gates. I don't like hurting people's feelings, so I allowed him to do it. Biggest mistake of my life."

"He can't be *that* bad."

"He let a Buddhist into Heaven last week. The guy took a wrong turn at Jannah, on his way to Nirvana. Michael thought he was being nice, because he didn't want the dude to have to travel all the way back. Do you know how awkward it is when you run into someone who doesn't believe in your existence?"

"Been there."

"It's very embarrassing."

"Bummer."

"Yeah. Bummer."

Hoboman and God came to a stop outside the gates and waited longer than they should have for Michael to look up from the logbook. God cleared His throat to expedite things and Michael finally noticed them. "And who might you be?" asked the archangel in a nasal monotone.

"Michael, you know who I am," sighed God. "I've brought Hoboman with me. Would you please open the gates for us?"

Michael glanced down at the logbook then squinted at God. "We're on high alert here. You're not the Devil, are you?"

"No. I just told you. I'm God."

Michael paused, glanced again at the logbook and sighed. "Go on ahead."

The gates opened with a 'Hallelujah' and God walked through them. Just as Hoboman went to follow, they suddenly swung shut. "Hey, what's the big deal?" Hoboman asked.

"I'm sorry, sir, but as I said, we're on high alert here. It's better to be safe than sorry. I'll need you to answer a few questions for me. Number one: are you the Devil?"

"No."

"Go on ahead."

The gates opened up again and Hoboman was granted access properly this time. As the gates shut behind him and the chorus ended, Hoboman turned and looked at Michael, who now had his back to them. He was like a robot that, having fulfilled its purpose, had switched onto standby mode. With no one coming into Heaven, Michael simply stared ahead, completely still except for the odd twitch of a wing.

"That must get tiresome," Hoboman noted.

"I haven't the heart to tell him to stand down," God sighed. "You know, there are some real downsides to being an all-powerful, mostly benevolent deity."

"I can relate."

God led the way and Hoboman followed in silence, taking in the view. It was like a ghost town in more ways than one: no one was around, and the infrastructure consisted solely of dead franchises. Hoboman wouldn't have been above making a Blockbuster joke, if he'd known what a Blockbuster was. Buildings Hoboman remembered from a much younger Uptown made up the streets. Over there was the plant nursery; there, a shoe repair shop. He couldn't believe his eyes when he saw Old Man Mulligan's corner store. The memories!

"How is Old Man Mulligan?" Hoboman asked. "Still giving out free lollies?"

"Oh, Old Man Mulligan isn't here."

"What? But he was so nice!" Hoboman paled. "Wait, I think I can piece it together. Old Man Mulligan handing out free lollies to little kids. He was—"

"Embezzling funds, yeah," God finished. "Why do you think the store shut down?"

"Oh. Makes sense."

They continued along companionably, striking up a conversation. The two spoke about the weather, each other's families, and how apathy and consumerism had contributed to the downfall of society and the values it used to uphold. By the time they stopped outside a dilapidated little building, the topic had naturally progressed to their individual opinions on the optimum temperature for storing butter so it didn't go too hard, but also did not melt.

"Here we are," God declared. "Raphael's Garage!"

"What? Do you need to get your car serviced or something?" Hoboman idly kicked a fuel bowser.

"This is our operations base." God smiled when He saw the dumbfounded expression on Hoboman's face. "You wouldn't expect it, would you?"

They pushed open the warped door and a bell jingled to announce their arrival. Hoboman saw the back of a man in greasy overalls whose wings, while stained with motor oil and bearing lubricant, were huge and beat steadily. At the sound of the jangling bell, the angel turned around, allowing Hoboman to examine his face properly. He looked as if he was straight from the 'fifties: short black hair combed to one side, a thin black moustache, and a flagrant disregard for laws prohibiting indoor smoking.

"Hello, hello, what have we here?" the angel asked, his cigarette dangling lazily from the corner of his mouth. He approached Hoboman, wiping his grease-covered hands with a rag, and extended one when it was a little cleaner. "Raphael's the name. How can I be of service?"

Hoboman shook hands readily; as his hands were constantly dirty, he didn't mind the leftover grease at all. Raphael's face fell on seeing God. He turned around, clapped his hands together and yelled at the sweatshop workers. "All right, get out of here, the lot of you! I don't pay you for standing about!"[52]

God raised an eyebrow at Raphael. "Did you forget about today?"

"Not exactly."

"How come you still have the shop open, given today's importance?"

"I was kind of thinking ... make a few bucks on the side?" Raphael offered. When he saw the look on God's face, he amended his excuse. "Actually, tell you what, I thought what a shame it would be if someone were to blow a gasket on their way to a picnic, seeing as it's so lovely out. Thought I might stay open until you arrive. Purely altruistic reasons, I assure you."

---

[52] Actually, he didn't pay them at all.

Hoboman sympathised as Raphael shrugged and smiled weakly. God, on the other hand, glared. "I'll deal with you later."

"Why don't we step into my office and go over the plan?" Raphael suggested. He held a screen door open for Hoboman and God, and pulled it shut as he followed them in.

The contents of Raphael's office left Hoboman gobsmacked. Filling up most of the room was a collection of highly polished chrome car accessories. They were everywhere, cluttering up the visitors' side of the desk so much that Hoboman and God barely had any elbow room. Raphael, however, had made sure there was plenty of room on his side.

"Not too shabby, eh?" Raphael asked when he saw the look on our hero's face. "I'm hoping to make a Hot Rod one day."

"Where did you get all the parts?" asked Hoboman.

"Yeah, Raphael," God said, picking up a shiny exhaust pipe. "Where *did* you get all the parts?"

"Not from taking them off my clients' cars and replacing them with inferior parts, if that's what you had in mind," Raphael stuttered.

"Hey, isn't this off my Kingswood?" God questioned, picking up a steering wheel.

Raphael frowned and crossed his arms, tapping his fingers along his forearm. "Kingswood? I don't seem to recall you ever bringing a Kingswood in here, boss."

"I think I did. Because the last time I brought it here was to get the side mirror fixed, and you didn't colour match."

"Nope, you definitely didn't."

"I'll just have to check your time sheets."

"You can't do that."

"Oh? I think you'll find I can."

"No, you *physically* can't. All my time sheets were burnt when some guy's Kingswood caught fire while I worked on it. It's okay, though. We put the fire out and gave it back to the guy, and He didn't even notice."

"I think I'll be swapping to Saint Christopher's Servicing and Maintenance after today. It's long overdue."

"That hurts, boss. That really hurts. We pride ourselves on being particularly professional here," Raphael said sadly, as he stubbed his cigarette out on his desk and lit a new one.

"This is getting pretty awkward, guys," Hoboman piped up, and God and Raphael suddenly remembered they had a visitor.

"Maybe we should get down to business," God concluded sheepishly.

"Sounds like a good idea, boss."

Raphael swept the contents of his desk onto the floor then sat down in his plush office chair. He indicated Hoboman and God should sit, too, but in the significantly cheaper fold-out visitors' chairs. Once everyone was seated, God leaned in conspiratorially and began, "I suppose you're both wondering why I've called you in today."

"Wait," interrupted Hoboman. "Are we doing this now?"

"Yes."

"But … what about the others?"

"You and Raphael are the only two who need to hear about the plan."

Raphael leaned in, frowning. "The only two who *need* to hear? I smell a technicality."

"Well …" God floundered. "There is … another."

Raphael kicked his feet up on the desk and leaned back in his chair. Clasping his hands behind his head, he stared accusingly at God, who remained impassive. "It's Michael, isn't it?"

"Of course, it's Michael!"

"We couldn't do something without your favourite, could we?"

"Hey, I'm not playing favourites with anyone," God bit back. "You know Michael. If I didn't tell him, we'd never hear the end of it. He'd just moan and moan, all day, every day. I did you a favour! Besides, I see him more as a scapegoat."

"He seems less intelligent than a brick, but surely you're exaggerating his shittiness?" Hoboman enquired.

"Do you know," Raphael butted in, "he once told me he was of the opinion that anyone in the Bible could come and go to Heaven as they pleased?"

"And you're telling me this same person is, at this very moment, minding the gates?"

"Unfortunately."

"And tell me, regarding this war with the Devil, will it be happening here?"

God shrugged. "Gotta happen somewhere."

"Hate to break it to you, but I'm pretty sure the Devil is in the Bible, too."

God covered His mouth in horror. "Oh, dear Me."

* * *

"Hello, good sir. Is this Heaven?"

Michael looked down from his pedestal. He found himself staring at a heavily sunburnt man who was busy hitching up his brown shagpile trousers, which gave the odd impression of his lower half resembling goat legs. Michael then glanced at the six geriatric men standing in line behind the newcomer before turning his attention back to him.

"It is."

The sunburnt man, who had expected a more verbose answer, cleared his throat. "As you may or may not be aware, there is a big event at the Stock Market today. My six sixty-six-year-old co-workers and I were hoping to gain entrance in order to conduct some business."

"You're not the Devil, are you?" Michael asked, scrutinising the Devil.

The Devil simply smiled. "Would the Devil be so bold as to walk right up to the front doors of Heaven and ask to be let in?"

Michael pondered this question. "I suppose not." He sighed. "Go on ahead."

"Thanks," said the Devil.

The Devil and his six sixty-six-year-old co-workers congratulated themselves on such a clever ruse. The Devil, toting his sceptre, gestured onwards. Their destination: the Great Stock Market in the Sky.

"Wait a minute!" shouted Michael in his monotonous whine. "That's the Devil's sceptre."

The Devil and his associates froze, their identities seemingly exposed. "You caught me," the Devil sneered.

"You *stole* the Devil's sceptre. Stealing is wrong!"

The Devil paused and, when it became clear Michael hadn't cottoned on, continued, "Right, is that all?" Michael nodded and the Devil muttered to his associates, "This is too easy. I genuinely feel bad about that. And I'm the Devil!"

"The Devil?" Michael stepped down from his pedestal and pointed past the gates. "Get behind me, Satan!" he blustered.

The Devil furrowed his brow. He looked at Michael, then looked at the open pearly gates behind the archangel and shrugged.

"It looks like you win again. I really didn't stand a chance against a mind such as yours, Michael." The Devil bade his associates to follow him, and they stepped across the threshold into Heaven.

Smirking, Michael flicked a switch and the pearly gates swung shut, locking the Devil in. But something didn't feel right.

"Uh-oh," the archangel moaned when the realisation hit him. "That *was* the Devil! Oh no, oh no, oh no!" He whipped around and jumped back onto the pedestal, which was the quickest he'd moved in a long while. He flicked through the pages of the log-book and wrote 'The Devil' in a blank spot. "Phew, that was a close one. I could have been in a lot of trouble for a second there."

* * *

Without warning, God's smartphone began to ring. He looked at the caller ID and grimaced.

"Michael," He said in response to Raphael's querying look. God put the phone on loudspeaker and said, "Hello, Michael. Where are you? You should be here by now."

"I was just wondering when we were heading over to the Stock Market to stop the Devil," Michael replied.

God shook His head silently. "Michael, I don't think you quite understand. You're my first port of call. The aim of our mission is to make sure the Devil never *makes* it to the Stock Market in the first place. We're simply backup in case he finds a back door in."

Silence on the other end of the line. "Oh, okay then," Michael said after a long pause.

God sighed. "What's the matter?"

"I don't want to panic you, but I could have sworn I saw the Devil walk into the Stock Market. I mean, I was just looking at the surveillance tapes, and it might *not* have been him, but I just think—"

"What? Are you still at the gates?"

"Yeah." Michael hesitated, and then probed, "You're not mad at me, are you?"

But God had already hung up. He, Raphael and Hoboman pushed their seats back in unison and raced out of the garage, not speaking a word. By the time they reached the pearly gates, they had to double over to catch their collective breaths.

Michael eyed them suspiciously from his pedestal and said, "We're on high alert here. You're not the Devil, are you?"

Raphael balled his hands into fists but said nothing, as much as he would have liked to respond. God decided He would handle the situation, seeing as He would use a little more tact than the others.

"That's why we're here, Michael," God hissed. "You said you saw the surveillance footage of the Devil but, in order for him to get to the Stock Market, he would have had to pass by *you*. These gates are the only way in and out of Heaven. Has the Devil come in?"

Michael pored over the logbook, tracing the entries with his finger. "Yep, I let him in," he said, glad he had written the entry; imagine if he had not been able to verify this.

God gritted His teeth, but Raphael butted in and nudged Him out of the way. "I really want you to try and follow me with this. Someone comes knocking on Heaven's door. What do we do once we verify the Devil, someone we *don't* want in Heaven, mind you, is at the gates?"

Michael considered the question. "We ... let him go on ahead?"

Raphael slammed Michael's face into the logbook – hard

"I'm afraid you picked the wrong answer, my friend."

"Ow!" whined Michael, rubbing his forehead. "What was that for?"

"I bet you let him in because he was in the Bible, huh?" asked Raphael.

"Yep."

Hoboman, God and Raphael moaned in unison. God punched the cast iron gates in anger and instantly regretted it. Hoboman had to resist the urge to take a leaf out of Raphael's book and inflict as much pain as possible on Michael – not because he understood the severity of the situation, but because everyone around him was angry and it was, well … contagious.

"Okay, okay," God intervened, trying to calm everyone down. "We can forgive a tiny little slip-up. No problem. But Michael, this is important. Did you let anyone else in?"

"No."

Everyone sighed in relief.

"Except for his six sixty-six-year-old co-workers."

*   *   *

When Michael regained consciousness, he found himself lying among a pile of steering wheels and gearsticks in Raphael's office, a bruise blossoming on his forehead. He woke up to hear Raphael asking incredulously, "This is the crack squad you've assembled? A hobo, a misfit and me?"

"*Hey*," complained Hoboman. "I'm *not* a misfit."

"God works in mysterious ways," God said defensively.

"You can't keep using that excuse," Raphael pointed out.

"So, the Devil is planning to take control of Heaven," elucidated God. "I have gathered you here today in an attempt to prevent that from happening.

"You see, today is the day the Stock Market opens for business. In this day and age, many people are turning away from religion. My stocks have never been lower. The Devil hopes he can gain a fifty-one percent majority stake of Heaven. We can't let that happen!"

God looked over at Hoboman to see how he would react to this news, only to find him picking his nose. "Have you been listening to anything I've been saying?"

Hoboman roused himself from his reverie and wiped his finger on his shirt.

"Huh? Yeah, of course. Hey, why can't Jesus do this instead of me?" he whined. He folded his arms and huffed. "I'm bored."

"Jesus is doing magic shows in Vegas," was God's tetchy response.

"That seems a bit out of character."

"Exactly. Who would expect the Son of God to be in Vegas for the Second Coming?"

"Touché."

Before everyone became even more distracted, Raphael interrupted with, "All we need to do is stop the Devil from buying stock? Piece of cake."

"We still haven't come up with a proper plan," God pointed out.

"Sorry," Michael interjected. "I also have a question."

"*What?*" God asked, immediately irate.

"Does anyone want a coffee before we start?"

God leaned back in His chair and did His best not to scream. "*Now?* You want to do this *now?*"

Michael looked at the three irritable expressions he was garnering and nodded, more to psyche himself up. "I think we could all use a nice cup of coffee."

"Okay, just hurry up!" seethed God.

"Do you think the Devil might want one?"

God, who had resorted to drumming His fingers on the desk impatiently, stopped. He turned His head slowly until He met Michael's blank gaze. "I don't know, *Michael.* Do *you* think we should make the Devil some coffee?"

The angel brought a finger to his lips and tapped repeatedly as he considered the question. "He *is* putting a lot of effort into this hostile takeover. You know what? I think I *will* make him one. Does anyone know how he takes it?"

"How about black, like his heart?" Hoboman chimed in.

"A triple shot without milk?"

God slammed His fist on the desk. "Can you please hurry up?"

Michael looked hurt. He went to walk out and turned at the door. "You're not mad at me, are you?"

"Just ... *go!*" Michael hesitated before leaving the office. The room was silent. "What do we do now?" God mused.

Hoboman leaned forward and suggested, "What if we just go in ... and punch him?"

God shook His head. "Michael? No. He's too thick to respond to violence."

"No! The Devil!"

"We can't. If people saw me doing that, I'd lose even more credibility."

"But what if I do it?" Hoboman offered. "Maybe it's exactly what I was put on this Earth for. You can just say I broke into the Stock Market and beat him up!"

God mumbled to Himself as He thought it over. He nodded. "Yes, yes, I think this could work. We have no time to lose! Ready, angels?"

"Ready, Charlie," Raphael simpered as he lit a fresh cigarette.

"I've warned you about that," God retorted, pointing threateningly at Raphael. "Let's go."

As they all stood, Raphael only half-heartedly asked, "What about Michael?"

"I'm sure he'll find us," God said, waving a hand casually.

"Before we leave, we might need some equipment," Raphael reminded them all. He upended his desk to reveal a hidden crate. He popped the locks as he explained, "Not that I've been looking at the schematics, boss, but I'm assuming the Stock Market is password-protected."

"It is."

"Thought so. The electronic locks are the real heavy-duty stuff. Lucky I have this decryption device then," he said, nonchalantly passing it to God and ignoring the look of suspicion directed his way. "There are fences forming a perimeter around the building itself. Anyone can see that," he added hastily. "They're more for show, so these bolt-cutters should make easy work of them. Here you are, my friend."

"Oh boy!" Hoboman squealed, accepting the bolt-cutters.

"Raphael ..." God hesitated. "Why do you have all this?"

"Don't ask, boss."

They piled out of the office and into the store proper. Hoboman asked a pertinent question. "Are we walking to the Stock Market? Because I *really* don't wanna."

"All good," Raphael said. He checked a corkboard holding a collection of keys on hooks and removed the set belonging to a Holden Kingswood. "I'll drive."

"Is that—?" God began.

"Of course not," Raphael cut him off.

In the garage, Hoboman jumped into the tray of the vehicle while Raphael and God climbed into the cab. Hoboman could have sworn he had seen this vehicle before, maybe in some distant memory, except the side mirror was different to the one he remembered. Probably just a coincidence.

Raphael was more forceful with the Kingswood than God would have liked. When the engine failed to turn over, a good whack on the dashboard seemed to do the trick. The ute finally coughed into life and Raphael floored it, tearing out of the garage.

The Stock Market loomed tall, towering over the other buildings. Fashioned like a modern skyscraper, its colours were muted and its windows glazed, forbidding anyone from seeing in. It stood in the middle of a square patch of grass, taking up a whole city block. It was perhaps the most unholy thing housed within Heaven.

"Watch your driving," God could be heard saying inside the cab.

"Oh, like it matters if I run over anyone. They're all dead already," Raphael responded tersely.

"If you crash the car, can *I* die?" Hoboman called.

Raphael swerved to miss a pedestrian and almost ended up on two wheels. "That is a very good question, Hoboman, and I don't have an answer for you right now," the mechanic yelled back.

They promptly pulled up outside the Stock Market and Hoboman leapt from the tray. He looked up at the chain-link fence spanning the entire block and scratched his chin. "Seems easy enough."

"We could have tried the gate up ahead, but there's a guard on duty," God explained. "We have to cut through the fence here and sneak into the underground carpark on foot."

"Should have put Michael on security," Hoboman joked.

God slapped Himself on the forehead. "Why didn't *I* think of that?"

"Work your magic," Raphael instructed Hoboman. "You know what to do with those, yeah?"

Hoboman glowered at the angel before he cut a hole in the wire and wormed his way through. God clambered through the space next, while Raphael brought up the caboose. Once in the grounds, they snuck over to the side of the building and inched along until they came to a fork in the road. One direction sloped down towards the underground carpark; the other ended in a cul-de-sac with a footpath leading to the Stock Market's main entrance.

The trio descended into the carpark and crept through it as quickly as possible, although God had to turn back and urge Raphael on after he slowed down to admire the automobiles. They reached a large elevator, cordoned off by painted yellow lines, which Raphael explained indicated only select personnel could use it. Hoboman had to believe him: it wasn't like he could read the 'Authorised Personnel Only' notice written in stencilled letters. God called the elevator down and they all stepped inside. Hoboman let one of the others handle their ascension, having never, not once in his life, operated an elevator.

"This is huge!" Hoboman exclaimed in wonderment. "You could fit a car in here!"

"That's sort of the point," Raphael replied, as he pressed a button.

"What he means," God explained, "is these maintenance tunnels are used for security vans to drive in and deposit safes inside the Stock Market. Saves workers having to manually lug them everywhere. See, this elevator only travels between two destinations: the carpark and the tunnels. You drive in, the doors shut behind you, and the doors in front allow you to keep on trucking. That way, someone who drives in doesn't have to reverse all the way down a tunnel."

Hoboman nodded. He had no idea what God was talking about, but if our hero had learned one thing, it was that pretending you knew what someone was talking about, and nodding confidently, encouraged them to shut up sooner. The elevator came to a halt, the front doors opening this time instead of the back doors, and Hoboman lost his damn mind.

Exhilaration coursed through our hero's veins as the trio moved closer towards their goal. It could not even be curbed by the fact he now stood at the mouth of a very long tunnel with a light at the end. What was there to worry about? He was in Heaven: it wasn't like he could die.

They dashed down the corridor, only to find their path blocked by a heavy metal blast door; however, a monitor mounted on the side wall gave them hope. A keyboard positioned underneath it indicated it would grant them access with the right password. From behind the door came the muffled sound of thousands of people deep in conversation. Hoboman rocked on the balls of his feet excitedly. Somewhere behind this door was someone he could beat up.

"Ooh, my hands are tingling," God whispered excitedly. "I've got chills." He squatted and played around with the wires and cords underneath the monitor until He found a cable He could attach to the decryption device. Once plugged in, both the decryption device and monitor lit up. Lines and lines of code ran across the screens as the computer cracked the password.

Then something happened to stop their progress dead in its tracks. Michael burst out of the elevator, laden with coffee in a cardboard cup holder. In his rush to be helpful, he was clocking a surprising speed. At this rate, there wasn't a snowball's chance in Hell he would slow down quick enough. He skidded on the smooth stone floor, lost his balance and, in order to free his hands to soften his fall, threw the coffee tray into the ether.

Hoboman, God and Raphael watched as, in apparent slow motion, the coffee spilled everywhere, raining down and splattering the computer monitor. Sparks flew as the circuits shorted. Smoke billowed from the now-dead monitor. It seemed things *could* die in Heaven.

God, a breakdown imminent, stared at the blank screen in disbelief. He collapsed, sobbing. Hoboman and Raphael, being of much
more volatile temperaments, turned towards Michael *very* slowly.
Contempt and, in Hoboman's case, pus, oozed from every orifice.

"Oh, my Him!" Hoboman shouted, pointing at God but
directing his righteous fury at Michael. "This never would have
happened if you could just hold onto your load!"

"But no, you just *had* to go and blow it, didn't you?" added
Raphael.

"All over the computer!"

"People use that computer!"

"Sorry, guys," laughed Michael nervously. "I couldn't help
myself."

Wordlessly, with Raphael in tow, Hoboman walked towards
Michael. Hoboman lifted Michael's legs off the ground while
Raphael hefted his torso. Michael, utterly confused, made no
effort to resist, even when the archangel found himself being held
horizontally. "That was very co-ordinated," he observed.

"I've been dreaming of doing this since I met you," Hoboman
let him know.

"Me too. We're going to use you as a battering ram," Raphael
explained.

"Won't that hurt?" Michael asked.

"Of course not. We're in Heaven, silly," Raphael reminded him.
"We're already dead, remember?"

"Oh, that's right! I forgot."

On that note, they began charging Michael at the door blocking their way. Michael's head made contact; the door refused to
yield. Michael crashed to the floor, screaming in pain.

"You said it wouldn't hurt!" Michael moaned, as he clutched
his bald pate.

"We lied," Hoboman admitted, leisurely chewing a fingernail.

"Now that's out of our system, let's take a look at this computer," Raphael instructed.

They leaned over the blank monitor. Hoboman scratched his chin and ran his hand through his hair. He finally nodded wisely before saying, "I hope you have some idea about what you're doing, because I'm a hobo. I haven't legally owned a computer in my life."

"I might just have an idea," Raphael replied, snapping his fingers. "Michael, get over here!"

Michael stood, rubbing his head and looking woozy. "This isn't going to involve me getting hurt, is it?"

"No, no, of course not. That was one time." Raphael urged Michael to hurry over. "Is it just me or does that look like a bit of colour on the screen? Because if it *is*, it means it's a pixel. And if there's a pixel, there's power. If there's power, there's a chance of rebooting the system."

Michael squinted. "I'm not too sure."

"Take a closer look."

Michael's face was just inches away from the screen when Raphael grabbed the back of his head and rammed it into the monitor. Michael fell to the floor, moaning, but found himself ignored as the screen suddenly lit up.

Hoboman stared at Raphael, a mixture of admiration and awe on his face. "How did you know that would work?"

Raphael considered him seriously. "I didn't."

Turning around, Hoboman nudged God's shoulder. "The computer's working. You can stop being a big baby and try decrypting the password again."

God wiped His bleary eyes and blew into His handkerchief. "Okay," He mumbled. "We may as well put an end to this."

Raphael stood aside as God approached. Hoboman took his place by the door, ready to run out with his arms windmilling. God adjusted the decryption device and ran the program. A row of asterisks blinked onscreen, indicating the parts of the code being resolved.

"Are you ready?" God asked Hoboman. The decryption had been completed. His hand hovered over the 'enter' key.

"Ready!"

God struck the button and everybody held their breath. The screen briefly flashed green before changing red. "Virus detected, systems shutting down," an automated voice announced through a set of speakers.

"He placed a virus on the computer to make sure we never made it!" God shouted.

"Who?" Michael asked. He was not graced with an answer.

Hoboman fell to his knees and began pounding on the locked door. "You gave me hope and took it away at the last second! You truly are the Devil!"

"Oh, *now* I know," Michael realised. "Wow, that Devil isn't a very nice fella."

"That's it! Heaven's gone!" God moaned. "There's nothing we can do! We are never, ever, ever—"

Raphael left God to have His meltdown and instead focussed his attention on Hoboman. He lifted our hero up by the shoulders and said, "I have one last idea before we give up. Are you in?"

"Does it involve me smashing faces and shattering bones?"

"Subtlety be damned."

"I don't know the meaning of the word."

"That's the spirit!"

"What?"

God and Michael were left behind in the maintenance tunnel while Hoboman and Raphael rode the elevator back down to the carpark. Raphael rummaged through his pockets and found the keys to the Kingswood. "I'll bring the car around. Can you intimidate the security guard so I can drive onto the grounds?"

"I thought you'd never ask," said Hoboman in response.

When Hoboman reached the security booth, he flew into a rage, demanding the gates be opened. Sobbing, the security guard complied. Hoboman watched Raphael glide by in the Kingswood and then bolted to the car. He buckled himself in and Raphael sped up the road.

"You putting your seatbelt on?" queried Hoboman, noticing the angel was unrestrained.

"Should be right," Raphael replied with a shrug.

"So ... what? Are we going to joyride this and wreck up the Stock Market?"

"Couldn't have put it better myself."

"Radical. This day just keeps getting better and better."

"I just wish we had more time," Raphael mused. "I totally would have used Samson's tank. Unstoppable, so long as you don't cut the fuel line."

"What about this? Is this going to be able to smash down the door?"

"I'm banking on it. This car is unstoppable as well, but in a different sense."

"How so?"

"I was adjusting the brake lines when I was servicing it. Never got around to putting them back in. There is literally no way to stop this car."

"Well, we're in Heaven: not like we can die again."

Raphael glanced at Hoboman and bit his lip, but Hoboman remained blissfully unaware. Raphael coasted down the slope into the underground carpark in angel gear and used the momentum to idle into the elevator without ever touching the pedals. He cracked open a window, leaned out, and pressed the button to ascend. The doors shut, the elevator rose, and the doors before them opened.

"Where did God and Michael go?" Hoboman asked.

"No idea," Raphael responded. "Seems an odd time for a toilet break. Never mind. Are you ready for this? We're doing this on a wing and a prayer!"

Raphael slammed the vehicle into gear, revved the engine and released the clutch. The two sped down the corridor, accelerating with each second, shortening the distance between them and the door. Hoboman found some junk in the footwell, leaned out the window as they neared the computer terminal, and destroyed it by pegging a solenoid at it. This seemed to slightly release the locks on the door; every bit helped.

"I should probably mention," Hoboman shouted as they neared the door, "I don't actually believe in God!"

Raphael turned and stared at Hoboman in disbelief. He was still doing so when they hit the door.

Hoboman blacked out.

The next thing he knew, he was upside-down, held firmly in place by his seatbelt.[53] He unbuckled himself and fell onto his head. Delirious, he crawled out of the smashed passenger's window and leaned on the side of the car to pull himself up. Covered in shards of glass, he studied the Kingswood and noticed it was resting on its roof, the wheels still spinning. He shrugged, hav-

---

[53] Seatbelts save lives, kids.

ing made a habit of suppressing traumatic experiences. He had no recollection of the Kingswood crashing through the maintenance tunnel door, flipping over and skidding across the Stock Market floor. All he sported was a cut lip and the beginnings of a bruise under his left eye.

It occurred to Hoboman that the room was very quiet. Too quiet, seeing as how a massive supernatural buyout was supposedly about to go down. He turned, to be greeted by a crowd of angels who waited a beat before yelling, "Surprise!" Confetti showered down from the ceiling and the champagne began to flow.

"What the hell is going on?" Hoboman shouted over the noise.

God stepped forward, a flute of champagne held aloft in His hand. "Are you surprised, Hoboman?"

"I think I'm concussed, to be quite honest."

"Would you like me to explain it all to you?"

"I'll admit it would make things a little clearer."

God laughed and sipped some of His champagne. "There's really not much to it. You see, sometimes I get a little bored, and I like to interfere with ordinary people's lives. Take Job, for example."

Job, covered in boils and with his arm in a sling, raised his glass in acknowledgement.

"So ..." Hoboman thought this through. "There was really no point in me being here?"

"Not really."

"Heaven isn't actually under threat?"

"Nope."

"There was absolutely no need for me and Raphael to crash the car through that door?"

"Negative. I don't even care about that car."

"I think Raphael might be dead. I haven't seen him since we crashed." Hoboman checked the smoking vehicle and scratched his head in confusion. "That's a really mean thing to do."

"I'm God," He smiled. "I can do anything."

Something nagged at Hoboman, deep down in the long-forgotten part of his brain that still actually functioned. Everything was not as it appeared. "If you can do anything, let me see you curl your tongue!"

God rolled His eyes but obliged. He stuck out His tongue and proceeded to curl it up. "Satisfied?"

"I am," Hoboman crowed. "Because there's nothing I enjoy more than proving people wrong. You're not God!"

God's smirk faltered, and He lowered His glass. "What do you mean?"

Raphael crawled out of the wrecked Kingswood with a bleeding forehead, having smashed into the windscreen when they crashed. "God can't curl His tongue! You're an imposter!"

God started to laugh, normally at first, but gradually evolving into something much more maniacal. He threw back His head, and when He looked at Hoboman again, His whole face had changed. Instead of flowing white locks, this man had shaggy black hair, a curled moustache and a goatee. The Devil removed the counterfeit robes to reveal his outfit of cloven black shoes and brown shagpile pants. He wore no shirt, and his body was totally, horrifically sunburnt.

"Oh, very clever," the Devil congratulated. "I have to admit, I underestimated you. Appearances *can* be deceptive. Nevertheless, I'm afraid you've run out of time. I have kept you distracted long enough for this merger to begin. You have failed, Hoboman."

"Yeah but ... those pants," Hoboman critiqued.

"They are very in right now, I'll have you know," the Devil replied defensively.

"Dude, where's your shirt?"

"I was holidaying on a beach. I've become accustomed to walking around shirtless."

"Have you ever heard of sunscreen?"

"I don't need this." The Devil clapped and the six angels nearest him stepped forward, their disguises melting away to reveal their true identities: sixty-six-year-old lawyer demons.[54] One passed the Devil his sceptre and he brandished it with a flourish.

"Nice fork," Hoboman commented.

"It's a sceptre!"

At this point, God and Michael emerged from the maintenance tunnel. "I had to go to the toilet," God explained. He stopped abreast of Hoboman and looked around, struggling to comprehend what was going on. "What did I miss?"

"The Devil tried to trick us into thinking he was you, we're just about out of time to stop this hostile takeover, and all the angels and saints seem to be completely fine with everything."

"To tell you the truth, we're all a bit uncertain about what is going on," doubted Saint Thomas. "I mean, it could be the Devil, but we thought this might have just been a really intricate prank."

The Devil played with his goatee as he smirked at God's anguish. "I told you I would win this time. But you foolishly believed you could defeat me with this ragtag lot. I mean, Michael? Tsk, tsk."

"What do we do now? We're about to lose Heaven," God lamented.

---

[54] Yes, I am fully aware of the tautology.

"And your car is wrecked," Hoboman pointed out.

"My car is wrecked?"

Hoboman pointed at the crashed Kingswood and God screamed.

Michael looked at the wreckage and laughed. "I guess that's why they call it a Stock Market *crash*, huh?"

"Shut up, Michael!"

"Cassiel, isn't there something you can do?" God asked.

Cassiel merely stood there, watching the events unfold around him without interfering.

"I need some form of guidance!" God shouted, grabbing Hoboman's shirt and shaking him violently.

"Take a bloody chill pill, mate!" Hoboman shouted back. "Tell me, do you have Facebook on your smartphone?"

God didn't know what to think. He frowned in confusion but nodded regardless. "Yes. FaithBook, at least. Why do you need it?"

"There's no time, just log in for me."

God pulled out His phone and quickly typed His username and password. The Devil watched with an amused expression. "How, exactly, do you intend to stop me with a single phone? You can't expect to hack into the Stock Market computers. You are nowhere near intelligent enough."

"I've logged in," God murmured, passing the phone to Hoboman.

Hoboman took the phone and waved it in the Devil's face. "I may not have seemed like I was doing much while I was on Earth, but I think you'll find I made quite a few friends. And by that, I mean two."

"We're up in the sky though," the Devil pointed out. "You only made it up here because of God. How, exactly, are your friends making the trip?"

"You're living in the past," Hoboman chided. "The future is now, old man. This is the age of technology. We aren't going to blow you up. You see, all I have to do is write some FaithBook statuses about you, maybe about you holding charity picnics or giving puppies to sick kids, and then I let the magic work."

"There's no way to prove I host charity picnics or give puppies to sick kids!" the Devil spat.

"I know. They're just rumours. But once I post them online, there's no way to retract it. Observe." Hoboman typed something on the phone and showed the Devil as he hit 'post'.

"Right now," Hoboman explained, "a Roman Catholic Irishman and a hardcore Christian redneck are going to ensure this goes viral. You do realise these are the people who share all the religious stuff? It's the nature of the beast. Do you honestly think they are just loveable stereotypes to fluff out the plot? Get outta here!"

One of the lawyer demons was looking at a laptop. He adjusted his glasses as he peered more closely at the screen. "My dark lord, we have a problem."

The Devil's brow furrowed as he stared at Hoboman for a moment before turning his attention to the laptop. "What's going on?"

"All your stocks are dropping, and fast," the demon pointed out. "It's almost as if you're losing credibility."

The Devil saw Hoboman's smug grin. "You did this! You're ruining everything!"

"We don't need to raise your stocks," Hoboman explained to God. "We just need to lower the Devil's to the point where they're worth less than yours. I think I might have to write another status about old mate helping out in soup kitchens."

"I'll kill you!" The Devil lost all pretence of finesse and ran at Hoboman.

Michael chose this moment to do what he did best: absent-mindedly get in the way. The Devil crashed into the lump of a man and was sent sprawling by the impact. He rolled onto his back and tried to rise, but Michael placed a foot on the Devil's chest. The Devil's sunburn was so tender, he dared not shift.

"Have a nice trip, Lucy," Michael quipped. "See you next fall."

"Shut up, Michael!" the entire congregation chorused, now just absolutely sick of the guy.

The demon looking at the laptop was shaking his head. "My dark lord, it would be imprudent to proceed. Your stocks have fallen so low you would be unable to achieve a majority. Heaven is no longer yours for the taking."

The Devil stopped struggling on the floor and lay there silently, all the fight gone out of him.

Hoboman smiled and chucked God's smartphone back to Him. "Did you just cyberbully the Devil into submission?" God asked, amazed. "I would never have thought to do that."

"It just seemed like the right thing to do," Hoboman replied simply.

"But how did you even manage that? I didn't think you could write."

"Oh, I can't. My conscience taught me how to type. It's a different thing altogether."

"That doesn't make sense."

"How so?"

"Never mind." God pocketed His smartphone and leaned over the Devil. "It looks like you've failed again. Why am I not surprised, Lucifer?"

The Devil's rage could hardly be contained. "I will take over Heaven and overthrow you, God! Just you wait! Even if it takes eternity, I will beat you!"

"I look forward to it. But, for now, I think you ought to leave."

Michael moved his foot away. The Devil stood, flipped them all the bird and walked over to his six demons.

"Hey, guys." Hoboman addressed both God and the Devil. "Anyone seen Jean around?"

"Jean?" asked the Devil.

Hoboman held his hands apart and said, "About yea big. Brown. Brushed. He's a potato."

"I haven't seen a potato in Heaven," God said.

"Me neither," the Devil said.

"What about in Hell?" Hoboman asked.

"That's what I meant, you moron." With that, the Devil and his six sixty-six-year-old demons all disappeared in plumes of smoke.

The Stock Market became silent and then, suddenly, applause broke out all around. God wiped tears of joy from His cheeks. "This is a PR miracle!" He cried. "Where's my messenger? Gabriel!"

Gabriel Messenger, of Channel 4 Shadowing News fame, appeared on the scene with a notebook in one hand and a pen in the other. "You called, God?"

"Everything worked out miraculously! For the Third Testament, I want you to mention how Heaven was saved by a homeless man. He isn't extraordinary. He's just a normal person. It's like what I said in the Beatitudes and all that, but, like, *real*. Quick, spread the word!" Gabriel nodded and disappeared into thin air.

"Oh, sometimes I amaze myself with how clever I can be," God continued. He found Hoboman among the ruckus and wrapped an arm around his shoulder. "You have done well, my son. I am proud of you. The odds will be ever in your favour."

"Don't you mean 'forever'?"

"I know what I said."

"It's all in a day's work. Can I have some money now?"

"Hoboman, I have something better than money for you," God explained. "I have knowledge."

Hoboman eyed God warily. "One certainly would debate the importance of knowledge in a materialistic society."

"I know who has your trolley," God said and, suddenly, Hoboman was paying attention. God leaned in and spoke the name of the trolley thief into Hoboman's ear.

"That means literally nothing to me," Hoboman whispered back harshly.

God drew back, perplexed. "You might know them by a different name. Here, try this." He leaned in again and revealed the thief's alias.

"Impossible. Just impossible."

CHAPTER 11

An Uneasy Conscience

The woman was looking out of her tiny apartment window, but not really seeing much. Tears had partially blurred her vision; alcohol had put paid to the rest. Dregs pooled at the bottom of her glass, but she had reached the point where she neither knew nor cared how much was left. The bottle of mixer rolled out of her limp hand and hit the worn floorboards with a dull thump. She leaned forward in a drunken stupor until her head came to rest on the windowpane, which became the only thing keeping her upright.

She could still hear her voice echoing through the empty apartment. "I can't do this anymore, Whitney. You told me we would have a better life here in the city, but you were wrong. I'm moving back to the farm. My parents have already said I can live with them. I'm taking our son with us."

"Don't," Whitney had pleaded. "I love you."

"And I love you, too," her wife had replied. "I'm not leaving our marriage, I'm just moving home, where you ought to be. Come back to the farm with us. Keep the family together."

"But your parents hate me."

"They don't *hate* you."

"Your sister threatened to stab me."

"That was one time, and it was a joke."

"She was passing it off as a joke, but she meant it."

"She just told you not to walk into the knife she was drying when we were doing the dishes."

"And then went into great detail as to how it would pierce my femoral artery and make me bleed out!"

"I think you're just trying to pit me against my family!"

"Why would I even do that? It's free accommodation! I wouldn't pass that up without good reason! Anything is better than paying an exorbitant amount of rent for this tiny little apartment!"

"I don't know what you want from me, Whitney," her wife had sighed. "I'm leaving. You can come if you want. If you love us, I'll see you at my parents' house."

The voices faded from her mind. Whitney managed to lift her head and turn to stare at the wall, which was stacked to the ceiling with tubs of baby formula.

"And you can keep the baby formula," her wife had added before she walked out of her life.

"That answers that," she slurred.

Whitney staggered over to the tiny kitchen bench and set about making a Baby Russian.[55] She misguidedly believed the caffeine in the coffee liqueur would revive her somewhat ... but hey, points for initiative.

Her phone buzzed and she clumsily reached into her pocket to check who or what it was. She had forgotten the Channel 4 Shadowing News app sent push notifications whenever there was breaking news. She opened the app and half-listened to the news report being livestreamed.

---

[55] A White Russian, with baby formula substituting the cream.

"For those of you only just joining us," Gabriel Messenger was saying, "baby formula prices are going through the roof."

"Baby formula prices are going through the roof?" Whitney parroted.

"That's right. Baby formula prices are going through the roof," Gabriel repeated. "On the black market, that is. New statistics have emerged citing baby formula now has a street value equal to, and in some cases, greater than, pure cocaine. If anyone is hoarding tubs of baby formula, it's your lucky day."

"I'm hoarding tubs of baby formula," Whitney told her phone, drunkenly believing she was carrying on a conversation.

"It *would* be your lucky day, that is, if police weren't cracking down on those trying to sell said formula on the black market. For every one innocent person attempting to make a mint offloading excess formula, there are around five drug dealers trying to sell huge batches of cocaine in baby formula tubs. You just never know what you're buying.

"The skyrocketing price of baby formula is a direct result of the upsurge in veganism. As vegans do not want to drink the milk of animals, baby formula is considered the best alternative, providing it is soya-based."

Whitney squinted at the tubs of formula, struggling to see the brand, 'Soy-a Boy-a,' with with her swimming vision. "I think we have that."

"I am also legally obliged to remind viewers that baby formula is artificial milk, not a recipe to make babies, as some have been led to believe," Gabriel clarified. "It is also not made from actual babies being crushed into a powder."

Whitney wasn't listening anymore. She threw her phone aside, which she would later regret when she sobered up and it took her twenty minutes to find it again. "I guess that settles it. I'll just sell everything on the black market!" Whitney paused. "But wait! I don't want to be caught by the police. Think, Whitney, think!"

She was on the verge of an epiphany when the sound of someone going through the rubbish skips below caused her to lose focus. Irate, she stumbled over to the window and opened it, ready to go off her tree – until, peering down at the alley, she saw the hobo, happily rummaging through the trash.

A new, even better thought occurred to her. Although the logistics were a bit of a concern. How was one to convince a run-of-the-mill, everyday hobo to become a superhero? She'd probably need a fake business as a front. That would require an ABN, signage, office supplies.

But what could she use as motivation? Refraining from yelling in case she spooked the homeless man, Whitney opted to spy on him instead. She watched, confused, as the hobo left the skips he'd been searching through, then proceeded to sit on a red-and-white-checked tablecloth as if it was a picnic blanket and start romancing a shopping trolley.

"I think," Whitney slurred to herself, "I may have found my leverage."

*   *   *

"You come to me on the day of my daughter's christening to tell me ... what, exactly?"

"There is an Irish farmer on a property bordering Uptown," Whitney explained over the phone. "His potatoes have been afflicted with a fungal disease capable of causing untold havoc to the ecosystem."

"I appreciate ya informin' me," the Godfather replied. "My family will take steps to rectify this. I am, however, a little confused as to what this farmer's Irish heritage has to do with anythin.'"

Whitney laughed her best customer service laugh. "I just thought it provided a bit of context. For the potatoes, you see?"

"I was not aware only Irish people could farm potatoes."

"Anyone can, I suppose."

"Exactly."

Whitney didn't know where to go from here. "I'm a woman, you know?"

The Godfather abruptly terminated the call.

"Whit...?" Whitney's second-in-command probed as she knocked on the door and leaned inside.

Whitney stashed the *Phytophthora infestans* sample she had just unleashed on Seamus Mann's farm in her desk drawer.

"Could you hold on for just a minute, Jane? I have an important call to make." She dutifully closed the office door and waited outside. Whitney dialled a number and waited for it to connect.

"Hello, is this Papa Razzie?" she asked. "I'd like to make a report that Flam Bam Buoyant, of Bubba and the Jugettes, is homosexual."

"Do you have any proof?" Papa Razzie asked, slimily.

"None at all."

"Okay, I'll run that story."

"You don't want any evidence?"

"I'm a paparazzo. I don't need evidence."

"Thank you for your time." Whitney hung up the phone and bade Missus Jenkins to enter.

"I feel we need to talk about Tim," she began.

"Who?" Whitney asked.

"The really average guy. Phone drone. Forgettable face."

"Don't remember him. Is it important?"

"He seems highly strung. I figured we'd better pretend we're supporting him somehow. Plausible deniability if he snaps."

Whitney's gaze drifted to the window and, as she looked down into the alley, she was shocked to see her quarry talking to an elderly gentleman who looked mysteriously like God. "I'm quite busy at the moment."

Missus Jenkins looked down at the notes she had been compiling on Tim and shrugged. "Yeah, it can probably wait." She ducked out of the room and went on with her day.

At that point, Whitney opened the office window. "Missing something?" she called from on high.

* * *

"It sucks about me woife, ya know," Irishman was saying, "but at least Oi can always get a new kid from me cabbage patch."

Bubba slammed down his porcelain jug of moonshine and stared. "Jus' what in the Lord God's name are ya talkin' about?"

Onion Jack, busy wiping out glasses with a rag, sensed the tension in the room but decided not to say anything: he might ruin the atmosphere and then people wouldn't buy any more drinks. He noticed Whitney step through the saloon doors and winked at the newcomer. Whitney nodded in acknowledgement and took a seat between Bubba and Irishman.

"Gentlemen," Whitney said. "How are you today?"

"No good," Bubba replied.

"Feckin' terrible," Irishman responded.

"I know the feeling," she agreed. "Though I'm hoping tonight, I can make you both feel a lot better."

"You solicitin' me?" Bubba asked, looking interested.

"No," Whitney replied, shutting that avenue down straight away. "I need both of your phone numbers so Hoboman can contact you."

"Whoiy would he need to contact us?" Irishman asked.

"I know the nature of the discussions you had," she explained.

"You been spyin' on me?" Bubba asked, flaring up immediately.

"Don't flatter yourself," Whitney answered coolly. "I've been keeping tabs on Hoboman. That man is worth more than his weight in gold to me."[56]

"Ah, ya must be his agent," Irishman deduced. "Makes sense. He didn't seem focussed enough to be able to remember his own appointments. In that case, Oi'll give ya me number."

Whitney removed a phone from her pocket and Bubba burst out laughing. "You only got one o' those cheap burner phones?" he snorted.

"I'll have you know, I was trying to teach Hoboman how to type on my own phone and he ran off with it. Twice."

Irishman and Bubba entered their numbers into the contact list and Whitney pocketed the phone again. "Thank you, gentlemen. I'll make sure Hoboman keeps in touch. You probably won't be seeing me again."

"But wait," Irishman called, just as Whitney reached the saloon doors. "Ya do realoise what ya want Hoboman to do isn't exactly gonna sit well with the law?"

She did not turn around. She paused with her back to the two and retorted, "That's the plan."

* * *

She stood on the rooftop, overlooking the alley where she had first laid eyes on Hobart Mann. It seemed like years ago. Then again, it also seemed like it was last week. Whit W. Omen caressed the

---

[56] Probably because, with the street value of pure cocaine, she had several times more than Hoboman's weight in baby formula sitting in her apartment.

cool metal of Hoboman's trolley as she watched the sun rise on the horizon.

Suddenly, something hurtled from the sky and landed behind Whitney with such force it shook the ground. Unperturbed, she removed her hands from the trolley and clasped them behind her back. "I've been expecting you for a long time ... Hoboman!"

"How did you know it was me?" asked Hoboman, as his skunk tail coiled back up into his pants. "That effect was really good. You haven't said that to some random, thinking they were me?"

Whitney quickly turned and replied, "Of course not. Why?" [57]

"I can't believe you would do this to me. My own conscience!"

"I'm Whitney Omen."

"That means *literally* nothing to me."

"I knew you would come in search of me ... once you learned the truth."

"I'm doing my best not to kill you right now. If you just give me back my trolley, I can return to my normal life, and I may only hurt you a little – but I make no promises!"

"You still don't understand, do you, Hoboman? I did you a favour by stealing your trolley. I plucked you out of the slums and elevated you to a level you would never have achieved on your own. I made you the first superhero Australia can call its own. Think of all the good you've done."

"Destroying Deddrich?"

"I wouldn't use that as an example."

"Turning Jean into a potato, ultimately resulting in him being fed through a spud gun and killed?"

"I guess you could say that was a public service."

---

[57] Actually, she'd said it to the cleaner earlier when he'd come to sweep the rooftop.

"Using contraband fireworks and a flaming hobo to blow up the only institution in this town devoted to law and order?"

"Ah, but that assisted me in selling baby formula for inordinately high prices to vegans on the black market without the risk of getting caught." Whitney watched Hoboman frown, then added, "It makes sense in context, I swear."

"Does it though?"

"Well, aside from everything else, you've been doing all right."

"Only all right?"

"Only all right. Look, I had hoped you never found out this way. I was heading to come clean when I saw the explosion at the police station. Can you imagine my surprise when I saw you take off into the skies on a flying lawnmower ... with God?"

"You're right," Hoboman acknowledged. "Context *is* pretty important."

"I was concerned that if I told you, you'd give up your pursuit of justice—"

"Heh, justice. Good one."

"—and return to your normal life!"

"Yeah, probably."

"Could you do it?" Whitney probed. "Go back to being just another homeless person, rather than remaining a famous superhero?"

"I think 'notorious' is a better description," Hoboman corrected. "But if anyone was going to decide if I became a superhero, it was me! It wasn't your right to choose! Give me back my trolley!"

"That's it, then? You're convinced if you regain your trolley, your superhero career will be over?"

"Why does it even matter to you? You sold all your baby formula, didn't you?"

"But what if I want more? What if other opportunities arise? What if I need you to destabilise more governments?" The glint in Whitney's eye was manic. "Why don't I just sort this problem out for you? Right here, right now?"

Whitney heaved with all her might, tipping the trolley and causing it to topple off the top of the building. Hoboman's eyes widened in shock. He ran to the edge of the roof, then hesitated.

"There's no point!" Whitney rationalised.

But Hoboman refused to listen to his conscience, his voice of reason. He climbed up onto the precipice. Just before he made his leap, the flask of Chekov's vodka dropped out of his coat.

He jumped.

Whitney shook her head, disappointed in Hoboman's choice. But there would be more to exploit, if necessary, she was sure. Suddenly, she spied the flask on the ground and raised an eyebrow. "A victory drink? Why not?"

She unscrewed the top off the flask and took a swig. As soon as the concentrated alcohol touched her tongue, She knew she had made a mistake. All her tastebuds burnt like hellfire and her tongue went completely numb. Falling to the ground, she clawed at her throat in distress. Her vision blurred. Her throat felt as though the flesh was seared. Her insides squirmed in agony.

Meanwhile, Hoboman was fast approaching his trolley. He managed to grab the handle and cheered with delight. That delight, however, was quickly replaced by fear, as he realised that at the rate he was falling, the ground was approaching far too quickly. Even with his skunk tail to pull him out of the descent, he would never halt in time.

All of a sudden, the winds slackened. The oncoming pavement seemed to stop rushing towards him. As if by a miracle, Hoboman came to a complete stop in his alley without a single scratch on him.

"Thanks, God!" Hoboman yelled to the heavens. The clouds shifted in the sky to form a hand giving the thumbs-up ... or potentially a giant pelican.

"I have something else you might like," announced the voice of God.

On the rooftop, Hoboman's conscience was struggling for breath. "Of all the ways I pictured myself dying, I didn't expect it to be methyl poisoning," she lamented between shallow breaths. "Someone help! I think I'm haemorrhaging."

A low rumbling sound, almost like a V8 engine, grew louder and louder, although with her blinded eyes, Whitney was hardly in a position to identify it. When it sounded like the engines were right next to her, she summoned every last ounce of strength she could muster and turned in the direction of the noise.

"You made it, didn't you?" she asked.

"Damn straight," Hoboman replied. He revved the engine that was now welded to his trolley and yelled, "Get a load of my Hobomobile!"

"I can't see anything!" she shouted back.

If Whitney *could* have seen, she would have been extremely impressed with all the chrome attachments adorning Hoboman's trolley, along with the set of monster truck wheels replacing those flimsy little ones that are always spinning out of control.

Meanwhile, in Heaven, Raphael had returned from hospital to find all his Hot Rod parts missing from his office. It was said the scream of absolute despair could be heard as far as Nirvana. Although, Raphael had to admit, on the plus side, the space was now immaculately clean.

"I have a question," Hoboman went on. "If you needed to sell baby formula for money, why waste funds on your company?"

"It was just a front."

"Not unsuccessful, from what I hear."

"It was quite good, yes."

"That's what I mean. Why not work honestly?"

"It was only ever a means to support myself while I convinced you to help me."

"Why not keep the company and just become a business entrepreneur?"

"... Hell."

"Anyway, you're about to learn the consequences of messing with someone's trolley!" screamed Hoboman.

Hoboman's conscience was doubled over, gasping for breath. Her vision now almost gone, the best she could do was hold out a hand in the direction she thought Hoboman was. "Please ... don't you have a conscience?"

Hoboman's face contorted with fury. "Not anymore."

He revved the engine so loudly, it roared. The monster truck wheels began to squeal and smoke, despite the fact that Hoboman and the trolley were levitating. Hoboman lined up his conscience, let the clutch out and rammed her over the edge of the building. Whitney Omen went flying, but Hoboman did not bother to wait around to see the outcome. Because that's the superhero way.

Our hero clambered into the basket of the Hobomobile and strapped himself in. Smiling at being reunited with his faithful trolley, Hoboman took the controls in his hands and flew off into the sunset.

CHAPTER 12

Getting Trolleyed

"**P**arty with a superhero? When we return from the break, Gabriel Messenger gives us the exclusive, live from Hoboman's wedding."

"I met him!" Tim reported excitedly, gesturing wildly at the television screen.

"As if, Dad," his son, Monte, replied, rolling his eyes.

"No, I really did! He stopped me from walking down a dark and destructive path."

His daughter, Gaiety, folded her arms. "I wish he hadn't," she muttered.

"Where's your mother?" Tim asked, as he turned the volume up on the TV. He leaned in closer to listen for the name of the venue.

"She's putting baby Pizza Shapes to bed."

"Tell her I'm going out."

"I'm sure she won't mind."

* * *

"Dearly beloved, we are gathered here today to join Hobart Darwin Mann and Mary Jane Ettic in holy matrimony." God stood at the altar, having exchanged His flowing white robes for a black set with a clerical collar.

Hoboman, dressed in a scruffy black tuxedo, complete with black silk fingerless gloves, stood next to Miss Ettic. She glowed in a beautiful wedding dress, and everyone had commented how radiant she looked now Jean was out of the picture. When Hoboman had knocked on her door to tell her the 'bad' news of Jean's demise, she had proposed to him on the spot. No one had ever done anything so nice for her. Such was the nature of their love.

"How did Hoboman get the actual, real-loife God to do the service at 'is wedding?" Irishman whispered to Bubba as they sat in the pews.

"Don't ya follow God on FaithBook?" Bubba whispered back.

"Yeah. Oi just sorta assumed it was a religious organoisation posting on God's behalf."

"Nah, it's got the li'l blue tick. Means He's real."

"Doesn't mean much these days though, does it?"

"Please be seated," God said, "as we contemplate a reading from the Bible. Today, we have a special guest speaker."

Saint Paul made his way from the front pew to the lectern and opened the Bible to the appropriate page. "A reading from the letter of me, Saint Paul, to Hoboman. Ahem. Love is patient, love is kind ..."

"Oi t'ought he said this to the Corinthians," Irishman muttered.

"Prob'ly. Y'know how it is. Say sumthin' clever once and ya always repeatin' it to whoever'll listen," Bubba replied.

"... always trusts, always hopes, always perseveres," Saint Paul concluded. He closed the Bible and paused solemnly. "The word of the Lord."

God nodded as Saint Paul returned to his seat. "What wonderful words. I mean, I'm pretty sure we were all hoping for something new, but it seems Saint Paul, like most other authors, has no idea what a deadline is." He smiled to the crowd and ushered Hoboman and Mary back to the altar. "We now have the exchanging of the vows."

Bubba sniffed and dabbed at his tears with a hanky. "Beaudiful. Jus' beaudiful. I ain't ever seen a better weddin' in ma life."

"Oi have," sighed Irishman.

*   *   *

"How do you like the music?" Hoboman asked Mary.

"It's ... different," she commented in return. "Who did you say they were again?"

"Bubba and the Jugettes! They're my favourite band. I may have convinced them to get back together. Their reunion tour is actually kicking off with our wedding. Cool, huh?"

"Um ... sure," Mary replied uncertainly.

Bubba and the Jugettes finished serenading everyone with their love song, 'Porcelain Skin, Porcelain Jugs', and all the guests put their hands together, Hoboman and God clapping the loudest.

"Thankin' ya," Bubba said into the microphone. "Ladies and gen'lemen, it's real swell to be with ya this evenin'. This is the firs' time in months that myself, Trout, Gay Gayle, Flam Bam Buoyant and Grandmumma Bubba have been on stage together, and we never woulda been here if it weren't for that man right there." Bubba pointed to Hoboman and everyone applauded politely, even if they had no idea what he was talking about. "So, if it's all the same to the band, I'mma dedicate this next song, 'Gator Ate Ma Baby', to him."

The Jugettes stepped out of the spotlight as Bubba began belting out his power ballad in dedication to Hoboman. Sadly, not very many people noticed. Jesus had arrived late to the party and was entertaining the guests by turning water into wine. Those who weren't drinking watched on in amazement; those who were drank the transfigured water enthusiastically.

Bubba strummed out the final chord on his electric banjo to huge applause, completely unaware it was in response to Jesus' antics. "Thank ya. An' now for what I'm sure ya been waitin' for all night: the weddin' cake!"

Hoboman *had* been waiting all night for this. As well as for dinner. A waiter wheeled a trolley laden with an enormous wedding cake from the function centre's kitchen. It was bigger than he'd thought.

"It's bigger than I thought," he told Mary.

"Come on," she said, grabbing his hand. "I think it's time for us to cut the cake."

Irishman, who was sitting with them at the bridal table, leaned over. "Oi'd refrain from using a knoife on that cake, if Oi were you," he advised when he heard what the couple were planning.

"Irishman, I can't exactly just collapse into the cake and eat it from the inside," Hoboman chided. "Believe me, I've asked."

"That's not what Oi mean," Irishman said.

"Then what—"

Without warning, cake exploded everywhere. A strange-looking apparition was emerging from it, covered in frosting and laughing like an absolute loony.

"Surprise!" shouted the man in the cake. The voice was shockingly familiar.

"Flaming Eddie!" Hoboman shouted with delight. "You're the stripper in my cake?"

"Yeah, mate," Flaming Eddie slurred, as he scanned the room for a matchbook. "I'm not a Christmas pudding anymore. I'm a wedding cake!"

"Good for you, Flaming Eddie." Hoboman smiled – although his smile soon faded when he realised there was now no cake for anyone to eat, in particular, himself.

"I'm heading over to the buffet," he told Mary.

"Bring me something. I've got the munchies something fierce."

Hoboman decided that, as it was his wedding, he could cut in front of everyone else waiting in line. He watched as a plate was loaded up for him, salivating at the sight of the delicious food getting ever closer. It was only when it was being handed to him that he noticed the chef.

"We meet again, Hoboman!"

"Wiener Munch!"

"No, it's *Werner!*"

"Hey, how did you end up out of prison?"

"Oh, that," Wiener Munch waved it off. "They only gave me community service. I mean, all I did was steal a few sausages here and there. I finished my sentence and ended up working the barbecue at Bunnings. I've never been happier." Those in line shifted about uncomfortably as they waited for the only worker to finish talking and serve them their meal.

"No way! Wait, didn't you literally murder your father?"

"In Germany. What are they going to do? Extradite me?"

"I genuinely don't know what that means. Anyway, what are you doing here?" Hoboman asked.

"I heard you were having a function and I thought I would stop by. If it wasn't for you, I would never be where I am today."

"Yeah, cool," our hero replied, then walked off before Wiener Munch could continue the conversation.

"Who was that?" Mary asked when Hoboman returned to the table with his food.

"I dunno," said Hoboman with a shrug.

She looked longingly at his plate. "Did you forget mine?"

"Hoboman," Irishman interrupted, just as our hero went to take a bite. "There's someone here wants to see ya."

Our hero sighed and set his fork back down. "Who is it?"

"Someone called 'Tim.'"

"Who or what is a 'Tim'?"

"I'm Tim!" a stranger declared, approaching the table.

Hoboman was thoroughly whelmed when he looked up and saw the most average-looking person he had ever seen in his life. Well, he *may* have seen him before, but this Tim character had such a forgettable face.

"Right, so what can I do for you, Tim?" Hoboman asked.

"I just wanted to say, what you did for me really helped, and I am greatly indebted to you," Tim explained.

Mary squeezed Hoboman's hand with one of hers, while the other one surreptitiously sought one of his party pies. "You never told me about this. I never knew how nice you were to people."

"I mean, I would have told you if I knew what he was talking about. You know how boastful I am," Hoboman told her. He turned his attention back to Tim. "Are you sure you aren't confusing me with another superhero hobo?"

"No, no, definitely not! I remember sitting there, at Onion Jack's, about to have a drink and probably ruin my life. Then you came along. You sat down, you told me everything was going to be fine and—"

"Look, are you going to pay me?"

"What?"

"You said you were indebted to me."

"I meant, like, figuratively."

"If that's the case, go back to your boring life with your boring kids and stop interrupting my wedding, you jerk!"

Tim opened his mouth to speak, but his innate meekness won out again. He shut his mouth, turned on the spot and left the function room. (Later, he would go home and tell his wife. She would only vaguely listen while reading her erotic novel, wishing her life had turned out differently, that maybe she'd experience something exciting like what she was reading about. They would go to bed with their backs to each other, dreaming about what could have been.)

"What ended up happening to Onion Jack?" Hoboman asked Irishman. "I sent him an invite, but he didn't RSVP and, come to think of it, I haven't seen him about."

Irishman swallowed his mouthful of Guinness before replying, "Oi heard 'e went bankrupt. His bar closed down."

"That's awful," Hoboman responded, upset that now he was probably never going to get free drinks again, as all the other bars in Uptown had what they referred to as 'ethical standards'. "How did he go bankrupt?"

"Turns out he was advertoising a singing, dancing potato, complete with a little top hat. Everyone was keen t'see this novelty. We knew Jean had doied, but Jack didn't get the memo. Everyone turned up. No potato. Jack lost all his money. What 'e didn't lose immediately, he lost when he was sued for false advertoising." Irishman shook his head. "It's sad."

Hoboman heard his wife sigh and glanced over. "You have *another* visitor," she muttered. "This is meant to be *my* big night, too."

"I can't help being a celebrity," dismissed Hoboman. "Right, who do we have next?" He instantly regretted asking. A girl from Chapter Two approached the table – which would have been fine except the last time they'd met he'd collapsed a makeup shelf on her. "If you're looking for money, I don't have any," he said, beating her to the punch.

"I'm, like, not looking for money," Trish said. "I just wanted to, like, thank you for what you did."

"You ... you do?"

"At first, I was, like, *so* mad, because, like, I lost all my cosmetics. Then I started going to therapy, and I ended up finding out, like, the reason I was lashing out was because of my own insecurities. I was just given everything I wanted. My dad, like, gave me things because he wasn't there all the time, and he thought they would be, like, a good substitute for his presence. But everything just, like, spiralled out of control. That trip to hospital in the back of an ambulance was the most quality time we'd spent with each other in ages. We now have, like, a normal relationship and stuff."

Hoboman was touched by the story. "Aw, get out of here you little scamp, before I smother you with more makeup."

Trish left and Hoboman finally went to start on his dinner, sans multiple party pies and a sausage roll.

"Another visitor," Irishman announced.

Hoboman slammed his utensils down and pushed his chair out. "Why does everyone want to interrupt me while I'm having dinner?" he shouted as he stood up and walked around the table. "Who's the bouncer?"

*   *   *

"I'm here for the wedding reception," someone told the bouncer, the first in a long line of people waiting to get in.

"Do you have an invitation?" Michael asked, scrutinising the gatecrashers carefully.

"No."

Michael paused. "Go on ahead."

*   *   *

As soon as Party Fowl crossed the floor and stood in front of Hoboman, our hero lashed out and kicked the evil zookeeper in the groin. Party Fowl dropped to the floor, wheezing in pain, as Hoboman stood over him, expressionless. "Pretty sure I warned you that was going to happen if I saw you again."

"Why?" Party Fowl gasped.

"Because I don't like you."

"That was ... more rhetorical ... than anything."

"Call it what you want. It's all the same to me."

Party Fowl slowly made his way up. He had to roll onto his side, push himself into a squatting position and gingerly rise from there.

"All I'm here for is to give you this," he rasped, handing Hoboman a newspaper clipping bearing the visage of our hero. "We found it in the panda enclosure. Since you were there, we thought you might know what it meant."

Hoboman took the clipping warily and stared at the article. "Oh, how sweet. Those pandas had a son."

"How do you know?" Party Fowl asked, slowly regaining his voice. "You haven't even read the clipping."

"I couldn't read it if I tried. I just smell the furry-moans this thing is covered in."

"Whatever." As the zookeeper went to leave, he added, "By the way, all the animals are back in their enclosures, no thanks to you. It seems all that time on the street was too much for them. They returned because they knew they would have a regular routine of food and exercise. I guess you could say they're ... creatures of habit."

Hoboman processed the pun, decided he hated it, and made to kick Party Fowl again. Party Fowl flinched and hobbled away from the reception as fast as he could. Hoboman sniffed the paper a bit longer and frowned.

"Oh, no! Mumma Bear is trying to win custody of the kid. It seems they can't keep the relationship up any longer. Bummer."

A familiar face appeared and Hoboman was just about ready to snap when he realised it was his conscience.

"How?" Hoboman asked, when Whitney Omen stood in front of him. "I thought I knocked you off the roof of the apartment. You should be dead!"

Whitney shook her head. "Did it ever occur to you I lived in a two-storey apartment?" she replied, her voice scratchy from a burnt oesophagus. "I needed to go to the hospital for a couple of days, but that's about it. Concussion. Some bruised bones. Not to mention damaged self-esteem. Otherwise, I'm the epitome of health."

"Weren't you blinded due to methyl poisoning?" Hoboman asked.

"Temporarily."

"Lucky, lucky, lucky. You know kids going to schoolies in Bali can be blinded for life?"

"I was lucky. I'm rich from selling all my baby formula. I paid for the best doctors and they had me sorted out in no time." Whitney placed a box and some documents on the table. "You might want to sit down. I have some things for you to look at."

"Hot diggity dawg," Hoboman exclaimed, thinking he could finally eat his dinner. Also, the box looked like it might be a wedding present, and he was all for free stuff.

"First up, we have a pardon from Sergeant Bolbusta."

"He survived?"

"She. Sergeant Bolbusta prefers to identify as female."

"Cool."

"Apparently, Flaming Eddie tackled her when he came running into the evidence room and all the fireworks went off. Flaming

Eddie absorbed all the heat and Justin Bubba ended up rescuing her from the rubble."

"Get out of town!"

"I will eventually, don't you worry. However, Bolbusta linked you to the death of some guy called Dave. She overturned your sentence when they were going through Dave's assets and found a note. The gist of it was that it was only a matter of time before he ate himself. Bolbusta stuck her neck out for you and you're off the hook."

"What a swell chick."

"Next order of business is this piece of legislation being considered by local council. It seems there's a new mayoral candidate who has appeared out of nowhere. The first item on his agenda is to rid the city of what he calls 'the homeless problem.'"

"He wants to eliminate all the homeless people?" Hoboman asked.

"I'm getting that vibe. Of course, he might just mean he wants to eradicate homelessness in the city, not go on a homicidal rampage."

Hoboman shrugged. "I'm not worried. I won't be Hoboman for much longer anyway. From this day on, I will be known as 'Homeownerman'!"

"Don't be too sure," Whitney said. "We still have this to talk about." She gestured to the box that had been hidden under all the documents. "Don Bradman of the Downtown Mafia found this at Mario's Italian Cuisine when he heard about the shootout. He said he wanted you to have it as a gift."

Hoboman had to refrain from squealing as he looked at the box, which was dotted with air holes. Something was scrabbling about inside and he could barely contain his excitement. "A puppy?"

Whitney said nothing. She remained impassive as Hoboman lifted the lid. Contrary to what he had been hoping, when Hoboman peered inside he found seven living potatoes bumbling about, bumping into each other in the darkness. They shielded their eyes from the light, and Hoboman's heart sank as he gazed upon seven Jeans.

"It turns out your little friend threw some sprouts into a pot plant. They grew. Many happy returns," Whitney congratulated.

Mary shifted curiously in her seat to see what her husband was looking at and her smile instantly vanished. "Seven? That's my son. And there are *seven* of him?"[58]

"It seems that way."

Mary stood abruptly and glared at the seven potatoes with a look of absolute loathing. "I'll be filing for annulment in the morning. I married you because you killed my son. Now, because of you, he's back, seven times more annoying. Goodbye, Hobart."

Mary left the reception without another word. No one paid her any mind, thinking she was just ducking to the bathroom; it would only be when the party wound down that people would start to notice the blushing bride had left but the groom was still around, getting trashed on free beer.

"Ah well, it was good while it lasted," Hoboman lamented. He tipped the Jeans out onto the table and lectured, "Listen here, matey potateys, you're like the seven dwarves, except not as charming. I like the seven dwarves. I don't like you. You guys are more like the seven letdowns. Scram!"

For those wondering what became of the Jeans, six did nothing remarkable. Jean Five was the exception, building a rocket

---

[58] God later explained Jean had not appeared in any form of afterlife due to this inadvertent cloning.

using only corn chips held together with French onion dip. He christened the rocket 'Spudnik' and blasted off into space. It is widely believed he landed on Jupiter and populated the planet with potato people, though no one can confirm this as they don't live on Jupiter.

Hoboman wrapped his arm around his conscience's shoulders. "What a bumpy ride, eh? But we made it, you and me. It was always us, right from Chapter One, and we made it to the end. I'm glad you're alive. It means I still have my moral compass."

"Speaking of morals ... what's the moral of your story?" Whitney asked.

"My story?"

"Your story. If someone had hypothetically compiled your past few weeks and expressed it in the form of, say, a book, what would people take away from it? All I'm picking up from this is 'beat up people you dislike and marry into wealth.'"

"Isn't that the great Australian dream?" Hoboman winked and gave the thumbs-up.

"What are you doing, Hoboman?"

"Winking and giving the thumbs-up to the audience. Obviously."

"What audience?"

"If this were a book or, say, a movie, you said it would be documenting my past experiences. If that's the case, I want to acknowledge the readers or viewers."

"But we *aren't* in a book or movie."

"No. Not *yet*," Hoboman said, winking and giving the thumbs-up to the audience.

And that, my dear friends, is where Hoboman's story ends. Pretty sure I tied up all the loose ends flapping about. I hope your mind wasn't too blown by the legendary adventures of one Hobart Darwin Mann.

And they all lived happily ever after.

The end.

Story's over.

Go home!

About the Author

Liam Higham is an Australian author who has still not won any awards and is still not a bestseller. He has previously written a short story, *Drop Dead Gorgeous*, published by Spineless Wonders. While he first published *Hoboman* in 2017, *Hoboman – The Higham Cut* supersedes the original in that it is truer to the author's vision (read: he could afford proofreading and editing).

Liam enjoys thinking of concepts for future works, although he is a bigger fan of procrastination and often fails to write these ideas down before they leave his head forever.